Praise for Diane Jeffrey

...... good thriller' Lisa Hall

'Brimming with tension, riddled with doubt and suspicion, insidious and compelling with a terrifying ending that had me catching my breath' Sue Fortin

'A tense, gripping domestic noir that shows just how fast the dream of a new life can turn into your worst nightmare' T.M. Logan

'With twists and turns that will wrong-foot you all the way, a dash of dark humour and a strong emotional punch' S.J.I. Holliday

'A thought-provoking and gripping read' Roz Watkins

'Superb . . . Maps the complex territory of female friendship with great insight, and kept me gripped from the very start' Kate Rhodes

'Heartbreaking and nuanced – with a clever twist but so much more than a thriller . . . beautifully written and gripping' Catherine Cooper

'An intriguing concept and an addictive read' Annabel Kantaria

'A thoughtful drama exploring an unlikely friendship' John Marrs

DIANE JEFFREY is a *USA Today* bestselling author. She grew up in North Devon, in the United Kingdom. She now lives in Lyon, France, with her husband and their three children, Labrador and cat. *The Couple at Causeway Cottage* is her fifth book.

Diane is an English teacher. When she's not working or writing, she likes swimming, running and reading. She loves chocolate, beer and holidays. Above all, she enjoys spending time with her family and friends.

Readers can follow Diane on Twitter, Facebook, or on Instagram, and find out more about her books on her website:

🐦 www.twitter.com/dianefjeffrey
f www.facebook.com/dianejeffreyauthor
📷 www.instagram.com/dianefjeffrey
www.dianejeffrey.com

Also by Diane Jeffrey

Those Who Lie
He Will Find You
The Guilty Mother
The Silent Friend

The Couple at Causeway Cottage

DIANE JEFFREY

ONE PLACE. MANY STORIES

HQ
An imprint of HarperCollins*Publishers* Ltd
1 London Bridge Street
London SE1 9GF

www.harpercollins.co.uk

HarperCollins*Publishers*
1st Floor, Watermarque Building, Ringsend Road
Dublin 4, Ireland

This paperback edition 2022

1
First published in Great Britain by
HQ, an imprint of HarperCollins*Publishers* Ltd 2022

Copyright © Diane Jeffrey 2022

Diane Jeffrey asserts the moral right to be
identified as the author of this work.
A catalogue record for this book is
available from the British Library.

ISBN: 9780008547943

This book is produced from independently certified FSC™ paper
to ensure responsible forest management.

For more information visit: www.harpercollins.co.uk/green

Printed and bound in the UK using
100% renewable electricity at CPI Group (UK) Ltd

In loving memory of my grandfather, Granda Tom.

I have so many fond memories of you in Belfast, Ballycastle and Devon, some of the settings for my book, that it seemed fitting to dedicate this one to you.
xxx

"He who seeks revenge should remember to dig two graves."
Asian proverb, attributed to Confucius

Chapter 1

It's only when I'm on the ferry, minutes before arriving, that it hits me how isolated I will be. Standing on the deck, using my hand to shield my eyes from the sun, I glimpse the island for the first time. The cliffs, imposing and impressive, even from a distance, then the port, a speck bobbing in and out of view, becoming bigger and more distinct as we approach. Until now, I've only seen images of Rathlin from googling it: a map of a small island shaped like a boomerang or an upside-down sock, pictures of its two churches and its white seafront cottages as well as – and this was the clincher when Mark tried to talk me into moving here – numerous photos of seals and birds.

When I announced I was going to live on a tiny island I'd never been to before, everyone was astonished. I still can't believe it myself. But new home, new start. The decision wasn't as rash as it sounds. As I explained to my friends, my dad was from Northern Ireland, so it feels a bit like going back to my roots. And it's familiar territory for Mark. He grew up eight miles away in Ballycastle, where he recently secured a place for his mother in a nursing home. It was the best thing to do – the only thing to do, but he's riddled with guilt. An only child who has lost his father, Mark is very close to his mum. I can certainly relate to that. It's only natural he should also want to be closer to her geographically, especially as she's so ill.

At the time, it felt like the right decision for me, too. The right move. For several reasons. I mentally tick them off on my fingers as I try to curb the uneasiness swelling inside me. Thumb: I grew up in Devon and I miss the ocean. Index: I was desperate to escape the frantic rhythm of London. Middle finger: I've always wanted to be an outdoor photographer – wildlife or landscapes. Rathlin will provide the perfect playground for me to pursue this goal. Ring finger: with its tight-knit community and tiny primary school, Rathlin Island strikes me as an ideal place to bring up our children when they come along. Little finger: the smallest digit on my hand, but an important consideration nonetheless – both Mark and I needed to get away from his ex-wife.

But enumerating all the advantages of this move does nothing to allay my agitation. I'm out of sync with the calm sea.

'Mark, show me the photos of our house again,' I say.

'You'll see it with your own eyes in a few minutes.' He hands me his mobile, an amused look on his face, clearly mistaking my jitteriness for excitement.

The estate agent showed Mark around the house while he was over three months ago visiting his mother, who has dementia. He took lots of photos and I've swiped through them on his phone so many times I can visualise in detail the place I'll call home from now on. But I had to make do with a virtual visit of the three-bedroom detached cottage we've bought. It doesn't have a garden, but neither of us is green-fingered, and with it being so close to the beach, that didn't bother us.

We'd initially been looking for a house on the mainland, but when Causeway Cottage went up for sale, our plans changed. Mark has always had this romantic notion about living on an island and this was the chance of a lifetime. It was the only suitable place for sale on Rathlin – the others were new builds, social housing – so we had to snap it up quickly. I was terrified we'd be gazumped – a word I didn't even know before Mark made a verbal offer on the house – and delighted when all the paperwork was finally signed and Causeway Cottage was officially ours.

But it feels disconcerting now, moving into a house I've only ever seen in photos. Is it because I don't like the idea of living in a house where someone died? I shudder, then berate myself for being morbid. I'm on my way to a beautiful island, where I'll be living the dream. It's not like I'm being ferried across the River Styx.

I give Mark back his mobile. He smiles at me, his turquoise eyes blazing in the sun. A rictus stretches across my face as I force myself to smile back.

'The finish line's in sight,' Mark says, as we make our way to the car, which is laden to the hilt with our mattress strapped to the roof rack. His Northern Irish accent is already more pronounced, even though he hasn't talked to anyone except me since we left London.

As Mark starts up the car and drives slowly off *The Spirit of Rathlin* and onto the island itself, I sigh with relief. We travelled for nearly fourteen hours yesterday – getting up at six a.m. and driving from London to Liverpool to take the ferry to Belfast, driving north from there as far as the coastal town of Ballycastle, where we stayed overnight at the house my mother-in-law lived in until very recently. Our crossing this morning – from Ballycastle Harbour to Rathlin – was mercifully short. The first boat of the day and the last leg of the journey.

Causeway Cottage is barely a minute's drive from the harbour, halfway up a steep hill. I throw off my seatbelt and leap out of the car before Mark can even turn off the engine. Standing at the front gate, I take it in. Now I'm here, I can finally get a feel for the place. The house is quaint and perfectly symmetrical. Red roses climb up the pure white walls on both sides of the front door and, for a second, I picture the cottage as a child might draw it, like a face, the flowers depicting red lips curling upwards as if the house is smiling at me. Or maybe it's laughing at me. The upstairs windows are eyes, their sills thick lines, pencilled with black kohl. I wonder what they see when they look down at me.

'It needs a bit of work on the façade and on the roof,' Mark says, materialising beside me, 'but other than that, the property's in pretty good shape.' I wonder if he's repeating the estate agent's words. 'So, what do you think?'

'It's beautiful. Like a cottage in a fairy tale.' I turn to look at him, but instead my gaze is drawn to the old, stone building behind him. 'I hadn't realised the cottage was so close to the church.'

'We don't have to go,' he says jokingly. 'Apparently there's no bell-ringing, so we can still have a lie-in on Sundays.'

'I was thinking more of the graveyard.' My imagination fills in what I can't make out, even with my neck craned: tombstones, scattered across the hillside, overlooking the sea and exposed to the elements. Frosty fingers walk down my spine as I wonder if the previous owner of our cottage is buried there.

'The estate agent assured me our new neighbours are only noisy one night a year.'

Mark's jovial mood is infectious. 'Let me guess,' I say, playing along. 'Hallowe'en.'

Mark chuckles. 'You got it.'

I laugh, too.

'That church doesn't actually have a graveyard,' Mark adds. 'The island's only burial ground is at the other one.' As he says that, I remember reading it online.

Mark whisks me up into his arms and carries me up the path to the front door. 'I didn't think this through,' he says, setting me down to fish the key out of his jeans pocket. Then he opens the front door, picks me up again and carries me over the threshold, the two of us giggling like newly-weds.

The first thing I notice is the smell. A stale odour only partially masked by disinfectant and bleach. It's because it has been shut up for a few weeks, I tell myself. I walk through to the living

4

room, past what I know from Mark is a working fireplace, and fling open the windows to let in the sea air.

'Wow,' I breathe. The village sprawls below us and, beyond that, the sea stretches to the horizon.

'The views are even better from upstairs.' Mark grabs my hand and leads me upstairs to the front bedroom – the master bedroom.

A cool breeze wafts in through the window when Mark opens it and I shiver.

'Cold?' Mark asks.

'Not really. I was wondering which room the last owner died in. It wasn't in here, was it?'

'I don't know, Kat. I didn't think to ask.' He combs his fingers through his wavy, salt and pepper hair. 'He was an old man. He died peacefully in his sleep.'

'It probably was in our bedroom, then.'

'Does it matter? I don't think the house is haunted.'

I'm being ridiculous. The house doesn't feel creepy. It's smaller than it looked in the photos, but it's massive compared to the flat we were renting in Hammersmith.

We spend the next half an hour or so walking around the house, upstairs and downstairs, opening cupboards and doors and planning where our furniture will go when it arrives. The removals van won't make it as far as the island – we'll unload everything at my mother-in-law's house, then we'll decide what to keep and bring over on the ferry and what to get rid of or replace.

Mark's mother had a lot of stuff in her house – she's a bit of a hoarder – but Mark cleared out most of it when he was offered a place for her in the care home. She insisted Mark should sell her house, and anything in it that would fetch some money, to cover the fees. The house wouldn't have suited us, not permanently. It's a very small bungalow with no sea views. On top of that, it's on a busy road. So we didn't see ourselves living there. We'd intended to stay there temporarily and take our time finding our dream home. But when Causeway Cottage came onto the market, everything happened more quickly than we'd anticipated and now we're about to become islanders.

Secretly, I was relieved we wouldn't be living in Ballycastle itself. As my mind wanders to the fortnight I spent there the summer I turned fifteen, Mark provides a welcome interruption to a painful memory and snaps me back to the present.

'Shall we do some unpacking?' he says. 'Then we can go for a pub lunch.'

*

McCuaig's Bar is on the seafront. Sitting outside at the wooden picnic table, I tuck into my scampi ravenously, enjoying the squawking of the seagulls. I take a sip of Mark's beer. I'd love a glass of wine, but I've resolved to cut back on drinking. When I stopped taking the pill a few months ago, we hadn't discussed moving to Northern Ireland. I suppose, with the stress and upheaval of the move, it's just as well I didn't get pregnant before now, and there was little chance of it happening with Mark away so often for work. But now would be the perfect time for me to get pregnant and I know too much alcohol could affect my fertility.

I finish my meal and put down my knife and fork. Feeling the sun warm my face, I close my eyes and tip back my head. Then I open them and look around me. At the table next to ours, two tourists are chatting animatedly, their backpacks on the ground by their feet. At another table, a man is sitting by himself, but there's an empty plate and pint glass opposite him. He's wearing a checked shirt with his sleeves rolled up and he's holding a hamburger with paint-stained hands.

Mark drains his beer. 'I think I'll have another one,' he says. 'Sure you don't want a drink?'

'I shouldn't.'

'I don't suppose one will hurt,' Mark says. 'We should be celebrating!'

'Go on, then,' I say, cursing myself for being so weak-willed. 'I'll have a glass of white wine.'

Mark gets up to fetch our drinks from the bar. He clambers over the wooden bench and walks straight into a man carrying a pint of lager in each hand.

'I'm so sorry,' Mark says. 'That was terribly clumsy of me.'

'Don't worry, mate. No harm done.' His voice is deep and sonorous. He's at least six foot two and towers over Mark, even though my husband isn't short.

'I've spilt beer all down your T-shirt.' Mark is clearly mortified.

'It's no big deal. It was dirty anyway. These are work clothes.'

As Mark continues to apologise profusely and insists on replacing the pints, the stranger glances my way briefly, although I don't think he takes me in. When he turns back to Mark, his expression has changed, as if he's struggling not to lose his temper. Perhaps because of Mark's fussing, he's more annoyed now than when Mark collided with him. I watch, mesmerised, as a red flush spreads from his neck to his cheeks and a vein in his forehead bulges. I would find the transformation amusing if it wasn't so dramatic. But he looks as though he might punch Mark if his hands were free. Instead, he clenches his jaw and glares at him.

As Mark scuttles inside, the man makes his way over to his table. Taking his seat opposite the guy in the checked shirt, he looks so calm and collected I wonder if I imagined his change in demeanour. I sneak a glance at him over my shoulder. He has a large, slightly hooked nose. Huge biceps. His fair hair is unkempt and a little too long, framing his suntanned face. If not exactly handsome, he's certainly attractive.

Mark comes back, carrying a tray with four glasses on it. He puts the tray down on our table and takes the pints over to the two men, apologising again.

'His face is familiar,' Mark says when he has sat down. 'I'm sure I know him from somewhere.'

7

I turn to look at the man again, but he's staring our way and, catching his eye, I whip my head back to face Mark.

'I've never seen him before in my life,' I say. 'Maybe you went to school together.'

'Maybe.' Mark sounds dubitative. 'I think I knew him when I was younger, but I don't think it was at school.'

'It's hard to place people out of context sometimes. Hey, maybe he's a celebrity and you've seen him on TV.'

Mark isn't listening to me. His eyebrows pinch together into a frown. 'I'm pretty sure I didn't like him.'

'What makes you say that?'

Mark shrugs.

'Oh well,' I say brightly, 'with a bit of luck, you won't bump into him again.'

I hadn't intended it as a pun, but Mark laughs wryly. 'If I do, next time I'll make sure not to knock beer down his front.' But then his face clouds over. He leans towards me and lowers his voice. 'I've got this strange feeling about him. Sort of gut instinct. Like he's bad news. I can't quite put my finger on it.'

I remember the thunderous look that came over the man earlier, when I thought he wanted to hit Mark. Perhaps I didn't misread his expression after all.

Chapter 2

Standing on the pebbly beach of Mill Bay, a short walk from the pub, the incident at lunch is all but forgotten as Mark and I gaze at the seals lounging on the rocks at low tide. There are at least twenty of them, basking in the sun, their brown-grey skins blending seamlessly with the rocks. Behind them, graceful black and white eider ducks and guillemots cruise across the bay. We have the beach to ourselves. Seaweed glistens like emeralds all around us, lending a magical quality to the postcard-perfect scene.

On the way here, we walked past some glamping pods. A young man and woman were sitting on deckchairs in front of one of them, chatting happily and sharing a cigarette. We also passed a ruined building, without a roof, which Mark informs me was once a kelp store. I'm starting to get a feel for the place. With its rugged landscapes and coastline, this "wee island", as Mark calls it, is both peaceful and breathtakingly beautiful. I feel relaxed, as if I'm on holiday. It still hasn't sunk in that this is now my home.

Mark picks up a stone and leans backwards, his arm poised, as if he's about to skim it. I place my hand on his shoulder, a silent request for him not to disturb this moment, and he drops the stone and puts his arm around me.

'I wish I'd brought my camera,' I say. I unpacked it earlier and put it on one of the alcove shelves in the smallest bedroom, the room we've decided to share – it will be Mark's office and my studio. Mark earns a good living and I have some money of my own in the bank, an inheritance from my father and some savings, which will tide me over while I see if I can make a decent living from doing what I love most – taking photos.

'You'll have plenty of time to shoot animals.'

I nudge Mark playfully in the ribs. 'You make me sound like a hunter.' Then, as a thought occurs to me, I say, 'I suppose the seals here were hunted once for food and oil like everywhere else.'

'Maybe. But the islanders used to believe your soul was reincarnated in animal form. If you led a pure life, you came back as a bird, but if you were a sinner, you were reborn as a seal. Maybe that deterred them, the thought that if they killed seals for lamp fuel or cooking oil, they might end up burning the fat of their ancestors!'

That makes me laugh. 'How do you know that?' I ask. I narrow my eyes. 'Did you just make it up?'

'No, not at all! We used to come on school outings to Rathlin. With our history teacher. He was mad about the island and knew loads about it: legends, massacres, invasions, shipwrecks …'

I vaguely remember a school trip to Lundy Island when I was little. We took the boat from Ilfracombe, my home town, a seaside resort on the North Devon coast. The crossing was rough and interminable. We didn't see a single puffin, despite the teachers' promises, and the most memorable part of the whole visit for me was throwing up on the ship's deck, both on the outward journey and on the way back.

I look again at the chubby, lazy seals and the elegant ducks. 'I think I'd rather be a seal right now,' I muse. 'I could do with a nap.'

'Let's head home. We can have a snooze before we finish unpacking.'

I'm torn. I'd like to walk further around the coast and see more of the island. I remember from what I've read that it's four miles across, from east to west, and nearly three miles down, from north to south. There are three lighthouses, caves, a bird sanctuary. I'm keen to explore. But the strain of the move and the travelling yesterday have taken their toll and I'm exhausted. I have the whole summer ahead of me to get to know Rathlin.

'Hmm. I like the sound of a snooze,' I say.

It's strange, hearing Mark call Causeway Cottage home. I don't know my way around my own house very well and I don't have all my belongings. I feel like a tourist on this island. An outsider; an explorer. It's uncharted territory for me. I wonder how long it will take me to feel like a local. Mark will be away on business for most of next week and I plan to go for a long run and plenty of walks so I can familiarise myself with my new habitat.

We stop at the island shop to buy some groceries, enough food to see us through the weekend. We also walk past the other church – St Thomas's – the one with the graveyard. It's built with the same grey-brown stone as the Catholic church next to our house, and as the crow flies, they can't be more than two hundred metres apart. Church Bay, this part of the island is called, according to Mark.

Hearing hammering and voices to my right, I turn my head to see two semi-detached houses under construction next to St Thomas's. White with black window frames, they resemble our cottage. They're mirror images of each other, the two front doors almost touching in the middle. I spot a builder, standing on the scaffolding, armed with a bucket. He's tall and slim with muscular arms. But what grabs my attention is his red and blue checked shirt. I recognise that shirt from earlier.

Then I see him. The man Mark banged into at the pub, spilling beer down his T-shirt. He's on the ground, passing some sort of tool – a trowel, maybe – up to his workmate. He's in his late thirties, I'd say, about eight to ten years older than me. The sunlight seems to fall directly onto him, bringing out red strands in his otherwise fair hair. He laughs at something his mate says. It's a lovely sound – loud and infectious – and I find myself smiling. An instant later, I remember his face as Mark apologised to him and my own face falls.

He looks my way then, and my cheeks burn. I've been caught staring. I force myself to hold his gaze. Slowly, he lifts his hand and, without smiling, he waves. Pretending not to notice, I turn away, towards Mark, who is looking the other way, out to sea. The Sea of Moyle. He hasn't spotted the two men and I don't point them out to him. I quicken my step and Mark follows.

When we get back to the cottage, I put away the shopping. I'll work out another day where I want everything to go. For now, I cram everything into one cupboard apart from the milk and cheese, which I put into an old, noisy fridge that wasn't cleared out of the cottage when it was sold.

In the bedroom, I pull off my jeans and sweatshirt. The bed frame and headboard will arrive in Ballycastle with the removals van, but for now we have the mattress and the bedding. I dive onto the mattress and pull the quilt up to my chin.

I watch Mark get undressed, appraising his body. He's not particularly athletic and his shoulders are slim. He's not fat, but I can see his middle-aged spread is more perceptible than it used to be, although he conceals it under a shirt for work. Mark's a little self-conscious about his body, but not enough to make any real effort to get into shape.

When we first met, he was concerned about the age difference between us. He toyed with the idea of taking up football again. He used to belong to a club and played throughout his childhood and teens. Every now and again he would vow to get fit, but he never stuck to his resolution. He made a few perfunctory efforts – did a few press-ups, went for the odd swim, cycled once or twice while I ran, that sort of thing. But he has long since given up the pretence and doesn't do much sport at all anymore. It's one of the major differences between us, that I am addicted to running and Mark won't even go to the gym.

Yawning, I close my eyes. A short sleep will do me good. A power nap.

But Mark has other ideas. 'I think we should get to work,' he says.

'You carry on unpacking if you like,' I murmur. 'I'm having a rest first.'

'That's not what I meant,' he says, lying beside me and pulling me to him. 'We have – ooh, the kitchen, living room, two of the three bedrooms, the bathroom – that's at least five rooms to christen and I'm going away for work the day after tomorrow.'

'Quite a challenge,' I say. I'm tired and not in the mood, but we are trying for a baby.

'Indeed.' Mark nibbles my ear and kisses my neck. 'I'm up for it, though.'

'Yes, I can sense that,' I say, my body responding to his touch.

We make love for the first time in our new house. Afterwards, I lie on my back, resisting the urge to grab Mark's pillow and use it to elevate my legs to increase our chances of conception. I'm dozing off when Mark's phone, on the floor by his side of the mattress, pings with a text. He picks up his mobile and puts it down again, heaving an exaggerated sigh.

'Who is it?' I ask.

His answer comes a beat too late. 'It's work.'

I'm wide awake now. *On a Saturday?* It's on the tip of my tongue to call him out, but I say nothing. I don't want to pick a fight. But I can tell he's lying. I know who it's from. Mark has that furtive look that comes over him whenever he talks about her or someone mentions her name.

Fiona.

I thought we'd get away from her here, but it seems Mark hasn't left his ex-wife behind.

Chapter 3

The rain is relentless the morning Mark leaves and it continues to batter the island for three days after that. It's early June and I feel cheated. It should be warm and sunny, as it was when we arrived. From my bedroom window, I can barely make out the front gate. Even so, I decide to brave the elements for a short walk, but I don't make it as far as the church next door before my umbrella turns inside out and I'm soaked. I'm desperate to get out for a run, and I don't usually mind the rain, but this downpour is so violent I might end up injured. Or lost. It feels deliberate and vindictive, as if the island has reserved this wild weather for my arrival, as a warning I'm not welcome here.

I spend those days stuck inside the cottage, alone. I can't tidy away any more of our things until the removals van arrives. Our clothes are in piles on the floor, waiting for the wardrobe. I'd like to paint the walls in our bedroom and in the baby's room, as I already think of it, but I'll have to go to the mainland to buy what I need and Mark has the car. It's his company car, a BMW, which he doesn't often let me drive, so I need Mark, too.

I read my book, exchange text messages with my best friend Charlotte in London and chat on the phone with my mum in Devon, telling them about the seals and birds we saw at the weekend. I don't mention I'm stranded by the rain. For one thing, I don't like to complain, but the main reason is I don't want to admit to them – or myself – the feeling I have in the pit of my stomach that I might have been wrong to come here. I've never felt so lonely or so far from home.

The rain stops pounding on the roof and windowpanes in the middle of the third night, but my heart is pounding instead, as if something has woken me up. Usually, I sleep soundly all through the night, even when Mark's not there, and for a few seconds, I'm disorientated. I reach out for Mark, only to find a cold, empty space next to me. I panic as the realisation hits me that I'm not in our Hammersmith flat. Then I remember where I am and my breathing and pulse slow to a normal rhythm.

Perhaps it was simply the silence that roused me. It's so dense I can't get back to sleep. I'm used to the frenetic bustle of London, where at all times of the day and night, passing cars provide white noise, punctuated by horns to which you become immune over time. When Mark is next to me, his light snoring rocks me back to sleep on the rare occasions I awake in the night.

I turn my head and read the red digital numbers of the radio alarm clock, sitting on a cardboard box that serves as a temporary bedside table – 3:32. It's half past three in the morning. I've only been asleep for about four hours. I decide to open the window a crack. Maybe if I can hear the sea or the seagulls, I'll be able to nod off again. I fumble around in the dark on the floor by Mark's side of the mattress, but I can't find the switch for the lamp. I can't see a thing. We don't have curtains up yet, and if there were streetlamps in front of the house, that would offer some light. But it's pitch-black, both outside and inside.

I get up and run my hands along the wall until I locate the main light switch. The bulb, hanging bare from the ceiling, dazzles me. I walk over to the opposite wall. Pulling the latch, I push the awning window outwards. Then I turn off the light and crawl back under the covers.

I close my eyes tight. I can hear the sea, albeit faintly, but it's no good. I'm wide awake now. After a few minutes, admitting defeat, I get up and make myself some tea. Our sofa isn't here yet, so I go back upstairs and sit on the mattress in the master bedroom, holding my mug in one hand and my book in the other. I finish reading the last chapter as the sun climbs into a clear blue sky.

After eating a light breakfast, I finally get out for the run I've been itching to go on. I'm about to discover my new home. As I scrape my shoulder-length dark hair back into a ponytail, strap my water bottle in a belt around my waist and tie up my trainers, I almost squeal with excitement. I feel like a child on Christmas Day, about to open her presents.

Full of energy despite a short night, I'm tempted to sprint up the road to get away from the house I've been trapped in for the last few days. But I need to pace myself. I plan to run to the lighthouse on the westernmost point of Rathlin and back again, an eight- or nine-mile run. It's very hilly, too. If I start off too quickly, I'll burn myself out.

The smell of the sea and the screeching of birds accompany me as I run up two steep hills. I pause at the top and take a swig of water from my bottle. Looking behind me, I have the most incredible view over the harbour.

A couple of miles further, I stop again. The narrow road I'm running along is blocked. There are brown cows roaming freely on the grass either side of the path, but one of them is barring my way. My instinct is to turn around and flee. I went over a cattle grid a minute or so ago – if I can make it back over to the other side, the cow won't be able to get me. But I've just passed a sign informing me I've entered Kebble National Nature Reserve and I know I'm not far from the West Lighthouse now.

The cow starts to walk towards me. I was chased by a bull once, years ago, across a field in Devon, and I'm terrified of cattle. It hasn't got horns, though. And it's probably used to people walking along here. But it's getting closer. I run. Not away from the cow, but onto the grass and around it. Glancing over my shoulder, I see the cow continuing its sedate walk in the opposite direction and I laugh at myself.

Rounding the next bend, I spot the lighthouse. A huge, white structure, it consists of a vertical, rectangular tower attached to a horizontal block, which I suppose must have been the lighthouse keeper's accommodation. It is built into the cliff rather than on it. As I approach, I notice the light itself is at the bottom of the lighthouse instead of on top. Inverted and unusual, it is unlike any lighthouse I've ever seen.

The cliffs around the lighthouse are dotted with birds – puffins, kittiwakes, guillemots and other species I can't identify, and I'm struck not just by how many of them there are, but also by the resounding din they're making. There's a seabird centre here, which I intend to visit another day before the summer is over. For now, I take a few shots with my phone, but I'm definitely coming back with my camera.

The run here was hard – it was quite a climb, so there's a lot more downhill on the way back, thankfully. I expect I'll have stiff legs tomorrow or the day after – DOMS, as runners call it: delayed onset muscle soreness. I know I'll be on a high for the rest of the day, though, and that makes me smile. I plan the rest of my day as my feet pound on the narrow, tarmacked road: a long bath, lunch, maybe a nap, followed by a trip to the local shop to buy what I need to make a delicious meal for this evening. Oh. And a bottle of wine. I'll limit myself to half a glass, but Mark will appreciate some wine with his dinner. He'll be back this evening. I don't feel nearly so isolated now I've been able to get out of the house, but I can't wait for my husband to come home.

*

I spoon against Mark and kiss the back of his neck, my arms around him. I'm so happy he's home and we've had a lovely evening. But as I reach inside the boxer shorts he wears in bed, he gently removes my hand.

'Not tonight, Kat,' he murmurs. 'I'm really tired.'

We don't make love every night, obviously, but we've always had sex on the evenings Mark gets back from business trips. Every time, without fail. Even the time I had a stonking cold. I don't think Mark has ever refused my advances before. In fact, he's usually the one who initiates our love-making. He has an insatiable sexual appetite. The rejection stings a little, but I tell myself there's nothing amiss. Then I remember the text message he received last weekend. Do I know exactly where he was and who he was with while he was away? Can I be sure he wasn't with his ex-wife?

'Night, then,' I say, silencing the voice in my head. I'm over-thinking all this. If I read something into it that isn't there, I'll never get to sleep.

He rolls over and cuddles me, giving me a peck on the cheek. I hug him back, feeling a pang of guilt for doubting him. He works hard, as head of research for Campbell & Coyle, a phar-maceutical company with its headquarters in London and offices in Belfast. He had to go away on business just a couple of days after the long drive here. It's hardly surprising he's exhausted. If he doesn't want to make love, it doesn't mean he has made love to someone else. I need to trust him. I need to let it go. It only happened once.

'Do you mind if I open the window a little?' I ask Mark.

'Are you hot?'

'No. It's just that I find it so quiet here. You can hear the sea with the window open. I think it might help me sleep better.' Mark's snoring will also lull me to sleep, but I don't say that out loud.

'Sure. Go ahead.'

Mark flicks on the lamp and I walk over to the window. I only see it for a split second out of the corner of my eye. Letting out a cat-like yowl, I flatten my body against the wall.

'What's wrong?'

I don't answer. I can't find my voice.

'Kat? What's wrong?' he repeats.

'Outside. I saw …'

'What? What did you see?'

Mark gets up and comes over to me. Standing next to me, he looks out of the window. 'I can't see anything,' he says. 'It's dark out there. Come here and look.'

I shake my head. 'There was something out there, Mark,' I say. 'I'm sure there was.' But even as I say those words, doubts gain ground in my mind. Could it have been my imagination? Or the light from our room casting shadows into the dark night?

'What is it that you think you saw?'

Mark doesn't believe me. That in itself reassures me at the same time as it angers me.

'I thought I saw someone out there,' I say, trying to sound dismissive.

Mark's hand is on the handle of the main window.

'No, don't.' My voice sounds childish and I'm ashamed of myself.

Ignoring me, Mark opens the window and leans out. I try to muster up the courage to look out of the window. It takes me several seconds. When I do look, there's nothing there.

I walk back to our mattress on the floor and get under the covers. 'Please shut the window,' I say. 'I'm cold now, anyway.'

To my relief, he closes it. Then he lies down next to me and turns off the lamp.

'There was nothing there,' he says, planting a kiss on my forehead before rolling onto his side, his back to me. 'It must have been a trick of the light.'

'What light?'

'The light from our bedroom.'

I came up with that explanation seconds ago, but I only believe it now Mark says it. He's right. I got spooked by a shadow. And yet, closing my eyes, I see behind my eyelids what I thought I saw outside: someone standing by the front gate, staring up at our bedroom window.

Chapter 4

I get into position, crouching as close to the edge of the cliff as I dare. It's a three-mile walk from our cottage to Altacarry Head, so I didn't bring my tripod. I need to invest in a lighter, carbon-fibre one that I can carry around. Resting my elbows on my knees, I peer out to sea through the lens of my camera. On the horizon, the sun is glowing from behind two stretched wisps of cloud, suspended over the Mull of Kintyre. I hadn't realised you could see Scotland from Rathlin Island until Mark pointed it out, and I'm surprised how close it is. On the way here, Mark acted as my tour guide, but I think he regretted offering to come with me when the alarm went off at five thirty. He isn't a morning person.

'Why don't you go back to sleep?' I said. 'I don't mind going alone.' It's true. It wouldn't have bothered me. In fact, I would probably prefer to be by myself. Without Mark, I could appreciate even more the feeling of being at one with nature, inhaling the crisp, pure air and listening to the only sounds breaking the silence – the sea and the birds.

But my husband insisted on accompanying me. I found that touching, although he took so long to get up and get dressed that we almost missed the golden hour, that moment

21

shortly before sunrise or after sunset when the light is softer and redder. I'm glad he came, though. I think he is now, too. He admired the spectacular views of Fairhead and Torr Head on the mainland, his face lighting up with childlike wonder. He's sitting a few feet away now, sipping coffee from his flask. I can feel his eyes on me as I hold my camera steady and shoot a few frames, capturing a panoramic scene thanks to the wide-angle lens.

And suddenly there it is. The moment I've been waiting for. Through the parallel streaks of cloud, the sun bursts like a star, its orange reflection bleeding into the water. It's so bright it's hard to avoid a glare. My gaze focused on the viewfinder, I move my body slightly to adjust the angle at which the sun enters the lens. To the right of my image in the foreground, the East Lighthouse stands proudly and patiently on top of the cliff, duplicating the short, vertical brushstroke of the sun's reflection and contrasting with the long, horizontal lines of the clouds and the skyline. This is it. Here's my shot.

I hold my breath, gently squeezing the shutter release button with my finger. In such low light, if I move even a tiny bit, the photograph will be blurred. But before I can take the picture, something bowls into me, knocking me over. My left hand breaks my fall while my right hand holds my camera into the air. Sprawled on my back, I'm inches from the cliff edge. The sea seems louder all of a sudden, as I look to my left and take in the sheer drop, realising how close I came to going over.

I'm aware of two men running towards me, shouting. One of them is Mark. Then my view is blocked. I find myself face to face with a Border collie. I'm not scared of dogs. Cows, yes. Dogs, no. I grew up with a golden retriever and a German shepherd, but my heart races as I get a close-up view of the collie's teeth. I think it's going to bite me, but it starts licking me. It has terrible breath. In spite of that, I laugh.

'Dexter. Bad boy! Here!' The dog owner reaches me before

Mark does. He calls off the collie and stretches out a large, calloused hand to help me to my feet.

'Are you all right, Kat?' Mark asks. He throws the other man a dark look, but it's quickly replaced by one of recognition. He opens his mouth to say something, but then closes it again.

I can almost read my husband's mind. He wants to shout at this man, swear at him, tell him that he should have his dog on a lead, that I could have been knocked over the cliff. But the dog owner is none other than the constructor that Mark banged into at the pub that day, spilling his beer all over him, and Mark's words die on his lips.

The corners of the dog owner's mouth twitch, as if he's suppressing a smile at the irony of the situation.

'I'm fine,' I reply.

'You could have gone over the cliff.' Mark says this to me, but I can tell it's a thinly veiled criticism levelled at the dog owner. 'You could have died.' Mark's going too far, and I shake my head almost imperceptibly, a signal for him to stop there.

'It was an accident,' I say. It sounds brave, but I'm still slightly shaken. I take a few more steps away from the edge.

'I think Dexter here thought you were about to throw a ball or something.' The man bends down and strokes the dog's head. 'I'm afraid he's still a pup.' As he offers these excuses, I realise he hasn't apologised.

To my surprise, he then turns to Mark and introduces himself.

'Er … pleased to meet you, Darren,' Mark says.

My heart clenches. Mark has misheard him. But I haven't.

'Not Darren,' he corrects. 'Darragh.'

'Oh. Pleased to meet you, Darragh. I'm Mark.'

Darragh looks at me. He's waiting for me to introduce myself, but my mouth has gone dry. 'Is that a common name?' I ask. Perhaps it's not the same Darragh, although it is possible – the one I knew – or, rather, knew of – was from Ballycastle, just across the Sea of Moyle.

'It's not that unusual. There was another one in my athletics club when I was a teen,' he says. 'It's an Irish name. It means oak and fertility, apparently.'

I need to get a grip. That Darragh probably wouldn't know me anyway.

'So, you're Kat, is that right?' Darragh says. My heart is thumping so hard it feels like it will burst out of my ribcage.

Shit! He knows me! How can he possibly know who I am? Then I remember Mark used my name a few seconds ago when he asked if I was OK.

'Yes. Nice to meet you.' I can hear the quiver in my voice. Only Mark calls me Kat, but I don't want Darragh to know me as Katherine. I can hide behind a truncated version of my first name.

Mark puts his arm around my shoulder proprietorially.

'You're new to the island, yeah?' Darragh says. How does he know this? We could be tourists. As if reading my thoughts, Darragh adds, 'Rumours and news tend to spread like wildfire around here. You're obviously local,' he says to Mark. 'How are you finding it here, Kat?'

He's looking at me. I need to pull myself together and act normal. 'It's beautiful,' I manage. 'I'm slowly learning my way around.'

'Shouldn't take long.' He chuckles. 'It's pretty small. Have you met anyone since you've moved in?'

When I don't answer, Mark steps in. 'Not yet. I've been away on business and Kat was stuck indoors because of the rain. But we plan to get involved with the community, that sort of thing.'

'How about I invite you both over to my place for a meal one evening? I love cooking and I have some great wines.'

'That would be lovely,' I say, trying to sound more enthusiastic than I feel.

'That's very kind,' Mark says dismissively. I can tell he's also reluctant to socialise with Darragh. He took an instant disliking to him in the pub. This incident will do nothing to make Mark change his negative first impression of Darragh. As far as Mark's concerned, Darragh's dog nearly killed me.

'We should get going,' I say to Mark, then to Darragh, 'We've got a long day ahead of us. We're fetching our furniture today.'

'Good luck with that!'

'See you around,' Mark says over his shoulder, steering me away.

We probably will, even if we try to avoid him. As Darragh said, Rathlin is pretty small. An area of nearly three thousand five hundred acres and a population of around one hundred and fifty, according to Wikipedia.

I would like to take some more photos, but we do have a lot to do today. Mark has rented a small van and we'll load it up, as well as the car, with our stuff. Once we've brought everything over on the ferry from my mother-in-law's house, we plan to spend the rest of the day assembling our furniture. Mark will take back the van on Monday.

*

By the end of the day, we're exhausted, but Causeway Cottage already feels more like home. We did some shopping at the Spar on the mainland and brought it over with everything else, but neither of us can be bothered to cook, so we have a sort of ploughman's lunch for dinner – bread, Cheddar, grapes, boiled eggs, coleslaw and Branston pickle. I allow myself a bottle of lager to wash it all down.

After dinner, we drop onto the sofa in the sitting room, happy to have recovered it at last and relieved we've got through the bulk of the unpacking.

'At least we managed to get away without giving him our address,' Mark says.

I don't need to ask who he's talking about. Darragh has obviously got under Mark's skin. Neither of us has mentioned Darragh all day, but although I've been trying not to think about him, he has been lingering in a recess of my mind since his dog sent me flying this morning. It's only now, when Mark alludes to him, that I realise he's been invading my husband's thoughts, too.

'He'll know where we live,' I say. 'This was the only place on the market apart from the social housing, remember?'

'Aye, maybe. Well, with a bit of luck that invitation to dinner won't amount to anything. He probably said that out of politeness.'

'Maybe.' I sound dubious. 'Have you remembered who it is he reminds you of?'

'He doesn't remind me of anyone. I said I thought I knew him once.'

'OK. Has it come back to you how you knew him?'

'No. I must have been wrong.' I look at Mark and raise an eyebrow, motioning for him to elaborate. 'It's highly unlikely our paths would have crossed, isn't it?' he continues. 'Not with a name like Darragh.'

'What do you mean by that?'

'Only that with a name like Darragh, he must be a Catholic. We wouldn't have attended the same school.'

Mark is a Protestant. The two religions might coexist more or less peacefully now, especially in a mixed area like Ballycastle, but Northern Ireland was a different place when Mark was growing up in the Eighties.

'He's around my age right enough,' Mark continues. 'But now I think about it, I can't see how I'd have known him. And his name doesn't ring a bell at all. I've never known anyone called Darragh before.'

Mark might not have done. But I have. His name rings a bell for me. A deafening alarm bell. It's ironic. Mark thought he knew him. He was convinced he'd seen him somewhere before. Now he thinks he was mistaken.

But I've heard of a Darragh. A long time ago. I didn't know him personally, but I knew someone who knew him well. I never met him, so I have no way of telling if this Darragh is the same

26

person. I hope not. And even if he is, there's little chance of him recognising me or my name – my full first name or the abbreviation. There's a strong possibility he never knew anything about me. About what I did.

And, more importantly, what I didn't do.

Chapter 5

It's a full week before I go back to Altacarry Head to try to get a shot of a vibrant sunrise like the one I can still visualise clearly, even though I glimpsed it for only a second or two. The weather conditions haven't been suitable, but the forecast was promising when I checked last night. It's hazy this morning, but hopefully the mist will lift.

Mark didn't offer to accompany me this time. He actually pouted when I said I was going to get up early to take some photos. Having been away all week, naturally he wants me to spend some quality time with him this weekend. I feel as if I'm indulging in a guilty pleasure. I try to quash the stab of guilt and savour my few hours of solitude. After all, Mark will probably still be in bed when I get back. And we're going to the local arts, crafts and food market together this afternoon, so it's not like I'm leaving him on his own all day.

As I come round a bend, I see something in the middle of the field. I peer across the carpet of green, peppered with purple and yellow heather. At first, I don't know what caught my attention, then, as I look, two hares leap up from the tall grass. The smaller one has dark fur; the bigger hare has an unusual light tan coat. This, I realise, is the legendary Irish golden hare. I've

28

read that it has striking light blue eyes, due to some genetic mutation, but even though the hares are surprisingly close to me, I can't make out their eye colour from here. Standing still, careful not to make any noise, I watch the hares play together, oblivious to my presence.

I contemplate getting out my camera, but I don't want to scare them off. The light is too soft at this time of day, anyway. Instead, I enjoy the show. This is likely to be one of their favourite haunts, so I'll come back another day and make a hide under the trees from which to photograph them.

After a few minutes, I tear myself away. I need to get out to the point before sunrise, so I leave the hares to their game of chase. When I get to the spot, I set up my camera and tripod. I've ordered a new travel tripod online, but it hasn't arrived yet, so I've lugged the commercial one I used for my work in London out here with me. I don't want to risk ruining my photos with unsteady hands.

But as I wait for the sun to come up, a growing sense of pessimism rises in me. The mist hasn't dissipated and now clouds are hovering threateningly, making the visibility even poorer. I can hardly make out the Mull of Kintyre. I won't be able to take the picture I wanted. With the sky overcast, the shades will be too subtle, the colours muted.

Scanning the scene, I settle on the lighthouse itself. An isolated subject could still look good in cloudy conditions. But as I look through the viewfinder, I know the tones will appear bland. I decide to convert my photos to black and white later in the hope that a monochromatic picture might convey more drama and beauty.

I've taken a few photos when something makes the hairs on the back of my neck stand up. I stop and glance behind me. There's nothing. Did I hear something? See something out of the corner of my eye? I try to brush off the unsettling feeling that has crept up on me and concentrate on taking pictures. But I'm still tense. My hands are trembling and I can't seem to press the shutter release button.

I need to pull myself together. I'm imagining things. I wanted to come out here alone, but now I'm scared. I tell myself I'm alarmed because there's no one else out here, but I'm convinced it's the other way round. I'm panicking because there *is* someone. I can't shake the impression I'm being watched, just as I watched the hares earlier. Except they weren't aware I was there and I *know* someone is here. I can sense a pair of eyes on me. Turning around again, more slowly this time, I examine my surroundings. There's no sound, no movement. But I don't feel reassured.

Trying to appear unruffled in case I really am being observed, I collapse the tripod and stuff it and my camera into my rucksack. I'd intended to make a detour on the way back to take some photos at Portawillin Bay. But like the hares and the starburst sunrise, I shelve this plan for now. I set off, aiming for a purposeful stride, but as I reach the road, I break into a sprint. I no longer care if whoever is spying on me knows I'm panicking. Despite the heavy bag on my back, I don't stop running until I reach the cottage.

Mark is still asleep, as I thought he would be. I shower and, once I've calmed down, I berate myself for letting my overactive imagination run amok. I won't tell Mark I got spooked. He'll only laugh at me.

My stomach growls and I realise I'm ravenous, so I wolf down a bowl of cereal. While I drink my tea, I boot up my laptop and import my photos. The pictures of the lighthouse do look good in black and white and I edit a couple of photos before uploading them to my social media accounts. I'm pleased with the result, although I'm still gutted I didn't get the shot of the sunrise I was hoping for. Maybe next time. Another thought jostles with that one, a question I can't answer. Is it safe for me to go out there alone?

*

The artisan market is being held in the Richard Branson Activity Centre, a renovated barn at the Manor House, a Georgian edifice overlooking the harbour at Church Bay.

'Why is it named after Richard Branson?' I ask Mark as we step inside.

'He crashed his hot-air balloon into the sea here after his transatlantic flight. A few of the locals were involved in the rescue,' Mark says. 'He donated some money to the island to thank them. The money went on restoring this place.'

At a stall selling handmade jewellery and candles, I buy a necklace with brightly coloured, hand-painted beads that I think my mother-in-law will love – we're going to visit her soon.

There's a long wooden table where three pupils from the local primary school are selling greetings cards to raise money for sports equipment. Their teacher is a woman about my age with sleek, copper hair and emerald eyes and a spattering of freckles like a star constellation across her nose and cheeks. I look at her, then do a double take. I recognise her. It's Erin. We lost touch years ago and I wondered if she'd moved away or if I'd bump into her around here. But then I realise I'm mistaken. It's not her. Just someone who resembles her. A lot.

'Did you make these?' I ask one of the boys.

'I made this one.' He points proudly at a birthday card with what looks vaguely like a teddy bear holding balloons on it.

'It's very good,' I say. 'Did all the pupils at your school make cards?'

'Yes,' the teacher answers for him, flashing me a wide, white smile. 'All fifteen of them.'

I glance at Mark. Only fifteen pupils! It will be perfect for our children when they come along. Mark turns to me and winks, which I take as a sign we're thinking along the same lines. I buy two birthday cards and a get-well card.

At another stall, I buy a walking guide and a couple of books on Rathlin Island – one about its history, the other about flora

31

and fauna – both by local authors. I wonder if this arts and crafts market is an annual event and if I might be able to sell my photos here next year.

'Are you the couple who have just moved into Causeway Cottage?' the vendor asks, breaking into my thoughts. He's a frail, elderly man with bushy grey eyebrows billowing over sparkling, slate-grey eyes.

'That's right,' Mark says. 'How did you know that?'

'Everyone knows everyone else's business on this island,' the man replies, tapping the side of his bulbous nose before holding out his hand. He has a surprisingly firm grip. 'I knew Mr Kelly, the previous owner.'

'I'm Mark Fisher and this is my wife, Kat. Pleased to meet you.'

'I'm Billy Duffy. Likewise.' He shakes my hand and then Mark's. 'How are you settling in? Beautiful wee cottage, isn't it?'

'It's grand. It needs a bit of work, though, on the roof and façade,' Mark says.

'You'll want to see Darragh about that,' Mr Duffy says.

'Darragh.' The look on Mark's face is inscrutable, but his voice has a hard edge to it as he spits out the name.

'Aye. Lovely man. Best builder around these parts. Reliable. He's an excellent painter, too, so he is.' From a pocket in a jacket around the back of his chair, Mr Duffy fishes out a mobile phone. 'I've got his number, if you'll bear with me.' He rummages around in his jacket pockets again and this time extracts his glasses and a pen.

'Don't worry about it,' Mark says. 'The repairs aren't urgent.'

'I'm holding you up,' the old man says apologetically. 'I'm no good with these mobile yokes.'

'We're in no hurry,' I say. 'Take your time.'

Rather than read out the number to Mark to punch into his own phone, the old man jots it down for him on the back of an author's business card. I thank Mr Duffy as he hands the card to Mark.

Mark takes my elbow and leads me outside. He's in a bad mood now, I can tell.

'You don't have to get in touch with him, you know,' I say.

'You've read my mind.' His voice is dripping with sarcasm. 'I'll fix the bloody roof myself.'

'Is that wise?' Mark's no handyman. 'There must be other building contractors around,' I add more tactfully.

Mark glares at me. He has grasped the subtext. 'I can do it. I'm good at DIY.' He's not, but I'm not going to argue. 'There's something strange about that man Darragh,' he continues. 'I don't trust him and I don't want him coming anywhere near our house.'

As we pass a litter bin, Mark takes the business card out of his pocket to dispose of it, but it falls on the ground. Picking it up, I glance at the spidery scrawl in blue ink on the back of the card. A phone number under a name. Darragh Moore.

My heart clenches, as if it has been squeezed by an invisible, cold hand. I recognise his surname. It *is* him. It's the same Darragh.

Ripping up the card and dropping the pieces in the litter bin, I say, 'I don't want to have anything to do with him, either.'

Chapter 6

From the outside, the place looks forbidding. A huge, austere building stands in the middle of a gated, concrete compound, surrounded by spiky, black railings, whose purpose is to keep people in as much as out. But inside, Marconi Care Home is welcoming and warm. A vase of fresh flowers sits on a table in the thick-carpeted foyer; the staff speak with mellifluous voices to residents and visitors alike. Even the receptionist, who looks bored, pastes a smile on her face as she gestures to the visitor book and asks us to sign in.

My mother-in-law's bedroom has a single bed and a large window. Three of the walls have been painted off-white and the fourth is mauve. Mark has put his mother's own ornaments on the chest of drawers, along with a few photos, mainly of him, some of them with me or with his mother. I recognise the rug on the grey, linoleum floor. It used to be in the sitting room of her house.

The last time I saw Mark's mum was several months ago and I am shocked by how diminished she has become. As she gets up to greet Mark, I notice she's hunched over. She was once a tall woman, but she has shrunk. She's as small as I am now. She used to be perceptive, her eyes – the same blue as Mark's – boring into me, giving me the unnerving impression she could see inside my mind and read what I was thinking. But when she lowers herself back into the armchair next to her bed, she observes me through dim eyes that are glazed over. I don't think she recognises me.

'Are you cold, Mum?' Mark wraps her cardigan around her brittle shoulders, without waiting for an answer. The mother-son roles are completely reversed.

When she talks to Mark, her voice is thin, raspy and accusing. 'I don't know why you put me here,' she says. 'I was much happier in my own home.'

Mark has told me this is her opening gambit at every visit since she moved into the care home. It upsets him, but I repeatedly tell him he has done the right thing and that he shouldn't allow himself to be guilt-tripped. She couldn't have stayed in her house by herself anymore. She was getting too forgetful, leaving the gas and the oven on and the washing in the machine. She was also eating food that was well past its sell-by date.

My mother-in-law turns to me. 'It's been such a long time. It's so nice to see you again, Fiona.'

'Mum. This is Kat, not Fiona.' Mark has the decency to look abashed.

'Where's Fiona? What have you done with Fiona?'

'She's in London, Mum. We're divorced, remember? I'm married to Kat now. We live on Rathlin Island. We bought a cottage there so we can be nearer to you and look after you better.'

Mark's mum tuts, shaking her head. 'Such a nice girl, Fiona,' she says.

'I've got you a present,' I say, holding out a paper bag containing the necklace I bought from the artisan market the other day.

'That's kind of you.' She takes the bag and puts it on her lap without opening it.

'Why don't I go and rustle up some tea and biscuits from somewhere?' Mark says.

I can't blame him for wanting to get out of the room. I'd like to get out of here, too. It feels claustrophobic. An unpleasant smell pervades the air, like rotten vegetables.

Once Mark has left, my mother-in-law talks for a while about the weather, then about her husband. He died of a heart attack four or five years ago, just before I met Mark, but she talks about him as if he were still alive. I don't correct her.

Suddenly, she stops mid-sentence, knitting her eyebrows. I wonder if she has forgotten who I am or what I'm doing there, but then I see a flash of recognition in her eyes.

'Be careful, young lady,' she says, wagging a bony finger at me. 'If he was fooling around with you while he was married to her, he'll cheat on you one day, too. A leopard never changes its spots.'

I hold back my irritation. I can't tell if it's directed at my mother-in-law or my husband. I want to set her straight. *I did not fool around with Mark when he was married to Fiona. He fooled around with Fiona when he was married to me!* But the words stay in my head. Even if I did say them, the point she's making wouldn't change. Once a cheat …

She smiles at me, as if she has completely forgotten what she was saying. She probably has.

'When are you thinking of starting a family?' Her intrusive question throws me. 'I would love to have grandchildren, so I would,' she continues. 'I hope you and Mark will have a few weans before I die.'

I nod, but it's not enough. She's waiting for an answer. 'We're working on it, Mrs Fisher,' I say.

It has always seemed strange, not calling Mark's mum by her first name. But she has never invited me to call her Margaret and I've never felt close to her, or welcomed into her family, so I'm reduced to calling her Mrs Fisher, a name by which I'm also known now I'm married. Fiona called her Maggie, of course. My husband's ex could do no wrong in my mother-in-law's eyes. Or my husband's.

Mrs Fisher leans forwards and places her hand on my knee.

As she does so, the bag with the necklace inside falls to the floor. 'Don't leave it too late, will you?' she says. 'I'm getting older, and so are you.' Her eyes fill with tears and it's as if they extinguish the spark of anger inside me. 'I'm going a bit senile,' she says, her voice conspiratorial. 'You always did want weans, didn't you Fiona, pet?'

She's confused. Fiona didn't want children, but that's of no importance now. 'I'm Katherine, Mrs Fisher,' I say, picking up the paper bag and getting to my feet. I take out the necklace and put it on the chest of drawers, scrunch up the bag and drop it into the waste basket. 'I'll go and see where Mark has got to.'

I find Mark talking to one of the staff nurses in the corridor. He's empty-handed, so he clearly hasn't got as far as fetching any tea or biscuits. I tell him I'll wait outside. He makes an apologetic grimace and promises not to be long.

When Mark finally emerges, his expression is grim. We walk down the hill towards the harbour, in silence, to take the foot passenger ferry – The Rathlin Express – back to the island. At the bottom of the hill, we walk right past the community hall. On the way to Marconi Care Home, we were on the pavement opposite and Mark and I were chatting, so I was distracted and didn't register the building. I couldn't remember exactly where it was. But as I see it now, everything threatens to come flooding back to me. I went to a céilí – an Irish folk dance – once in this building, a long time ago. It's a night I've tried to forget, although I've never forgotten my friend. I wonder if she has forgiven me. I shudder as we pass the hall, suppressing the memories before they can quite form.

Perhaps thinking I'm cold, Mark puts his arm around my shoulders, but he remains silent. He doesn't say much during the twenty-minute crossing, either. I can't tell if he's sulking or pensive.

As the catamaran docks, I ask him if he's mad at me.

'No, not at all,' comes the reply. 'I'm shocked at how fast her mind is deteriorating, that's all. I don't blame you for not staying any longer.' He sighs, then adds, 'I hate to think she might be unhappy in that place.'

'It's a lovely care home!' I hope Mark isn't going to ask if she can move in with us. I know he takes his filial duty seriously, but I couldn't cope with that.

'Was she awful to you?' he asks.

'She didn't mean to be. She wants us to get a move on making babies.' I don't add that she was under the impression she was talking to Fiona when she made this suggestion.

'Well, we can certainly redouble our efforts.' He looks at me for the first time since we left the care home. To my relief, I can see the familiar cerulean twinkle in his eyes.

We walk up the hill towards the cottage. Mark is smiling now, although it appears strained. He must be worried about his mum, I think. Then an ugly thought ploughs into that one. Perhaps he's morose because his mother has made him think about his ex-wife.

Mark sees it before I do. He stops at the front gate. 'What's that?'

He doesn't point. He's staring at the cottage, so I follow his gaze. Leaning against the front door is a large, rectangular parcel, wrapped in brown paper and tied with string.

'I have no idea.'

As we approach, I can see my name, written on the front of it with a black marker pen in neat capital letters. No surname, no address, not even my full first name. Just "KAT".

I glance at Mark, shrugging in reply to his raised eyebrows. I can't decide if he's acting or not. Is this some sort of house-warming present from him?

Once inside, I kick off my shoes and put the parcel on the table in the kitchen. I have to open two or three drawers before I remember which one I tidied the scissors into, then I cut the string.

Mark has flicked on the kettle and is putting teabags into mugs, his back to me, as I unwrap the parcel, uncovering a painting. For a few seconds, I stare at it, open-mouthed. Then I gasp.

'What?' Mark whirls round to face me.

'It's beautiful,' I say. And it is, although that's not what made me gasp. I look again at the two interwoven letters in the bottom right-hand corner – the artist's initials. I know who this present is from.

'Show me.'

I turn the painting round, resting it on the kitchen table, so Mark can see. My fingers conceal the artist's signature. The canvas has been mounted on stretcher bars and has no frame. A small, white envelope is taped to the back of the picture.

'Isn't that—?'

'Yes, yes, it is.'

It's a view of the Mull of Kintyre, at sunrise, from Altacarry Head. It's the exact scene that I was trying to capture that morning with my camera. The blinding burst of light as the sun erupted through the two stripes of cloud, the bright orange reflection in the water, and, in the foreground to the right of the picture, the East Lighthouse, its bottom half white, its top half black with red railings encircling the lantern gallery.

'It's very good,' Mark comments.

By his own admission, Mark knows very little about painting, or photography for that matter. But he's right. The acrylic paint has been applied in thin layers with precise brushstrokes to provide depth and build colour – cheerful orange and powerful purple hues. It's such a vivid depiction of that early morning scene that I can almost taste the cool, briny air and feel the warmth of the sun on my face.

'Why was it in our porch?' Mark asks. 'Did you order it?'

'Yes, yes, I did.' I'm shocked at how easily the lie tumbles out of my mouth. 'It's by a local artist. Someone at the arts and crafts festival recommended him to me, said he was a good painter.' That much is true, at least.

I have a quick image of the elderly man we met at the artisan market as his words come back to me. *Darragh* …

Best builder around these parts ... An excellent painter, too. Billy Duffy didn't mean a house painter. He meant Darragh was a talented artist.

Mark has already lost interest and is pouring milk into the mugs. He's probably still got his mind on his mum. Or his ex-wife. He doesn't see me slip the little envelope into the back pocket of my jeans. He hasn't seen the monogrammed signature on the painting, the intertwined D and M. Darragh Moore.

'The tea's ready. Shall we go into the living room?'

'I'll just pop to the loo.'

Carefully, I put the painting on the floor, propping it up against a cupboard. Once I'm sitting on the toilet, I open the envelope and take out a card. It's blank on one side. I turn it over and read the message, written in neat handwriting.

I promise I wasn't trying to push you over the edge!
Sorry if I scared you.
Dexter

I stare at it, perplexed. I'm not sure what reaction I'm supposed to have. Am I expected to smile at a message purportedly written by Darragh's dog? I don't find it amusing.

My heart is racing, but I don't know why. I look down at the card I'm clutching in my hands. "I promise I wasn't trying to push you over the edge!" Is that a pun? This has certainly put me *on* edge. "Sorry if I scared you." I wasn't scared when the dog sent me flying. I am now. It's not even a real apology. Sorry *if*. Perhaps I'm being pedantic. He painted this especially for me.

Of course! That's why I'm so uneasy. The dog knocked me over; Darragh helped me up. He gave us a desultory invitation to a meal at his place. That should have been enough. But he has gone to the trouble of painting the very picture I was trying to take with my camera. It must have taken him several hours, maybe even several days. It's too much. Not so much over the edge as over the top.

And that's not the only thing bothering me. I've just lied to my husband. I pretended I ordered this painting from a local artist. I've hidden in the toilet to open the envelope. I don't know why I'm being so surreptitious about this. Did I lie to Mark in order to protect Darragh? Mark can be argumentative and he has a quick temper. But he's not prone to violence.

Am I overreacting? Darragh's intentions might have been genuine and innocuous. Maybe he has simply given me a gift to make up for his collie's clumsiness. Hopefully, that's the end of it.

But no matter which way I turn it over in my mind, this doesn't feel like the end. On the contrary, it feels like the beginning of something dangerous.

Chapter 7

Sleep eludes me and, for once, instead of soothing me, my husband's soft snoring irritates me. But that's not what is keeping me awake. My mind seems to have gone into overdrive, a dilemma snaking its way around my head and demanding attention. Should I thank Darragh for his painting? Or do I stay well away from him? While I don't want to appear ungrateful, I'm troubled by his gesture, which seems almost romantic. I mustn't do anything that might encourage this behaviour. I'm married and Darragh is a stranger. I'd like things to stay that way. It will cause a row with Mark if I seek out Darragh to thank him. So, in the end, I decide not to. I also have my own reasons for keeping Darragh at arm's length.

I manage to sleep for a few hours, albeit fitfully, but then I'm woken by another thought. How did Darragh know how to spell my name? He wrote it in neat capitals with a black marker pen on the parcel: KAT. How did he know it wasn't spelt with a "C"? Was it a lucky guess? Or does he know who I am? Could he have read my letters all those years ago?

I get out of bed and go downstairs to make myself a mug of tea. Sitting on the sofa with my legs tucked up, I read my book until Mark gets up. It's a thriller, about a man leading a double life. The "other woman" reminds me of Fiona, but at least the novel takes my mind off Darragh for a while.

After breakfast, Mark says he wants to get some things done around the house. I ask him if he wants some help, but he must sense it's a half-hearted offer. I'm keen to get outside and Mark doesn't appear to mind, so I pack my camera and my new portable tripod into my rucksack and, armed with the walking guide I bought at the arts and crafts sale, I set off for Ushet Point. I haven't been there yet, but I've read online that it's one of the best places on the island to spot seals.

It's a good two-mile walk to Ushet Point, which is situated near the island's southernmost tip. On my way, according to the guidebook, I pass the site of the 1575 Rathlin Island massacre at the hands of Sir Francis Drake; a former police station with a hole in the ground that served as a jail; two lakes – Craigmacagan Lough and Ushet Lough; and two huge rocks called the Mac na Cheeries. Legend has it that should these boulders ever touch, the whole island will sink into the sea.

At Ushet Point, it's as if the seals are waiting for me – a large colony of both common and grey seals. I'm the only person out here and I don't imagine there are ever many people around, and yet, as I approach, the seals don't seem wary of me and allow me to get close to take my photos. I get a superb photo of a grey seal, stretching up from among the rocks and looking directly at the camera through large, inquisitive eyes. I find the common seals even prettier with their round, canine faces. I crouch down and get a few great shots of some of them, lying on the rocks, with the island's third lighthouse at Rue Point in the background.

As I straighten up, a puffin flies towards me, beating its wings rapidly. With its white body, black wings, and orange beak and webbed feet, it's a beautiful sight. I aim my camera at it and focus, and when it's close, I hold down the shutter button to take several pictures in quick succession, capturing the bird with its wings outstretched and its feathers splayed.

I spend an hour or so walking around Ushet Point and Rue Point taking photos. At midday, my stomach growls, urging me to head home for lunch with Mark. I'm feeling so exhilarated from the fresh air and the photos I've taken that I practically float all the way back to Church Bay, where I stop in the shop to buy eggs and bacon to make an omelette.

As I'm leaving the shop with my groceries, there's a woman at the door, about to enter. She steps back to let me come out first. Her long Irish-red hair is tied back this time, but I recognise her immediately. She's the local primary school teacher. She gives me a broad, white smile – she has recognised me, too.

'Hi, I'm Jenny,' she says. 'I didn't get a chance to introduce myself the other day.'

'I'm Katherine.' I realise instantly I should have introduced myself as Kat. If Darragh knows anything about me, anything about what happened all those years ago, he'll know me as Katherine. But it's too late now. 'It's lovely to meet you properly,' I say, turning my attention back to Jenny. 'Did you sell all the greetings cards at the crafts market?'

'Yes, we did, as a matter of fact. That should pay for a few ping-pong paddles!'

We exchange pleasantries. I warm to Jenny straight away. Like everyone else we've met on the island, Jenny knows we've just moved into Causeway Cottage. She tells me her family has lived on Rathlin for many generations. She's friendly and bubbly, but as I listen to her talk about her family, I can't help wondering if the islanders will accept a stranger like me or if I'll never fit in here.

'I should probably get back. We haven't had lunch yet,' I say after a minute or two, holding up the shopping bag. 'I hope we bump into each other again.'

'I'm sure we will. This is a pretty small place.'

Pretty small. The same words Darragh used to describe the island, I remember.

We say goodbye, but as I'm walking away, Jenny calls out to

me. 'Oh, Katherine, there's a pub quiz on Thursday evening. It starts at eight. Would you and your husband like to come? My other half – Tom – will be there. Teams of four.'

'I love pub quizzes, but you'll lose if I'm on your team! I have no general knowledge, except maybe in arts or history.'

'That will be perfect. Tom knows a lot about sports and I'm a bit of a science geek. And, sure, it's only a bit of fun. Check with your husband and let me know.'

I take out my mobile so I can type in Jenny's phone number. I'm already looking forward to the pub quiz and I'm so excited about making a friend here that I almost skip away. I'm halfway up the hill before I realise I didn't think to ask where the quiz was being held, but McCuaig's Bar is probably the only pub on Rathlin. Then I remember that Mark will be away for work next Wednesday and Thursday. Damn! I'll have to ring Jenny and cancel. I'm gutted, coming down abruptly from my earlier high. I'll feel better when I've had something to eat and have looked at my photos on my laptop.

At the front gate, I pause and stare. On the gatepost, there's a wooden sign with the name of our house carved on it: *Causeway Cottage*. The sign doesn't fit, protruding slightly on both sides of the pillar, and the wood itself looks tired and damp. When we moved in, Mark and I agreed we would replace it at some stage with something more elegant, a cast-iron or slate sign.

But the sign is not what has grabbed my attention. It's the metal plaque underneath. I'm amazed I've never noticed the plaque before, but the house sign does detract from it, I suppose. I run my fingers over the two names engraved on the square of stainless steel. K. Fisher. M. Fisher. So that's how Darragh knew to spell Kat with a "K" and not a "C"! Inwardly, I sigh with relief.

Mark is in the kitchen, where he has put up some shelves. Despite the spirit level lying on the table, the shelves look wonky. I'll put some ornaments on them rather than my heavy cookery books. I suspect Mark's burst of home decorating is to prove that he's fully capable of carrying out DIY jobs, even though I implied he wasn't. I dutifully admire his handiwork. I don't point out that standing on a chair to fix some shelves to the wall isn't the same as climbing on top of a house to fix the roof.

'Go and see what I've done in the living room,' Mark says, clearly pleased with himself.

He follows me into the room. At first, I can't work out what has changed in here. It's only when I turn to face Mark that I see it behind him. Darragh's picture. Mark has hung it above the fireplace.

'What do you think?' Mark is looking at me expectantly.

'It's the perfect spot for it,' I manage.

And it is. The fireplace is the focal point of the room and the painting complements it perfectly, its bright colours offsetting the neutral white of the wall. When the fire is lit, it will emphasise the dynamic oranges and yellows of the sunrise.

'Did you notice I've put up our names on the gatepost, too?'

For a second or two, I'm winded and I can't answer. Thoughts start rushing around my head, colliding with each other. I take a deep breath and tell myself this doesn't mean anything. 'Yes, yes I did,' I say. 'Sorry, when did you put the nameplate on the pillar?'

'This afternoon. While you were out.'

It does mean something. It means Darragh didn't see my initial on the plaque because it wasn't there when he delivered the parcel. 'Oh. I thought it had been there a while and I'd only just noticed.' I try to chuckle, but it sounds hollow. 'You have been busy.'

My mouth is dry. Surely Darragh can't know who I am. He can't have known how to spell my name. He must have guessed correctly. He had a fifty-fifty chance of getting it right. He can't possibly remember me. It all happened so long ago.

'Are you OK?' Mark asks. 'You've gone white.' He takes my arm and leads me to the sofa.

'I'm fine. I'm a bit tired, that's all. I didn't sleep very well last night.'

'I'll fetch you a glass of water. Stay there.'

Sitting obediently on the sofa, I stare again at the canvas, hypnotised by something about it that I can't identify. To my relief, I can't make out the monogrammed signature from here. Mark mustn't find out who painted this picture. He'd be furious. More importantly, Darragh mustn't ever discover who I really am. Two identities to keep hidden; two secrets to keep under lock and key.

Chapter 8

I am wearing a low-cut top that's sexy but not slutty. I have curled my hair with tongs. I've applied dark eyeshadow, eyeliner and, most importantly, waterproof mascara so that there's no risk of the smoky eye effect morphing into a tired panda look by the end of the evening. Not only has Mark put up shelves and the painting, he has also put up a mirror in the hallway and I can't resist a quick glance in it to appraise my appearance one last time before leaving the house. I grimace at my reflection, not because I'm dissatisfied with my efforts, but to check there's no lipstick on my teeth.

I haven't been out for a while and I'm insanely excited about going to the local pub quiz. I'm also a bit nervous – I barely know Jenny and I've never met her husband. I wish Mark wasn't away, although I'm also glad that Jenny insisted I should come even without him. I pull on my heeled ankle boots and tuck the hems of my skinny jeans inside. The extra two inches will boost my confidence, although I regret my choice of footwear as I negotiate the downhill walk.

The pub is packed and it takes me a few seconds to spot Jenny seated at a round table in the corner. There's a man opposite her with his back to me. Her husband, presumably. It's only as I reach their table that I recognise him. He's Darragh's workmate – the one I saw sitting with him outside this very pub that day, and standing on the scaffolding an hour or so later.

And then it dawns on me. Oh God, I should have known. Sod's Law. Or Murphy's Law, as Mark would call it.

Jenny confirms my fears. 'This is my husband, Tom. Tom, Katherine. Here, sit down next to me. Tom's mate has agreed to be our fourth quizzer, although he says it's not his thing. Isn't that right, Darragh?'

I look up and his eyes lock onto mine, sending a tingle down my spine. I'm not sure where that feeling has come from or what it is, so I ignore it. His eyes are light brown, the same colour as my own. Feeling increasingly uncomfortable, I lower my gaze and notice I'm fiddling with a cardboard beer mat.

'I can be persuaded to do most things for a pint or two,' he says to Jenny, setting down the drinks he has carried over from the bar. To me, he says, 'What's your poison?'

It's a strange expression and when Darragh says it, it sounds sinister rather than old-fashioned. I'd decided not to drink any alcohol this evening, but I change my mind and ask for a glass of white wine.

I chat to Jenny for a while about St Mary's Primary School. Jenny is the principal and teaches all fifteen pupils, from Primary One to Primary Seven. She's easy to talk to and I bet the kids love her.

Tom gets up to buy another round of drinks, followed by Jenny, who announces that we need crisps and I find myself alone at the table with Darragh. I down the rest of my drink. A knot has formed in my stomach even as the alcohol eases the tension from my shoulders.

'I wanted to thank you for the painting,' I say. Not quite true. I'd decided not to thank him so as not to invite similar gestures on his part. But it would be rude, now we're face to face, not to mention his gift. 'It's beautiful.'

49

'I hope it didn't cause any upset.'

I'm not sure what he means by this, but I shake my head. 'It must have taken you a long time to paint,' I say. 'It wasn't a big deal, you know, with your dog … you didn't have to go to so much trouble.'

'Och, it was no trouble at all. I enjoy painting. I sometimes feel like I missed my vocation. I was always destined to take over my dad's construction business. I didn't get to explore other avenues or work out if I had any other skills or talents.'

'I think you're very talented,' I say without thinking, although it is indeed what I think. I'd resolved not to encourage him and yet that's precisely what I'm doing. It's the alcohol talking, causing me to shed my inhibitions and lose my common sense.

He blushes, making me regret my compliment even more. I'm saved from embarrassing myself – and Darragh – any further, as Jenny and Tom come back, armed with snacks and drinks.

There's a high-pitched squeal as a microphone is turned on.

A male voice booms over the speaker. 'Good evening. And welcome. I'm your quizmaster for tonight. In a wee second, I'll give each team a pen and a piece of paper. At this point, can I please ask everyone to turn off their mobile phones. We can't have anyone slipping out to the loos to cheat, either, so if you need a pee, now's your chance. Otherwise, you'll have to wait until the break!'

Another squeal as the mic is set down for the paper and pens to be handed out. Jenny takes charge of writing the answers for our team. Tom suggests the name: "Builders' Team". No one can come up with anything better, so we go with that.

The quizmaster's voice comes over the speaker again. 'There will be ten questions in each round and six rounds altogether – general knowledge; sports; arts, literature and entertainment; science; music and, finally, a picture round. Let's get started on the general knowledge, shall we?'

For the first round, I know the answers to a couple of

questions, but I'm useless when we get to the sports round. So is Jenny. Neither of us knows the answer to a single question. Luckily for us, Tom and Darragh seem to know all the answers but one. I fare better on the arts, literature and entertainment round.

Between each round, we mark another team's sheets. Tom assigns this task to Jenny, saying it's part of her profession. No one laughs at his joke, but we all laugh when Jenny gives him the finger for it.

During the break, I get up to buy a round of drinks. I've already had two glasses of wine and I'm feeling tipsy, so I switch to fruit juice this time. Although I ate dinner before coming out, I'm hungry. I order two plates of chips so everyone can dig in. Darragh has come to the bar to help me carry everything and when we get back to the table, I find myself chatting to him again.

'So, how's Dexter?' I ask.

'He's a bit of a bad dog at the moment.'

'Oh?'

'Collies need a lot of exercise and Dex likes to come running with me, but I've an injury at the minute. My knee's banjaxed.'

'You're sure it's the knee and not the IT band?'

It slips out and I'm about to explain, in case I've used obscure running jargon – Mark wouldn't have a clue what I was talking about – but if Darragh's a runner, he probably knows what it is and I don't want to be condescending.

He smiles and leans across the table, closer to me. 'Hope not. I don't think it's that serious. Just need to rest it. Rest, ice, compression and elevation, you know the drill.'

It's my turn to smile. For the second time this evening, the wine numbs my brain-to-mouth filter and I hear myself offering to take Dexter running with me. I regret the words as soon as they come out of my mouth. I'd intended to avoid Darragh. I was scared he might know me. But he can't know who I am. Who I *was*. He'd hardly be so nice to me if he did.

Darragh crams a few chips into his mouth before replying. 'That would be great. If you're sure it's no bother.'

He gives me his number so I can let him know when I go for a run and I add him to the contacts in my phone. The same number, no doubt, that was scribbled on the business card I threw into the litter bin not long ago, as I came out of the crafts market at the Branson Centre. We chat some more, but I'm careful not to ask too many questions about his past or his background. He asks me about my photography, about Mark, about our decision to move here. He's attentive when I reply and I realise I'm enjoying chatting to him.

Then he says something that throws me completely. 'So, Kat, you're obviously English whereas your husband's a local. Had you been to Northern Ireland before you met him?'

I answer Darragh's question, but the quizmaster chooses that moment to start up again. I hope his voice coming over the speaker has drowned out the lie I've just told. He gives us the scores so far and we're in the lead – but only just. After the next three rounds, the final results are announced and we come second by half a point.

'What's the prize for the winners?' I ask.

'A free meal each,' Tom says.

'But the runners-up get a free drink each,' Darragh says. 'The only caveat is that prizes are not redeemable this evening.'

'Clever,' I comment.

A bell rings for last orders. Jenny and Tom offer to drop me home.

'I have to go for a wee first,' Jenny says. 'I've drunk far too much.'

'My thoughts entirely,' I say.

Tom pipes up with some comment about women always going to the toilet in pairs and Jenny sticks her finger up at him again.

As Jenny and I stand in front of the mirror in the ladies' loos, washing our hands at adjacent sinks, our reflections unleash a memory: my fifteen-year-old self, standing next to my friend

Erin as we looked at ourselves and each other in the bathroom mirror in the holiday cottage my grandparents had rented for the second summer in a row. We were getting ready for the céilí – the dance – that was being held at the community hall that evening. Erin wasn't used to wearing make-up. In fact, she didn't even own more than a lip balm. I showed her how to apply foundation, eyeliner, blush and lipstick, passing the make-up to her one piece after the other, and watching her in the mirror as she copied me, applying the make-up to her own face.

I lent her a short skirt for the occasion and a tight crop top. She said her mother would ground her for a month if she could see her. I imagine Erin staring at me now through accusing eyes in the mirror and I close my own eyes to erase the image.

'You seem to have hit it off with Darragh,' Jenny says, transporting me back to the present.

'Yes.' There's a pause until I come up with something to say. 'I've met him before … once before. His dog … well, he ran into me.'

'Ran into you?'

'Hmm. He knocked me flying, actually.'

'Oh dear. I'm sure Darragh was mortified.'

For some reason I don't tell Jenny about the painting, although that's what I'm thinking about. I can see it in my mind's eye as if it were on the wall, here, in the ladies' toilets.

'He was very apologetic,' I say. Remembering that Darragh didn't apologise in so many words, I add, 'Well, his dog was, anyway.'

I want to open up, to confide in Jenny about the picture that Darragh took the time and trouble to paint for me, about the card supposedly signed by Dexter. I'd love to get her take on this. I wait for her to prompt me, to ask what I mean.

But she says, 'In any case, Darragh certainly seems taken with you. It's strange, I thought maybe he was wary around women. Shy, you know.'

I pinch my eyebrows in question at her in the mirror.

'He has never been very friendly towards me. Oh, don't get me wrong. He's not unfriendly,' she amends hastily. 'I think he avoids me. I wondered if he was that way with women in general, but it would seem not. It's obviously just me.'

'I'm sure that's not true,' I say. 'Perhaps he keeps his distance because he's mates with your husband and doesn't want to cause a problem, you know, with them working together and all.'

'No, it's more than that. I don't think he likes me. I've no notion why.'

Jenny's reflection gives me a wistful smile before turning away and walking over to the hand dryer.

Jenny might not have a clue why Darragh is awkward around her, but I think it might have something to do with what she looks like. Or rather, who she looks like. With her beautiful green eyes and fiery hair, Jenny reminds me so much of my friend Erin. At least, she was my friend until I let her down.

Darragh must see the likeness, too.

Chapter 9

Before long, we've established a routine. I text Darragh in the evenings when Mark is away for work and Darragh stops off at Causeway Cottage the next morning. Dexter sits on the passenger seat of Darragh's van, his black and white head sticking out of the window and his long, pink tongue lolling out of his mouth. I wait by the gate. As soon as Darragh pulls up and opens the door for him, Dexter leaps out of the van. At the end of our run, I drop off Dexter at the building site in Church Bay.

This morning, though, Darragh arrives a little early and I'm still inside, drinking my coffee. Through the window, I see him striding up the short driveway to the house, the collie at his heels.

'I'll be ready in a second,' I say, opening the front door before Darragh can knock. 'You can leave Dexter with me, if you need to get on.'

'No, I'm not in a hurry.'

He eyes my espresso cup. I'm not sure if he's looking at it longingly or if he disapproves of drinking coffee before a run. He's standing on the doorstep and makes no move to walk away. I need to say something. It's my turn to speak and this is getting awkward.

'Would you like a coffee?' I ask, hoping he'll decline.

'Yes, thank you.' I wonder if he was expecting to be asked in and think he's presumptuous if that's the case, but he adds, 'I've left the engine idling. I'll just grab the keys.'

If Darragh realises I only take Dexter with me on the days when Mark's not here, he hasn't said anything. At some point, I need to tell Mark, but I keep putting off that discussion.

The exchange with Darragh is less stilted once he has stepped inside the house. For a few minutes, anyway. He tells me about an annual road run on Rathlin at the end of August and says I should enter. He's hoping to do it if his injury has healed by then.

'I'll think about it,' I say. 'It's two months away. Your knee should be better by then.'

Darragh also tells me Dexter is behaving better and his coat looks nicer.

'He's much happier,' Darragh says, bending down to fondle the dog's ears. 'Who's a lucky boy, going for three runs this week?'

He's serious as he talks to the dog and I get a sudden urge to laugh. As he straightens up, I hand him his cup of coffee, hiding my smile behind my own cup.

'I like what you've done to the place,' he says, looking around. 'It's cosier and more modern.'

'I didn't realise you'd already been inside.'

'Yes. I did some work for old Mr Kelly a while ago.'

Presumably not on the roof, I think. We're in the kitchen and other than a lick of paint, a few rickety shelves and our American fridge-freezer instead of the old refrigerator, we haven't changed anything in here. But with our stuff, it looks homely, I suppose.

'I should show you something,' I say.

Darragh follows me into the living room. He spots it immediately and his face lights up. 'Oh, you've hung up the painting!'

'Well, my husband did, yes. I think it looks great above the fireplace.'

'It does! It'll look even better when the fire's lit.'

'That's what I thought!'

His eyes stay focused on the painting as he asks, 'Did your husband … Was he OK …?'

He doesn't finish his sentence, but I know what he was going to say. He was about to ask how Mark reacted when he realised who had painted the picture. I've decided not to tell Mark who the artist is, but there's no way I'm telling Darragh that. It would be disloyal. But I'm already being disloyal. To both Mark and Darragh.

Darragh's attention is drawn to a framed photo of my parents on the mantelpiece. He bends towards it to examine it. 'Your parents?' he asks.

'Yes. My dad died a long time ago. It's an old photo.'

Darragh nods. 'It's horrible, losing a parent. Where does your mum live?'

'In the West Country. She runs a bed and breakfast in North Devon. I also have uncles, aunts and cousins in Somerset.'

'Sounds like a big family.'

'Not really. I'm an only child. What about you?' The question spews out of my mouth before I can swallow it down.

Darragh doesn't answer for a few seconds. I throw him a sideways glance and realise from his expression that I've dealt him a blow. I search for a way to cushion it, but I don't know the full story. Only part of it. The incomplete version I have isn't Darragh's side of the story. And I was never told the ending.

The silence that stretches between us is too long, too uncomfortable. 'Big family? Lots of aunts and uncles?' I add eventually. It's the best I can come up with to make up for my blunder.

'No.' His expression becomes less tense. 'Surprisingly small for a Catholic family in Northern Ireland. My dad retired a few years ago. He lives in Derry near his brother and sister.'

I notice he doesn't mention his mum. I assume she's dead, given his earlier comment about losing a parent. I don't know what to say. The next logical question – whether Darragh has siblings himself – is the one I'm trying to avoid, for my sake as well as Darragh's. If he wants to tell me, he'll tell me in his own good time. I'm scared of what he'll say if I ask him. And I'm not sure I'm ready to know what happened next.

'I should take off,' Darragh says, putting an end to our conversation. He drains his coffee and pats the dog, who stays firmly by my side. As I'm doing up the laces on my trainers, Darragh hoots his horn and drives away. I step outside, lock the door and put the key into the little zip-up pocket of my shorts. Then I'm off, too, heading in the opposite direction with Dexter dogtrotting next to me.

I have my earphones in as I run up the hill, but the voice in my head is determined to drown out the music from my playlist and make itself heard. I don't like keeping secrets from my husband, but I'm keeping three. And they're all tangled around Darragh. Mark has no idea who painted the picture; nor does he know I send Darragh text messages to arrange to take his dog for runs. Above all, he doesn't know that my path once came close to crossing Darragh's. Very close. Evidently, Darragh doesn't know that last secret, either. It has to stay that way.

When Mark gets home this evening, I'll tell him about my runs with Dexter. If he notices the monogrammed signature on the painting one day, I won't lie about it. That will have to do. That's as honest as I can be. This resolution muzzles my guilty conscience for now and I tune in to the music, lengthening my stride as I reach the brow of the hill and the narrow road flattens out.

We're in the middle of nowhere, following a waymarked route through the nature reserve to the west of the island, when Dexter pulls his stunt. He dives under a gate and into a field full of sheep. I call him again and again, but he won't come back. There's a farmhouse and some barns behind the field. Remembering an incident from my childhood in Devon, my pulse, already fast from the physical exercise, speeds up even more. Our next-door neighbour lost control of his dog while walking along a public footpath that cut through a field. The dog started chasing the sheep and the farmer fetched his shotgun and killed the dog to protect the pregnant ewes. Our neighbour and the farmer came to blows over it.

I look all around, but I can't see anyone. I've hardly seen anyone since I started out on my run. I stop calling the dog, partly to avoid drawing attention to myself and Dexter, but also because I'm shouting myself hoarse to no purpose. It's the end of June now, I reason. Lambing season is over. If the farmer does spot Dexter, hopefully he won't shoot him. Then again, there are loads of lambs in the field. The farmer might shoot Dexter to protect the lambs rather than the ewes. How would I tell Darragh his dog is dead?

Dexter eventually comes back, bringing me the entire flock of sheep that he has rounded up. He lies down at my feet and looks up at me through his big blue eyes. He seems to be proud of himself and waiting for me to praise him.

'I don't have any treats if that's what you're after. And you haven't earned one anyway.' He has earned my grudging admiration, though. I'm impressed Dexter knew how to round up the herd. Instinct, I suppose. 'Think you're clever, do you?' I continue and he wags his tail. I pat his head. 'You nearly scared me to death, you bad dog.'

Dexter lowers his head onto his paws, contrite. He knows the words "bad dog".

'Come on. Let's go.'

I wish I'd asked Darragh for a lead, but until now Dexter hasn't left my side when he's been out with me. We set off again, but just as I relax into my stride, he bolts off. I race after him, but I can't keep up. We sprint for five or six hundred metres until he runs into a driveway and makes a beeline for the front door.

This time the mutt comes when I call him, thankfully, and stays glued to my side all the way to Church Bay.

I greet Darragh with an outburst. 'So much for your dog being better behaved!' And the whole incident with the sheep spills out in one go, even though I'm out of breath.

'Aye. He's done that before. It's in his blood. Collies are sheep-dogs, you know. Amazing, really. He's never been trained to do that.'

'He hasn't been trained to come back when he's called either! He gave me such a fright! I thought the farmer would shoot him.'

I'm expecting Darragh to apologise on the dog's behalf. But he says, 'Oh, no. All the way out near Kebble Nature Reserve did you say? Big field on the top of the hill at Kinramer, was it? The farmer's my neighbour. He wouldn't shoot my dog.'

'But there were no houses around for … Oh!' It dawns on me why Dexter ran away from me. 'It must have been your place we passed. Was it? Dexter ran up the driveway. Big greystone house with no gate?' I don't add what I really thought. Completely isolated.

'Aye. That sounds like my place right enough. Listen, I know Dexter is grateful, even if he didn't show it today. I'll understand if you don't want to take him any—'

'No. I love the company.'

I only realise how tense and irritated I've been as those feelings evaporate, but I try to keep my face stern. I want Darragh to take this seriously. Does the man ever apologise properly? Without warning, a giggle bubbles up inside me. I try to swallow it down, but it escapes as an embarrassing honking noise. I think it's due more to relief than amusement, though.

'He looked so proud of himself, rounding up all those sheep for me.'

Darragh laughs. His laugh is highly communicable and it's impossible to stay mad at him. I bend down and kiss Dexter on the head before jogging home.

When I get to the cottage, I pause at the front gate, surprised. Mark is sitting on the doorstep. He's not due back until this evening and my first thought is that he's checking up on me, trying to catch me out. I immediately reject that idea. His body language is all wrong. He's cradling his head in his hands and he hasn't seen me. He looks utterly dejected.

A memory comes to me – the first time I met Mark. I'd done some headshots for his company late one afternoon and afterwards I wound up at their local pub with them. Like me, Mark was talked into going against his better judgement, or against his will. He looked then like he does now. Vulnerable. Sitting on his own, holding his head in his hands.

We got chatting. Mark's accent was similar to my dad's. My father had grown up in Belfast, where my grandparents had lived until they died. My grandparents liked to come for days out to Ballycastle, where Mark had grown up, and I'd spent a week there with them the summer I turned fourteen and another week the following summer. It was hardly a remarkable coincidence, but Mark and I liked to think we were destined to meet one day. We seemed to have a lot in common. Mark told me his father had died of a heart attack. Mine had died a few years previously of prostate cancer. He was an only child. So was I.

He talked a lot about his father and said how worried he was about his mum, who was getting forgetful and didn't have anyone to look after her anymore. I was touched at how much he cared about his parents. I thought he was pouring out all his troubles; I felt flattered he was confiding in me. I didn't know until much later the real reason he was so upset that evening. His wife had asked him for a divorce.

'Mark. What are you doing here?' I ask now, approaching him.

He looks up, startled. 'I didn't take my keys. I'm locked out. I rang you, several times, but you didn't answer.'

There's a spare key on the ledge of the kitchen window, behind a hideous garden gnome that my mother-in-law gave me for Christmas one year. But I don't remind Mark of that now.

'My phone was in airplane mode so it wouldn't ring while

I was running,' I say apologetically. 'I meant, how come you're home early? Have you been here long?'

'I don't know. I've lost track of time.'

I notice that his face is streaked with tears. This shocks me. I've never seen Mark cry.

'What's the matter?' I sit down on the step next to him and wrap my arms around him. 'Have you … have you lost your job?' It's the only thing I can think of. 'Has something happened, Mark?'

But he sobs into my chest and I can't make out his next words.

Chapter 10

Mark is inconsolable. I help him to his feet and he puts his arm around me, leaning onto me as if he's wounded, as I lead him into the house. It's only when I've made him sit on the sofa and held him for a minute or so that he's able to tell me coherently what the matter is. Then he spurts it out in one breath.

'My mum. She died during the night. She's dead, Kat. Gone. A carer found her this morning.'

'Oh no. I'm so sorry, Mark.' I make all the right noises and say all the things you're meant to say, but none of them seem to help. I make Mark a mug of tea with an extra teaspoon of sugar. I think that's what you're supposed to give someone who is in shock. Poor Mark. He was so close to his mum. He must be absolutely devastated.

'I need to get washed and changed, Mark,' I say. 'Then we'll take the ferry and go to the care home together. OK?' He manages a nod.

The day has got off to a bad start and it's likely to get worse. I have a headache, which I'd put down to Dexter's antics stressing me out, but now my stomach is bloated, too, and I know even before I dive into the shower that I've got my period. It's only been a few months since I stopped taking the pill, but it feels like

63

years. So much has happened in such a short time that it seems longer somehow. Looking back, I can't believe that five weeks ago, we were still living in London.

I shed a few silent tears in the shower, but I don't mention my period to Mark. I know he wants a baby, too, but it affects him less than me every month it doesn't work out. He doesn't build up his hopes the same way or feel as if his body is failing him. I'd like him to comfort me and tell me to be patient. But right now, with the terrible news he has just received, I need to be there for him rather than the other way round. He'll have more than enough to deal with today.

I get dressed as quickly as I can and wolf down some tea and toast. Then we take *The Rathlin Express* to Ballycastle.

'How are you holding up?' I ask, feeling distinctly queasy, as the catamaran bounces from the trough of one wave into the crest of the next one, spraying a small arc of water over us.

'It's so unexpected,' Mark says. His words are slurred and I attribute that to the shock, until he leans into me, putting his head on my shoulder and I smell alcohol on his breath. Whiskey. Did he pour himself a drink while I was in the shower? Under the circumstances, I don't blame him.

'Well, your mum *was* ill, Mark,' I say. 'That's the main reason we moved here.'

My words sound hollow and I feel hollow. We moved here to be closer to Mark's ailing mother. Now she's dead, I feel cheated, trapped, somehow, even though I'm settling in here. I berate myself for having such thoughts when Mark has just lost his mother, but I can't help it.

It's not far to Marconi Care Home – five minutes on foot, at most. We're asked to sign in, so we duly write our names in the visitor book. Mrs Gillespie, the manager, is expecting us and ushers us into her office. We sit down in uncomfortable wooden seats opposite her. It feels like being sent to the head's office at school, although that only happened to me once, after I was caught smoking behind the sports hall with some classmates.

Mrs Gillespie knows Mark, but this is the first time I've met her. She's wearing a cheap suit that emphasises her short, plump build. She has a kind, rotund face. Her long, dark fringe is uneven, and I wonder if she can see out from under it and if she cut it herself. She gives Mark a tentative smile, but he doesn't respond. I reach over and take his hand.

'Firstly, let me say how sorry I am about your mother, Mr Fisher,' she begins. 'We were very fond of her, here at Marconi.'

Somehow, I doubt that, but I keep my thoughts to myself. I glance at Mark, whose glassy eyes are fixed on our fingers, entwined in his lap. His eyebrows unite in a bewildered frown. He still can't take this in.

'Thank you,' he manages, without looking up.

She offers us tea or coffee, but Mark shakes his head, so I decline politely. I scan the room. The wallpaper – a hideous, retro design with greens and browns – is adorned with still-life prints. The time-travel vibe resonating from the decoration is at odds with the manager's black leather swivel chair, the black oak executive desk and the iMac on it.

'This must be a terrible shock for you both,' Mrs Gillespie says.

Out of the corner of my eye, I see Mark nod. He hasn't spoken much since he told me the news. It's only now that I realise he hasn't told me how his mother died. For Mark's sake as much as for his mum's sake, I hope she didn't suffer.

As if reading my mind, Mrs Gillespie turns to me. 'As I told your husband on the phone, Mrs Fisher, your mother-in-law passed away, peacefully, in her sleep,' she says. 'Her carer found her dead this morning and I rang your husband as soon as she alerted me.'

'What happens now?' I ask.

'Well, usually, the next of kin formally identifies the relative, then we arrange for the body of the deceased to be taken to the hospital mortuary, where a doctor will issue a medical certificate, which will enable you to register the death. The body is kept at the hospital until the funeral is arranged.'

Mrs Gillespie delivers this information, practically without taking a breath, in a matter-of-fact tone. Working in a nursing home, she must be used to death, but I find her explanations morbid and impersonal.

'So there won't be a post-mortem?' I ask.

'You can contact the coroner's office to ask for a post-mortem to be carried out if you so wish, although this is only necessary in the event of a sudden or suspicious death.'

'It *is* a bit sudden,' Mark pipes up.

Mrs Gillespie looks from me to Mark and back again. 'Would you like me to help you arrange for a post-mortem?' she offers.

'No!' Mark sounds horrified.

'No, thank you, Mrs Gillespie,' I say. 'That won't be necessary.'

'OK.' She gives me a tight, satisfied smile, as if I've given her the right answer. I notice one of her front teeth is badly chipped. She turns to Mark. 'Do you feel up to formally identifying your mother, Mr Fisher?' she asks. 'Then I can call the hospital.'

We get up and Mrs Gillespie leads the way out of her office. She leads us along the corridor towards my mother-in-law's bedroom.

'Ah, this is Nadine,' Mrs Gillespie says, stopping as a young woman with a blond ponytail comes out of the bedroom next to my mother-in-law's. Wearing a light blue tunic with *Marconi Care Home* embroidered on the pocket, she's easily identifiable as one of the carers. 'Nadine is the one who found Mrs Fisher this morning,' Mrs Gillespie continues. 'It was a bit of a shock for her, bless her. She hasn't been working here for very long. Nadine, this is Mr and Mrs Fisher.'

'Mr and Mrs Fisher, I'm so sorry for your loss,' Nadine says.

'Thank you,' I say. My voice comes out croaky, which surprises me. I'm not sad – I didn't like my mother-in-law much – but all of a sudden, I feel overwhelmed. I blink back tears and swallow down the lump in my throat. I have to keep it together. Mark has just lost his mum.

'I'm so sorry,' Nadine repeats, then, addressing Mark, she adds, 'At least you got to see her last night before she passed away.' I look at Mark, but he's staring at Nadine and says nothing.

'Thank you,' I repeat, as Mrs Gillespie opens the bedroom door.

*

I can't help feeling curious about the carer's comment, but it's not until we leave the nursing home that I get a chance to ask Mark what she meant.

'I was about to ask you the same question,' he says, to my surprise. 'You didn't visit Mum yesterday, did you?'

'No! Did you think that carer – what was her name? Natasha? Nadia? Nadine, that's it. Did you think Nadine was talking to me?'

'Well, *I* certainly wasn't here last night,' he says. 'I was at the Europa Hotel in Belfast, as you know.' Mark always stays in the Europa when he's in Belfast on business.

I remember signing my name in the visitor book when we arrived at Marconi Care Home about an hour ago. There had been only a handful of entries the day before – hardly surprising for a weekday, perhaps – and we were the first to sign in today. Mark's name definitely wasn't among yesterday's visitors. And neither was mine, obviously.

'Well, either way, she must have been mistaken,' I say.

'Clearly,' Mark agrees. 'Perhaps she saw me on a different day and got confused.' His voice breaks slightly as he adds, 'I wish I had seen her one last time before she died.'

'You know, maybe Nadine isn't the one who was mistaken. Perhaps your mother mentioned to the carer that you'd been in to see her. Your mum's mind was muddled and she got dates and people mixed up all the time. She might have genuinely thought you were with her shortly before the end.'

Mark manages a tight smile at that. 'I'll hold on to that idea,' he says.

On the way to the harbour to take the ferry home, we walk past the community hall. As we do, I imagine I can hear the loud Irish music and raucous laughter from that night all those years ago, drowning out the sound of someone calling for help, calling my name.

The sun elbows its way through the clouds. My headache has got worse and I close my eyes for a few seconds to shut out the light. Perhaps if I don't look directly at the place where that horrific incident took place all those years ago, I'll also be able to shut out the memory before it can fully take shape in my mind.

Chapter 11

Mark mopes around the house while I organise the funeral. When I take the ferry to Ballycastle to meet the funeral director or sort out paperwork at my mother-in-law's house, Mark tags along, wearing black clothes and a long face. He's uncommunicative and withdrawn, and he flinches when I touch him. I can't stand seeing him broken like this and I don't know what to say or do to help ease his pain. His mood is contagious and I feel very low, too. I had no intention of visiting his mother more than was strictly necessary and I won't miss her, yet her death has also affected me. I'm overcome with a sense of loss, although not for the same reasons as Mark.

He has taken a week off work and it's only now, when he's with me all day long, that I realise how lonely I am. I've left behind everything in London. We moved here so Mark could be near his mother to look after her. It didn't seem like a big sacrifice at the time. But now she's gone, it has left me bereft, as if I've lost not only my job and my friends, but also a big chunk of myself. My life has become directionless.

I had aspirations when we came here. I imagined setting up photography tours on the island for tourists, once I'd worked out the best spots myself. I planned to update my website and sell landscape photos of Rathlin Island. I also had a long list of attractions to photograph on the mainland – the Giant's Causeway, the Mountains of Mourne and, of course, some of the film locations for *Game of Thrones*.

I can still do all this, I reason with myself. I haven't been here long. I need to give it time. I've already made two friends, sort of, even though Mark wouldn't approve of one of them. But Darragh and Jenny are the only people on this island who go out of their way to make me feel welcome here. Both of them sent me text messages, asking if we're all right and if there's anything they can do. I didn't tell either of them that Mark's mother had died, but word has a way of getting out and about on this island and, somehow, they knew. I'm glad. Their messages have buoyed me up these past few days.

The morning after the funeral, I'm in the kitchen, making breakfast, and Mark is upstairs in the shower when my ringtone blares out. I grab the phone from the worktop and stare at the name on the screen. *Darragh Moore*. He has never called me on my mobile before. I hesitate for a few seconds only. Then I tap on the red circle to decline the call.

I'm suddenly annoyed with Darragh, but I'm not sure why. Did I expect him to limit his contact with me to text messages in reply to my own and small talk when I dropped off his dog? I've never told him that Mark doesn't know about him and Dexter. So why does it feel as if Darragh has crossed an invisible line or trampled down an imaginary boundary? I scold myself for being unreasonable. Darragh is being friendly. I'm a newcomer to a small community and he has welcomed me.

When Mark comes downstairs a minute or two later, I'm still holding the phone. Mark says something, but I don't register what it is. I'm wondering why Darragh rang and if he has left a message. Mark repeats his comment, something about the dodgy Internet connection in this place, but I'm distracted by the text notification sound on my phone. I glance down. It's from Darragh.

Fancy a picnic? Jenny's idea.
Sun, fresh air, good company, wine … sound tempting?

I sit down at the table and bite into a slice of toast. I'll answer his text after breakfast. I don't know whether to accept the invitation or not. I'd love to go for a picnic with Darragh and Jenny. Anything to get out of the gloominess that has descended on our cottage over the last week. Presumably, the invitation includes Mark, though, which means I'll be found out. Darragh is bound to bring up my runs with Dexter. As if on cue, the phone dings again. I can't resist picking up my mobile and reading the message.

Dex will be there. He misses you. He hopes you've forgiven him for herding the sheep.

I try to suppress my smile so Mark won't see.

'Who was it?' he asks, nodding at the phone.

It's my line. This is the part where I should fess up. 'Jenny.' I wince inwardly at yet another lie rolling off my tongue. 'She wants to know if we'd like to go on a picnic with them.'

'With Jenny and her husband? It's good of them to ask us. What did you say his name was?'

'Tom. Er … Darragh will probably be there, too. He's Tom's workmate.'

'Ah.' Mark's expression darkens.

'I know you two didn't exactly hit it off, but he's all right. He was in the pub on the evening of the quiz. I talked to him a bit then. I've taken his dog running a couple of times.'

Mark bends forwards, over his mug, and I think he's about to spurt out his coffee. But he manages to swallow it down. 'What?'

'I offered to do it. Darragh has a bad leg. The dog kept me company. It's desolate running around the island. Most days I don't see anyone at all.'

I observe Mark grappling with his emotions. His face reddens and his eyes blaze. He didn't want either of us to have anything to do with Darragh. I brace myself for his outburst. But he doesn't seem to have the energy to get worked up. He hasn't spoken this much all week and he appears to be losing impetus. Or interest.

'They're nice people, Mark. They sent sympathy cards and flowers to the funeral home.' I wasn't going to tell him that. It slipped out, like the lie just now. I detached Darragh's card from the flowers and threw it away. Along with the elaborate wreath and card from Fiona. I thought it better that Mark didn't see them. I didn't want him getting any more upset than he already was over his mother's death. That's how I justified it to myself, anyway.

'Oh, well,' Mark says with an exaggerated sigh. 'We may as well go on the picnic. Jenny seemed nice when we saw her at the crafts fair. And it sounds like Darragh owes you a favour. Maybe he'll give us mates' rates for the roof.'

I gape at Mark, incredulous, but I let it go. He knows about Darragh, Dexter and me. That's the main thing. And that conversation went a lot better than I thought it would. I just hope Darragh doesn't mention the painting when we're on our picnic.

*

We meet up at the aptly if unimaginatively named Sandy Beach. I introduce Mark to Jenny and Tom. Mark shakes their hands heartily as they offer their condolences and say all the right things. I thank them for the flowers. Mark is noticeably more aloof when he is introduced to Darragh. He must grip Darragh's hand too hard because Darragh grimaces and flexes his hand when Mark lets go. Mark looks uncomfortable as he finds himself sitting next to Darragh on the picnic rug that has been laid out on the sand. Dexter squeezes between Jenny and me and sits with his head on my lap.

Darragh is all smiles and charming with everyone, handing out plastic plates, cutlery and goblets, and pouring the wine. As we help ourselves to potato salad, crisps, sausage rolls and sandwiches, Darragh politely asks Mark about his job and the transfer to Belfast. Mark's initial animosity has dispersed. But in Darragh's hazel eyes, normally so like my own, there's something unrecognisable. As I try to read his expression, he puts on his sunglasses and I'm left wondering if the malicious gleam I thought I saw was due to my imagination or even the sun.

After lunch, we all swim in the sea, including Dexter. I can't help noticing Darragh's toned, tanned body. I try not to stare, even when Jenny voices my thoughts out loud. Everyone else's skin is white in comparison, especially Jenny's. She has inherited the Celtic pallor, although she quips that if her freckles continue to multiply, she'll end up looking suntanned. Darragh brushes off Jenny's compliments about his tan. I get the impression he's studiously avoiding having to talk to her alone and I remember what Jenny said about him being standoffish around her.

The water is cold and when we get out, my arms are pricked with goose bumps. I made coffee before coming to the beach and I pour it from the flask into the plastic cups. With the hot liquid and the sun, I soon warm up again.

Sitting cross-legged on the picnic rug, I look out to sea and admire the view while Tom dozes and Jenny talks to me. She tells me her grandparents lived on Rathlin Island and her parents still do, but until she started teaching here, she wanted to get away. She asks me about my photography and then tells me about a recent art class with her pupils where they came outside and painted or drew pictures of Church Bay.

I listen attentively until I overhear Mark mention my name. I try to eavesdrop on his conversation with Darragh. Mark is talking about my background. I hear him say that my dad was originally from Belfast. My heart misses a beat. I want to shake my head at Mark, warn him not to reveal too much, but I can't

73

catch his eye. I can hear from Darragh's intonations that he's asking Mark questions, but Jenny has asked me one and she's waiting for my answer. In trying to keep track of both conversations simultaneously, I haven't followed either of them. I ask Jenny to repeat what she said.

It's not until later, after another swim and during a game of ball with Dexter, that Darragh and I get a chance to chat. He tells me his knee is better and asks if I'd like to run with him and Dexter from now on. He's wearing only Bermuda shorts and I have to make a conscious effort to look up and not let my eyes linger on his broad, bare chest.

He changes the subject abruptly as we go back to the others and his expression is suddenly serious. 'Mark tells me you spent a lot of time in Ballycastle when you were growing up,' he says, his smile wavering as he sits down.

I glare at Mark, even though he can't possibly understand what he has said wrong. He couldn't have realised I didn't want Darragh to know I had any connections with Northern Ireland. But this is what I was afraid of. This could give me away.

I remember Darragh asking me on the night of the pub quiz if I'd been to Northern Ireland before meeting Mark. I'd hoped he hadn't heard my answer over the voice of the quizmaster, but now I wonder if he has caught me in a lie. Perhaps I've given myself away.

I weigh up my words before replying. 'No, not really. My grandparents lived in Belfast and they brought me to Ballycastle a couple of times on day trips when I was little.' I don't mention I spent a week here the summer I was fourteen and came back for another two weeks the following year, too.

'But you met Mark in London?' There's something I can't identify in Darragh's tone. Disbelief? Confusion? It feels as if he's trying to catch me out.

But I'm on safer ground here. I can tell the truth. 'Yes, that's right. I did some work for Mark's company and then we all went to the pub. Mark and I got talking and realised we both had roots in Northern Ireland, although I hadn't set foot there for years. My father moved to England way before I was born. I had no reason to come over after my grandparents died.' I can feel everyone's eyes on me. Jenny and Tom are listening in, too. I try to make a joke of it. 'I heard Mark's accent and I was smitten.' I smile. 'He had me at "bout ye".' Jenny and Tom chuckle politely and Mark beams.

Darragh's face is impassive. He turns to Mark. 'But you grew up in Ballycastle?'

'I did, yes.'

'And you never met Kat while she was here? Did you not have mutual friends or something like that?'

I try to get in first. 'I only came once or twice when I was really—'

But Mark interrupts me. 'No, as I told you earlier, the ties to Northern Ireland are just a coincidence. Kat's eight years younger than me. I don't suppose we moved in the same circles when she was in Ballycastle. She was probably at the beach building sandcastles while I was down the pub getting stocious.' Mark looks pleased with himself for that comment. I refrain from retorting that what he has said doesn't reflect well on him, and not only because of his flawed mental arithmetic.

'I grew up in North Devon,' I say to Darragh. 'I barely know Ballycastle and I didn't have any friends in Northern Ireland at all.'

Darragh shoots me a look and I get the disturbing sensation he can see through me. Somehow, he knows I've just told a lie.

Chapter 12

St Mary's Primary School is a long white building, perched on top of the hill overlooking the bay, and it takes me only a few minutes to walk there. Jenny has been looking out for me and greets me at the door.

'I owe you a huge favour,' she says, clasping her hands together in front of her, as if in prayer, to show her gratitude. 'I was worried you wouldn't be able to come at such short notice.'

Jenny rang me an hour ago to say that the photographer, who was due to come over from the mainland to take the school photos that day, was ill.

'I didn't want to have to postpone this,' she continues. 'The twins, Sinéad and Orlagh, went to the hairdresser's in Ballycastle yesterday to get French plaits and their mum told me this morning they didn't sleep well last night because they were worried about messing up their hair. I think some of the parents have even ironed the kids' shirts for today.' She grins.

I follow her through the school, which consists of only two rooms, to her classroom, where the pupils are busy writing in their exercise books. They look up at me curiously.

'This is Mrs Fisher,' Jenny says to them. 'She'll be taking your photos in a few minutes.' When they continue to stare, she adds pointedly, 'When you've finished your work.' They all follow her cue and get on with their writing. Jenny turns to me. 'Have you got any ideas?'

'What does your photographer usually do?'

'He takes individual photos of the pupils sitting at their desks, then standing against the white wall in the corridor,' she says. 'And finally, a photo of all the pupils together.'

'Well, that will be easy enough,' I say. 'Would you like me to take some shots outside? The weather is perfect today and we could sit the pupils on the wall just down the hill a bit and get the sea in the background.'

'Oh, that's a fantastic idea. We've never done outdoor pictures before! Last time the old guy came, it was bucketing it down, mind.'

I take photos of each child and of the two sets of siblings at the school, too. I set up shots indoors and outdoors and some photos of all fifteen children together with Jenny. Patrick, a Primary Three pupil, lost one of his front teeth this morning and flatly refuses to smile for his photos, but when I encourage the children to pose making funny faces for a couple of pictures, I catch him grinning gappy-toothed from ear to ear and capture the moment on camera.

'I can't wait to see the photos!' Jenny says when we've finished.

'I'll get to work on them this evening,' I say.

It's breaktime and we're standing in the playground, mugs of tea in our hands, talking while Jenny keeps an eye on the kids. I can't stop thinking how amazing this little school is and how happy my own children will be here.

'I'm not one to bad-mouth the elderly and the sick, but usually the individual photos he takes look like mugshots,' Jenny says. 'I don't know how he manages it. It can only be deliberate. However, I'm optimistic after seeing you work that we're going to have some great photos. I don't think we'll be commissioning our official school photographer again!'

'Are you offering me a permanent job?' I joke.

'Aye, absolutely. Are you available for sports days and nativity plays, too?' She doesn't wait for me to answer. 'You must let me know how much I owe you.'

'Oh, I have no idea. I'll need to—'

'And if you won't name your price, I'll pay you what I've always paid our former school photographer – a fortune, but the parents never complain. They're always relieved to have sorted out the Christmas presents for the uncles, aunts and grandparents in one fell swoop, though the kids will have changed a bit by December.'

'Listen, when the parents have ordered, I'll give you the exact printing costs. If you want to add to that, you can keep the proceeds for the school. It was a pleasure. I don't want any money for it.'

'Och, Katherine. That's not how it works. Either we come to an agreement or I'll take back my job offer!'

Jenny looks over my shoulder, distracted, and waves. I turn to see Darragh walking towards us. He's carrying a long canvas bag over one arm and what looks like a huge roll of fabric under the other one. He's wearing his work clothes – paint-stained jeans and an old T-shirt – with his sunglasses sitting on top of his head.

'Hi, Jenny,' Darragh says when he reaches us. 'Hi, Kat. I didn't expect to see you here.'

Jenny beams at him. 'I can't wait to see it,' she says, pointing to the thick, rolled-up material.

'What is it?' I ask.

It's Jenny who answers. 'It's the backdrop for the school play. Normally we only do a nativity, but some of the pupils are leaving us at the end of the school year to go to secondary schools on the mainland and they wanted to do an end-of-year play. Darragh kindly painted the backdrop for us. He's a terrific artist.'

'I know he is.' I can sense Darragh's eyes on me. We're both thinking about his painting of Altacarry Head. Before Jenny can ask how I know, I say, 'What sort of play are you putting on?'

'A musical. It's called *Pirates and Mermaids of Rathlin*.'

'Did you write it?'

'No. I adapted it. Cut down the number of parts. Changed the title and the characters' names. That sort of thing. The twins' mum plays the piano. She's going to accompany the pupils.'

'I could take photos on the night of the performance if you like?'

'I was hoping you'd say that!' To Darragh, she says, 'I'm afraid I can't help you put that up.' Darragh looks relieved, as if he was dreading finding himself alone with Jenny. She was right about him acting aloof with her. 'School's not out for another half an hour,' Jenny continues. 'I thought Tom would be with you.'

'He wasn't feeling very well. He had a headache. I sent him home.' Jenny looks concerned, but Darragh reassures her. 'I think he just got a bit dehydrated, you know, working in the sun.'

'I'll help,' I say. 'What do you need me to do?'

The play is being held in ten days' time in the parochial hall, situated next to the school. We fix the backdrop to the ceiling so that it hangs against the wall. Darragh does most of the work, using an efficient combination of hooks and PVC pipes from his bag. I notice he has machine-sewn sleeves along the top of the fabric to thread the pipes through.

Once it's up, I stand back and admire Darragh's handiwork. He has painted a bay – clearly recognisable as Mill Bay thanks to the rocks and the derelict cornmill – with the sea stretching to the horizon. A mermaid sits on a rock in the foreground and a pirate's ship sails in the distance. There are seagulls and kittiwakes, seals and dolphins. With its bright and cheerful colours and blend of realistic and fantastic elements, the scene is like an enlarged illustration from a children's picture book.

'Fancy a drink at McCuaig's?' Darragh asks. I look at my watch. Mark's coming home earlier than usual, but I've got over an hour before his ferry gets in. 'I'm buying,' he adds when I hesitate.

'Go on, then!'

The bell goes, signalling the end of the school day, so we ask Jenny to join us, but she's a little worried about Tom and says she has some lesson preparation to do for the following day.

Darragh's van is parked near the school. He throws his bag of tools into the back of it and drives us the short distance to McCuaig's.

'What are you drinking?' Darragh asks me as I sit down at an outside picnic table.

I'm still trying to keep my alcohol intake low and it's a bit early for me, anyway. Plus, it wouldn't do to be tipsy when Mark gets home. 'A lemonade, please,' I say.

Darragh fetches the drinks and some crisps from the bar and sits down opposite me. He clinks his pint glass against my glass of lemonade.

'It was good of you to make the backdrop,' I say.

'Did you recognise the scene?' he asks.

'Well, I have to admit, the mermaid threw me a bit,' I joke, 'but, yes, I recognised Mill Bay.'

Darragh looks pleased, like a schoolboy getting praise from his teacher.

'It's a great school, isn't it?' I say.

'Aye, it's grand. Jenny has done wonders there,' he says.

'It was one of the things that swayed me when Mark wanted us to move here. I love the idea of our children going to a small school like that.' Darragh says nothing, apparently lost in his thoughts, but he's looking at me attentively. 'You know, one day. When we have kids,' I add. I should stop, but Darragh's silence makes me blurt out more. 'Soon, hopefully. We're trying for a baby.'

Darragh still doesn't reply and for a moment I think I've embarrassed him as well as myself. I notice he has almost finished his pint already. I look down at the table, running my finger around a ring where a glass has stained the wood.

Eventually, Darragh says, 'My girlfriend, is coming to visit soon – she lives in America.' He has a huge smile on his face. 'She has been over a few times and loves the island. She's planning to move here one day.'

This is the first time Darragh has told me about his girlfriend. I didn't even know he had one. He has mentioned his strict Catholic upbringing a few times and occasionally mentions his parents – usually in throwaway, negative remarks – but on the whole he talks very little about himself. The beer seems to have loosened his tongue, though. Or perhaps because I've confided in him, he feels it's his turn to confide in me.

'I always wanted my kids to go to school there, too. Gloria and I … we're hoping to adopt a baby.'

I don't know what to say to that. I wonder if his girlfriend doesn't want to go through pregnancy and childbirth, or if either she or Darragh is unable to have children, but I don't want to pry.

I'm still trying to work out how to respond when Darragh says, 'I've always dreamt of having a little girl. I had so much fun growing up with my younger sister. I brought her up, really.'

Is it my imagination or is he studying me to gauge my reaction? The mood seems to have changed. The sun is still out, the sky almost cloudless, but I shiver, suddenly feeling cold. This is what happens between us. One moment, we chat comfortably and effortlessly, the next everything is serious and awkward, as though we're both playing a dangerous game, keeping our cards close to our chests to avoid making any wrong moves.

'I didn't know you had a sister,' I say. A complete lie, but I've become such an accomplished liar that I'm confident he can't tell.

'Yes.'

'Does she ever come to Rathlin?' Something I've wanted to know since I realised who Darragh is.

'No.' Almost inaudibly, he adds, 'She died.'

Every time his sister could have come up in the conversation, Darragh has skirted round the subject or changed it altogether. His reluctance to talk about her made me think something might have happened to her – something bad. But this news still winds

81

me, as if Darragh has thrown me a punch in the stomach. I didn't know she'd died. His eyes are burning into me. I try to hide my shock, transform it into sympathy. The words I should say go through my head. *That's terrible. I'm so sorry, Darragh.* But when I catch my breath, that's not what comes out.

'How?'

It's all I can manage. Did her death have anything to do with what happened that night? Could I have prevented it? Did I cause it?

'Car crash,' Darragh says.

Relief floods through me. She died in a car accident. I am blameless in that, at least.

'That's the short version, the official one, anyway,' he continues. 'It's a wee bit more complicated than that.'

His words compress my heart, making it beat erratically. I wait for him to elaborate. But he shakes his head, pensive. Although I'm rattled, I want to hear the full story. But he's not going to tell me any more than that.

Instead, he says, 'I'd like to name my daughter after her.'

This time I manage to say the right thing, even though I already know the answer. After all, I knew his sister. 'What was she called?'

I say it in my head at the same time as Darragh says it out loud.

'Erin. Her name was Erin.'

Chapter 13

'I don't trust him.' The smile that flickered on Mark's face a few seconds ago when I arrived home has inverted – *re*verted – into a frown. It has become his default setting since his mum died. 'I don't trust him and I don't like him.'

I've lost count of how many times Mark has said this since we first met Darragh. I could have lied, and almost wish I had now. But I've lost count of the number of lies I've told recently, too.

'Look, Mark, I know you and Darragh have some sort of personality clash, but he's my friend. We go running together and this evening I had a drink – a soft drink in my case – at the pub. You trust *me*, don't you? I've never given you cause not to.'

I instantly regret my barbed comment, but Mark doesn't pick me up on it.

'Of course I do, Kat. I don't trust *him*.' His face has turned crimson. 'I think he has an ulterior motive in befriending you.'

'He's got a girlfriend!'

'That's not what I meant.'

'What did you mean?' I feel slightly offended, although I'm not sure why. I hope Mark isn't spoiling for an argument. I'm not in the mood for one and I don't have the energy.

To my relief, he drops it. 'Nothing,' he says. 'I'm probably just jealous. I'm being irrational and unreasonable. Forget I said anything.'

I follow him into the kitchen, where he takes leftovers out of the fridge to heat up for dinner. While I sit at the table, a knot ties itself in my stomach as the news of Erin's death sinks in. Erin's dead. She may have died years ago, but I've just found out and a wave of sadness breaks over me. The knot tightens. I can't quite believe she's dead.

Mark turns around to face me just as I wipe away a tear. 'I'm sorry,' he says. 'I didn't mean to upset you.'

'You didn't. It's OK.'

He comes over, drags a chair round and sits next to me. He pulls me towards him. For a while, we stay like that, Mark holding me, stroking my hair. I pull myself together and push Erin to the back of my mind for now.

'How did the photo shoot go?' he asks, getting to his feet.

I'm glad he has changed the subject. As I tell Mark about taking photos at the school, the air between us clears. Mark says all the right things: he's proud of me, he's sure the photos will look perfect, Jenny and the parents will love them and this is a good way of making a name for myself through word-of-mouth recommendations.

But although we've warded off a row and now chat casually about my day and Mark's day, my mind is in turmoil. I oscillate between feeling sure that Darragh knows who I really am and then convincing myself that if he did, he wouldn't have confided in me like he has. If he suspected, even for a second, that I had something to do with what happened to Erin that night, he wouldn't want anything to do with me. He wouldn't have told me about his girlfriend and their plans to adopt a baby. He certainly wouldn't have gone to the trouble of painting the sunrise at Altacarry Head for me.

I hear Mark talking, but I can't work out what he's saying over the unanswered questions clamouring for attention in my head.

Was Erin's death recent? Or did it happen, as I now suspect, just after I lost touch with her? I wonder if her death was somehow connected to that fateful night, although this seems unlikely if she died in a car accident. I curse myself for not having the presence of mind to ask Darragh *when* Erin died. I can hardly bring this up the next time I see him. It's too sensitive a subject. Her death must be terribly traumatic for him, regardless of how long ago she died. It was untimely, unexpected. That much is clear.

When we've finished dinner, on the pretext of importing the school photos to my computer, I go upstairs to our study and boot up my laptop.

I drum my fingers on the desk as the computer whirs slowly into life. Then I type her name into the search bar: Erin Moore. There are hundreds of professionals with that name on LinkedIn. I try adding keywords such as "death", "car accident", "Ballycastle" and "Antrim", but I can't find what I'm looking for. I try Facebook and think of sending Darragh a friend request to see if there's any information about his sister's death on his wall, but he doesn't appear to be on Facebook.

I jump at the sound of Mark's voice behind me and hastily close the browser window before turning round. He has popped his head round the door. I'm pretty sure he can't see from there what I was doing on my laptop.

'Would you like a cup of tea?'

'Yes, please. That would be lovely.'

By the time Mark comes back, carrying a steaming mug in each hand, I've transferred my photos and I'm sorting through them. He looks over my shoulder and admires some of the photos.

'It's a lovely school, Mark,' I say. 'I can't wait for our children to go there.'

'In that case, let's get an early night and work on the first phase of that plan,' Mark says. Standing behind me, he strokes my hair. Although it sounds forced, he hasn't been this chirpy for a while.

'Hmm. I like the sound of that idea,' I say.

He goes downstairs to watch television and leaves me to label and retouch my photos. The pictures are great and Jenny will be thrilled. I'm pleased, too, but I can't keep my mind on the task in hand. I can't get Erin out of my head. I stare at a photo I took of one of the pairs of siblings. An eleven-year-old blond boy in Primary Seven – his last year at St Mary's – and his younger sister, aged four, in Reception. This shot was taken outdoors, with the two of them sitting next to each other on the wall. The sun enhances the Irish red of her hair, which falls in ringlets to her shoulders.

If I remember correctly, the age gap was bigger for Darragh and Erin. If they were at the same primary school at the same time, it can't have been for more than one year. And they certainly didn't go to St Mary's – they grew up on the mainland, in Ballycastle. But I can't help thinking that, as kids, Darragh and Erin would have looked a lot like the brother and sister in the photo I took. It crosses my mind, not for the first time, that if Erin were still alive, she would resemble Jenny now. No wonder Darragh is aloof around Jenny. She must be a painful reminder for him.

I sigh. I wonder if I should confide in Mark about Erin. There was a time when we told each other everything, or so I thought, but then there was Fiona. Lately, I seem to be keeping a lot from my husband. But I can't talk to him about Erin without revealing my role in what happened that night and I'm too ashamed to admit that. I can barely admit it to myself. I can't tell Charlotte or my mum, either.

The screen fades as my computer goes into sleep mode. I jiggle the mouse to make the screen saver disappear and the photo reappear. I stare at it again, transfixed by the school badge on the dark school jumpers the brother and sister wore for their photos despite the warm weather today. The island of Rathlin, in green, its inverted "L" like a boomerang over the pupils' hearts.

My thoughts jump to a documentary I saw once about Australian Aboriginal beliefs and traditions. Boomerangs were once used as weapons; they were used to hunt. They were made from bones before they were made of wood. All this comes back to me now. There are returning and non-returning boomerangs. If thrown correctly, returning boomerangs come back to you. Like a returning boomerang, I've come back to Northern Ireland. I've returned to the scene of the crime.

When Mark and I decided to move to Rathlin Island, it didn't occur to me that Erin would come back to haunt me like this. I thought I might try to find her, or at least find out what had become of her. I couldn't remember the name of her street in Ballycastle, even though I used to send her letters, but I went to her house a couple of times that summer and thought I might recognise it if I passed it. I even thought if she'd forgiven me, maybe we could catch up with each other. But it never entered my head that the past might catch up with me. Not once did I imagine Erin might be dead.

This time I hear Mark's footfalls on the stairs.

'Are you coming to bed?' he says, poking his head around the door again.

Remembering his earlier comment about going to bed early, I spin round in my office chair to face him, raising my eyebrows suggestively in the hope of eliciting a smile. But he has already turned away.

I shut down my laptop and follow Mark into the bedroom. I take off my clothes, then I walk across the bedroom naked, stand behind him and wrap my arms around him.

'Kat, do you mind if we don't?' he says as my hands move down his chest to his stomach. 'I'm tired and I have to get up early.'

It's not like Mark to suggest sex and not go through with it. In fact, it's not like Mark to refuse sex, even if I'm the one to initiate it. And yet, this isn't the first time he has rebuffed me recently. But he hasn't been in the mood for sex since his mother passed away, which is understandable.

Or perhaps it's the idea of having sex in order to start a family that's putting him off. Maybe that has taken the excitement out of it for him. If it has become a little more mechanical and a little less pleasurable for me in the few months since I stopped taking the pill, then it might be the same for him. Maybe Mark sees it as a chore now, no longer an activity where we can just enjoy the ride, to put it bluntly, but instead something our future as a family rides on.

'No problem,' I say. I'm not miffed. I'm not in the mood tonight, either. I've got too much on my mind.

I hope, though, even if Mark has gone off sex a bit, that he hasn't gone off the idea of starting a family altogether. My heart sinks as this occurs to me. I remember my conversation with Darragh and the longing look on his face as he told me he wanted a baby. A baby girl he would name Erin after the sister he'd more or less brought up himself.

I pull on my pyjamas and go into the bathroom, thinking about Erin, about Darragh's loss and my friend. As I remove my eye make-up with a cotton pad, I picture Erin, her cheeks streaked with mascara, the last time I ever saw her. She had a leaf and a twig in her hair and her skirt was torn. She was sobbing so hard I could hardly distinguish her words.

'I said no,' she told me. 'I kept saying no, but he did it anyway.'

I blame myself for what happened to Erin that night. I splash water on my face, trying to convince myself, as I have done many times over the years, that it's not my fault and I didn't do anything wrong. But I know that's not true. I should never have let her go off with a complete stranger. If I'd looked after her at the céilí, it wouldn't have happened. Erin wouldn't have been raped.

Chapter 14

The weekend in London has been planned for ages. I bought my plane ticket weeks ago and it's a special event – my friend Charlotte's hen party – but I can't go. Mark has gone back to work, but he comes home nearly every evening at the moment, getting out of any overnight stays in Belfast for work. He's been very down since his mother's death, so I don't want to leave him, even if it's only for three days. Right now, Mark needs me here.

It's a shame. I was looking forward to seeing my best friend again. It would have done me good. Even though I've been running with Darragh and Dexter and keeping busy, taking photos and updating my website, I feel marooned on the island and cooped up in the cottage, where an overbearing sense of sorrow seeps from the walls and permeates the air.

Forcing a smile so Mark can't see how disappointed I am, I tell him I'll ring Charlotte to say I'm not coming. But to my surprise, Mark insists I should go. I put up a cursory protest and then text Charlotte with my travel details.

On the day of my departure, Mark works from home so he can drive me to Belfast International Airport. When he drops me off, I hug him tightly, asking with genuine concern if he'll be all right. I feel bad about leaving him and promise to call and send texts, but as soon as I'm through security, the guilt dissolves and my face breaks into a smile.

Looking out of the window as the plane takes off, I feel as if I'm escaping. In a way, I suppose I am. This is a getaway – a short break to soak up a more joyful atmosphere, a brief respite from the gloomy climate at home.

I'm also keen to get away from Erin's ghost for a few days. When I moved into Causeway Cottage, I had no idea that Erin was dead. Even if, as I suspect, the car crash happened a long time ago, the news of Erin's death is recent to me. I need to let it sink in.

When the plane lands, I get the Gatwick Express into London. Stepping off the train onto the platform at Victoria, I spot Charlotte easily. She's tall and slim, and for as long as I've known her, she has worn her thick, black hair like a helmet – short bob, straight fringe.

'Hi. How was your trip? It's so good to see you! I've missed you!' she gushes.

Charlotte's originally from Braintree. She's bright and was educated at a girls-only public school, having been awarded a full bursary. She now works as a marketing and PR consultant. But her plummy accent sometimes lapses into an Essex one, especially when she's tired or drunk. It makes her a little less intimidating and even more inspirational.

Charlotte and her fiancé, Rupert, live in Hammersmith, not far from where Mark and I used to live. They're going to the Maldives in a week's time for both their wedding and their honeymoon. So, obviously, no one has been invited to the wedding. Charlotte tells me that although Rupert didn't want a stag do, he insisted on staying over at a mate's place tonight because he didn't want to get in our way. We take the tube and dump my suitcase at their flat.

We spend the day, the two of us together, reminiscing about old times as we stroll along the Thames, laughing as we pick out hen night paraphernalia in a party shop in Kensington and catching up over coffee and then lunch.

A few times during the day, a look passes over Charlotte's face, as if she's about to tell me something. But when I ask her what's wrong, she either smiles or shakes her head.

In the evening, we meet up with Charlotte's best friends and a couple of her colleagues. There are seven of us altogether. I know all her friends and one of her co-workers. They have booked a spy-themed escape game and we all end up wearing an incompatible fusion of fancy dress. Charlotte is wearing a bridal veil and a James Bond tuxedo; I'm sporting a trilby, and a trench coat over a short skirt that shows off the lacy garter around my thigh.

The gamemaster informs us that we are undercover agents and our mission is to work out the combination to a safe in which there is vital intel needed to prevent the escalation of the Cold War. We're then locked in a room and have a maximum of sixty minutes for our code-breaking and problem-solving. One of Charlotte's workmates – the one I didn't know – has smuggled in a bottle of tequila and some shot glasses. There's no lime or salt, but we all knock back a shot after each clue we solve.

At one point, I look around me and start to feel claustrophobic. We're confined to a small space, crowded into a tiny room, and I wonder if anyone other than the gamemaster knows we're in here. If the gamemaster had a heart attack or something, how long would it be before someone found us? How long could we survive with only a bottle of tequila between the seven of us for sustenance?

But we're having so much fun that this thought is only fleeting and we crack all the codes, find the combination to the safe and escape from the locked room with four minutes to spare. After we've successfully completed our mission, Charlotte, in her role as our self-appointed handler, gives us a new one that she code-names "Operation Pub Crawl".

It's not until we're back at Charlotte's flat and have made up my bed on the sofa that I find out what was on her mind and on the tip of her tongue earlier today.

'I've got something to tell you,' she says, plopping down on the sofa and ripping off her veil. She spills some of her tea onto the cushion as she does this, but doesn't appear to notice.

I sit down next to her. 'Oh, no. This sounds ominous.'

Charlotte pulls a face. 'Now, bear in mind, I may have put two and two together and made five or six,' she says, slurring her words slightly.

Charlotte is usually very astute and it's not like her to misread a situation. 'OK,' I say, bracing myself.

'I bumped into Fucking Fiona not long ago.'

This is Charlotte's nickname for her, not mine. Charlotte's fiancé, Rupert, used to work with Mark and although they were no longer working for the same pharmaceutical company when I met Mark, they were still good mates. That's how I met Charlotte. In turn, she and I became good friends. But because Charlotte knew Mark before I did, she also knows Fiona, Mark's ex-wife.

'Go on.'

'Well, she said she has finally moved on. She's with someone else now and—'

'Really?' I scoff.

Charlotte throws her head back and laughs. 'Oh, come on, Katherine. She's not that bad.'

My brain is addled from the alcohol and it takes me a few seconds to work out we're not on the same wavelength. 'No, I'm not surprised she has found someone else. It's just that she keeps texting Mark. If she has moved on, why is she still texting him?'

Charlotte shrugs, almost spilling her tea again.

I ponder my own question. Mark and Fiona's divorce was fairly amicable. They didn't want the same things, but they still cared about each other. A bit too much, in fact. Although she was the one who asked for the divorce, she would come up with all kinds of excuses to get him to come round to her place, where he used to live, too. Could he fix her dripping tap? Could he help her assemble a bookcase? It was almost laughable, especially considering how crap at DIY Mark is. Of course, he fell for the damsel in distress act every time and raced off to the rescue.

And one of those times, he ended up sleeping with her. "Only once", to quote Mark, as if that makes it negligible. It happened about a year ago and also about a year after Mark and I got married. When I found out, he promised never to see her again.

'Anyway, when I saw her, she was very pregnant, like huge,' Charlotte continues, making a gesture with her arms, mug still in hand, to show a massive pregnant belly.

'What? She and Mark got divorced because she didn't want children and he did!'

'I know. Right? Maybe she just didn't want children with him. Or perhaps she has changed her mind. She was quite young when they got married, wasn't she?'

It's true. There's an even bigger age gap between Mark and Fiona than there is between him and me.

'She said she and her partner were very excited and he was moving to London,' Charlotte says.

I wonder if Mark knows. They still have some friends in common. Someone might have told him.

'You said you put two and two together and made five … or six.'

Charlotte looks astonished that I remembered this in my inebriated state. 'Yes. I'm coming to that. Anyway, I congratulated her on her pregnancy, asked when it was due, that sort of thing.' Charlotte has dropped the h's from the beginnings and the t's from the ends of her words. 'Then I mentioned you and Mark were trying for a baby, too.'

I choke on my tea. 'Charlotte!'

'It sort of came up in the conversation.'

'You mean *you* brought it up! Why?'

'I don't know. I regretted it the second it slipped out. I'm sorry.'

'Oh, it doesn't matter. She probably knew anyway. Mark says he ignores her texts, but he obviously hasn't blocked her number. For all I know, he has already filled her in on our sex life.'

'I don't think so.'

'What makes you say that?'

'Her reaction.'

Before she elaborates, Charlotte takes a sip of her tea, which infuriates me. 'She went very red. Then she asked me to repeat myself, like she thought she'd misheard. I wasn't sure what I'd said wrong. I asked about her partner again, you know, where he lived. I … er … well, sort of to try and defuse the tension, but I expect it came over as an interrogation.'

Another sip. I wonder if Charlotte is doing this on purpose.

'What did she say?'

'She got all cagey and dodged my questions. She wouldn't say anything more about her partner, even though she was the one who'd mentioned him first. Except for one thing. Something strange.'

'Go on.'

'She said, "You don't know him, I can assure you." It struck me as really odd because it came out all defensive, like she was protesting, but it seemed completely out of context, like we'd got our wires crossed. And then she sort of scuttled off, like she was in a hurry to get away.'

Suddenly, I feel very sober. 'How long ago was this?'

'A month or so ago. Maybe a bit more.'

'And you're only telling me now?'

'I didn't want to tell you over the phone. I wasn't sure if I should tell you at all, actually. I wanted to be a good friend and I didn't know what a good friend would do.'

'How pregnant was she?'

'Seven months, I think she said.' She pronounces think as "fink". 'Do you think …?' She doesn't finish her sentence.

'I'm trying not to,' I say.

'Yeah, that's what I wondered, too. I had to tell you, in case I'd made the right assumption.'

I feel the colour drain from my face. Fiona would be around eight months pregnant now, if Charlotte saw her about a month ago. Eight months ago, we were still in London. Twelve months ago, Mark slept with Fiona and then swore he wouldn't see her again. He wouldn't have betrayed me, would he? Not again?

Charlotte is observing me. 'Forget I've said anything. I've obviously jumped to the wrong conclusion. It wouldn't make sense, would it? I mean, Mark moved away from London with you. And you're trying to start a family.'

'It can't be Mark's,' I say, more to myself than Charlotte. 'I don't know why Fiona behaved so strangely, but there must be some other explanation.'

'I'm sorry. I should have kept my thoughts to myself.' She waves her hand – the one not holding the mug – dismissively.

'No, no, you did the right thing.' I put my hand on her arm.

'I'm sure you're right, Katherine. There must be another explanation.' But Charlotte looks as unconvinced as I am.

Chapter 15

When we moved to Rathlin, I'd hoped that Fiona would fade into an unpleasant, distant memory. But, like Erin, Fiona has become a spectre, haunting my mind, and my thoughts flit from one to the other on the journey home. I put my forehead against the small, round window of the plane, but the window is not as cool as I hoped and does nothing to alleviate my headache. I groan, wishing I hadn't drunk so much last night. Looking vacantly at the clouds, I try to decide what to do.

I want to confront Mark. But if he has been true to his word and therefore true to me, that would demolish the trust we've been rebuilding since his "one moment of weakness", as he refers to it. There's nothing to suggest he has done anything wrong; nothing to indicate he's the father of Fiona's baby. It's no more than pure speculation on my part. A nagging suspicion. I'm probably being paranoid.

The problem is the timing. Fiona got pregnant four months after she and Mark slept with each other, supposedly for the last time. It doesn't seem long enough to find someone new, settle down and start a family. Of course, she may already have been seeing this guy the last time she saw Mark. Or perhaps she only met her partner a few months ago and got pregnant by accident. She might have run off because she didn't want to admit this to Charlotte. Am I being naïve? Am I refusing to face facts? I don't want to be one of those women who turns a blind eye, taking her husband's indiscretions lying down, so to speak.

I still haven't made a decision when the plane lands. I stay seated until nearly all the other passengers have got off. My hangover is clearing, but now I have a heavy feeling in the pit of my stomach. It's not only due to the alcohol swilling around inside me. I should be looking forward to seeing Mark and going home, but I'm not. He has been so depressed recently and despite my best efforts to lift his mood and help him through this difficult time, I feel instead as if I've been pulled down, too.

Mark has come to pick me up at the airport. He smiles when he sees me, a wide smile that hollows out cute dimples in his cheeks and makes the skin around his blue-green eyes crinkle. The look on his face instantly disperses the dread I was feeling. Mark is clearly happy to see me.

'I'm sorry I've been such a grouch,' he says in the car.

'That's OK. You were understandably down after your mum—'

'Yes, but you were very supportive, Kat. I should have made more of an effort. I was a grumpy git and you didn't deserve that.'

'It's fine, really. It's good to see you smiling again.'

Mark dutifully asks about my weekend and appears to take an interest in what I have to say. He's joyful, or at least trying to be joyful. This comes as such a relief. If I am going to broach the subject of Fiona, now is not the right time.

It's only as Mark drives onto the ferry in Ballycastle that a plan forms in my head. I know as soon as my brain runs through the idea that I'll do it, although I've never done anything like this before. I'll go through Mark's things. I'm going to snoop on my husband! I must still be in spy mode after the escape game. If I don't find anything to prove he's been unfaithful, I'll drop this and put it down to an overactive imagination. But if I find anything suspicious, anything at all, I'll tackle him about it.

*

The next morning is Monday. Before the alarm clock goes off, Mark wakes me up, nibbling my ear and stroking me between the legs. We're still naked from having sex the previous evening, but neither of us is sated, it would seem. After our love-making, Mark brings me a cup of tea. I try to drink it without sitting up too much as I know you're supposed to lie on your back for a few minutes after sex to optimise your chances of conception. Propping myself on my elbows, I watch Mark as he gets ready for work.

'I should go away more often,' I joke, as he buttons up his shirt.

He whips his head round to look at me and I can tell from his face that he doesn't find that amusing. 'Not too often,' he says softly.

He comes over to the bed so I can knot his tie for him. Then he goes back to the wardrobe to get his trousers. Suddenly, he seems to freeze, his back to me as he stares into the open wardrobe. Then he turns to me, holding a hoodie in his hands.

'Where did you find this?' he asks. His tone is reproving.

'Sorry?'

'This sweatshirt. Where did you find it?'

'I didn't. I haven't touched your clothes, except for the shirts I ironed and hung up. Why? Did it go missing?'

'No. It's my old football club sweatshirt, from when I was a teenager. But I didn't think I still had it. I haven't ...' Mark breaks off. He seems flustered, but it's hard to read the expression on his face in the dim light of the lamp with the curtains still drawn.

'Perhaps it was at the bottom of a drawer in London and ended up at the top when you unpacked your stuff here,' I suggest. 'You might never have found it if we hadn't moved.'

'Perhaps,' he repeats, but he sounds dubious.

'Or it may have been at your mother's. You've been clearing out some of the stuff from her house, haven't you?'

'Yes, of course. That must be it.' He smiles, but it looks forced.

He puts the hoodie back on the shelf in the wardrobe and comes over to the bed, a bemused look on his face, to give me a perfunctory peck on the lips before leaving for work. Then he thunders down the stairs and a second later, the front door slams behind him.

For a few seconds, I don't move, wondering what all that was about. I thought things were back to normal. Mark was cheerful yesterday and we made love last night and again this morning. But the tone of his voice and the expression on his face just now have stunned me. I get the impression there's more to this than an old football top turning up, something I didn't grasp.

I'd almost abandoned my plan to search through Mark's things – I'd even woken up during the night feeling guilty about the idea. But Mark's odd behaviour this morning has renewed my determination and reinforced my conviction that he's keeping something from me.

I jump out of bed, pull on my pyjamas and get to work. I start by riffling through his drawers, then I go through the pockets of his clothes in the wardrobe. I'm not entirely sure what I'm looking for. A receipt for a bottle of champagne? A secret phone? I realise if he does have a second mobile, he's likely to have it on him. Similarly, even if I did know the password to his computer, he has taken his laptop to work. I go through the bank statements online for our joint accounts, but nothing stands out. As far as I know, Mark doesn't have any other bank accounts, but he does have a company credit card for his business expenses and, of course, I have no access to the statements for that.

All my ferreting about takes less than an hour and turns up

nothing out of the ordinary. I should feel pleased – I've found no evidence that my husband is cheating on me – but I feel strangely disappointed, as if I've failed in my mission. Have I missed something? The fact that I haven't found anything doesn't mean Mark has nothing to hide. It might just mean he has hidden it well.

Eager to get out of the house for some fresh air, I text Darragh and at lunchtime, we go for a run. I'm not sure if it's a good idea. I'm anxious he might be dangerously close to unearthing a secret I must keep buried at all costs. But I enjoy spending time with Darragh, and as I discover the island on my runs with him, I'm growing to feel slightly less like an outsider here.

Darragh hasn't had time to fetch Dexter and for once it's just the two of us. We stick to a pace that enables us to chat. We're more relaxed around each other now. Most of the time. Sometimes our discussions get awkward and we tiptoe around each other, circumventing the question or changing the subject. But today, the conversation flows more or less freely – more for Darragh, who manages to talk without sounding out of breath; less for me as my sentences are punctuated with gasps for air.

'How was your trip to London?' he asks.

'A lot of fun. It was good to get away.'

I tell him about Charlotte's hen party – the escape game and the pub crawl. I'm tempted to confide in him about Fiona, but stop myself in time.

'It must have been hard, coming back to this wee island after the bright lights of the Big Smoke,' he remarks. Not for the first time, Darragh seems to have read my innermost thoughts.

'Not least because I had to travel home with a hangover,' I say flippantly.

We stop to admire the view. We're standing along the edge of the sheer, rugged cliffs, next to the ruins of Bruce's Castle and only a stone's throw away from Altacarry Head, where I tried to photograph the scene that Darragh then painted for me. As we look out to sea, across the water to Scotland, I wonder if Darragh is thinking about that, too.

My mind wanders to something from the guidebook I bought at the crafts market, but the details escape me.

'Robert the Bruce, right? Isn't there a cave named after him, too?'

'Yes. We're standing pretty much directly above Bruce's Cave, but you can only get there by boat.'

'I'm trying to remember what I read about it.'

'Well, Robert the Bruce holed up there for a while in exile. Legend has it he was inspired by a spider while he was hiding in the cave.'

'A spider?'

'Yeah. It was weaving a web. It tried six times to secure its thread to a rock, but only managed on the seventh attempt. Robert the Bruce had been defeated six times by the English, so he saw this as a sign.'

'A sign?'

'Aye. You know, if at first you don't succeed, try, try again. The spider got there in the end and Robert the Bruce took this to be a prediction of his own success. He decided to return to Scotland to fight for his country's freedom one last time.'

'And did he succeed?'

'Yep. Seventh time lucky. He defeated those troublesome English at the Battle of Bannockburn.'

I nudge him playfully. 'Oi! I'm English!' I take the sports bottle out of my waist pack and swig some water from it. 'I remember learning about that in history at school,' I say. 'The bit with Brucie at the Battle of Bannockburn, not the bit where Incy Wincy struggled to spin a web.' I shudder involuntarily.

'Are you cold? Want to get going?' Darragh asks.

'No, I'm not cold. I just bloody hate spiders.'

Darragh laughs loudly at that – a rich, throaty laugh that takes me back to the first time I heard it, as he stood by the scaffolding at the house at Church Bay, joking with Tom.

'We should head back anyway,' Darragh says. 'I need to get back to work or Tom will wonder where I've got to.'

Darragh doesn't allude to his sister and so I steer clear of that subject, too. Perhaps it's better for us not to discuss Erin. It might upset Darragh and I don't want to do that. I know it's difficult for him to talk about her. But there's another reason I'm keen to avoid mentioning Erin. Whether Erin died years ago or more recently, I'm in no way accountable for that, but I don't want Darragh to even suspect what I am accountable for, the role I played that night.

I steal glances at him on our run back and for the first time I think I can see the resemblance to Erin. His eyes are hazel whereas hers were green and his hair is fair whereas she was a redhead, but Erin's nose was ever so slightly hooked, just like Darragh's, and he also has a sprinkling of freckles across his nose and cheeks.

When I get back to the cottage, I feel tired out, although the run has done me good. The fresh air seems to have pushed Fiona and Erin to the back of my mind. I take a shower and heat up some leftovers from the previous evening for lunch. I decide to take a quick nap before going out to take some photos and I climb into bed, sleepy, but on a high from the run.

But my suppressed thoughts force their way into my dreams. Fiona is shouting at me, though I can't make out her words. The images are film-like, a close-up shot first, focusing on her face. There's no sound at all now, but her lips are still moving. Then the camera zooms out into a medium shot, showing Fiona with her hands cupped around her pregnant belly. Her features change and she becomes someone else. The image blurs, but not before I've seen who Fiona has morphed into. A beautiful teenage girl, her pale face dotted with freckles and framed with copper-coloured hair. Erin. She's holding her round tummy, too, or maybe it's just her head on Fiona's body. Unlike Fiona, she's not angry. Her wide, green eyes show she's terrified.

I wake up in a pool of sweat, panting more than I did at any point during my run earlier. I tell myself it's only a bad dream – I can barely recall it now I've woken up, anyway – and yet, I have the same feeling as I had earlier when Mark made a fuss about his football sweatshirt. There's something I should see, something important, but it's just out of sight and I can't bring it into focus.

Chapter 16

'I won't be home tomorrow night,' Mark tells me that evening. 'I need to stay over in Belfast. An early start the next day.'

This immediately arouses my suspicions, even though ever since I've known him, Mark has been away a lot for work. Is he working away from home or playing away in his hotel room?

'Can I come?' I had no idea that was going to pop out. I feel as surprised as Mark looks to hear my question. If he says yes, will I use it as an opportunity to snoop on my husband a bit more? And if he says no, will I assume he's up to no good?

I'm even more surprised at his answer. I expect him to refuse outright or at best fob me off with excuses. But he says, 'Of course. If you want to. I'm working all day, but I'll take you out for dinner in the evening, if you like.'

'Great!' I haven't been to Belfast since I was a child and I know the waterfront has had a massive makeover since then. 'I'll visit Titanic Quarter while you're working.'

'You can visit the Crumlin Road Gaol as well. It has become a really popular tourist attraction, and it's really interesting. All sorts of prisoners have been locked up inside the Crum.'

I've also heard good things about this attraction and want to visit it one day. But if the weather's nice, I'll take photos of

Belfast's murals instead – the political paintings as well as the more recent works of street art.

After texting Darragh to say I won't be available for a run in the morning, I pack my bag. I don't need much – my camera, obviously, undies, running kit, toiletries, a book and a smart casual outfit seeing as we're going out for a meal.

∗

I get up with Mark – early – and we take the first ferry to Ballycastle. Once we've disembarked, it's just over an hour's drive to Belfast, along the M2. Mark drops me off at the Europa Hotel, where I leave my bag.

I spend the day doing exactly as I'd planned. I start by visiting the Titanic museum. I can't decide whether the building itself looks more like an iceberg or a ship's prow. It's an expensive attraction, but I find it well worth the money and spend nearly three hours inside, learning all about the ship's construction and launch as well as the stories of the passengers who died and those who survived.

It rains while I'm in the museum, but the sun is shining when I emerge into daylight. I take my first photos of the day – of Samson and Goliath, the famous yellow cranes on the site of the former Harland and Wolff shipyard. I capture the gantry cranes reflected perfectly in the puddles on the ground around them.

As I eat lunch in a café in the city centre, I look up Belfast's murals on Wikipedia and decide to walk to the main Peace Wall that separates the Falls Road and the Shankill Road communities. From there, with the help of Google Maps, I walk in a wide loop around the wall, taking in the different areas and taking shots of the murals on both the Catholic and Protestant sides.

After that, I go back to the hotel and ask for early check-in, as Mark suggested this morning when he dropped me off. Briefly, I toy with the idea of questioning members of staff, but I feel ridiculous as I imagine myself flashing around a photo of Mark on my phone and asking if anyone has ever seen him in this hotel with another woman. I doubt anyone would tell me, even if they had. I should let this go. After all, I have very little reason to think Mark is keeping something from me, more a gut instinct than anything else, whereas I'm keeping a lot of secrets from him. I'm the one being deceitful.

I've been walking around all day so far and I'm tired, but I decide to go out for a run anyway, so I get changed. I map out a four-mile loop on a running app on my mobile and follow the route along the Ormeau Road over the River Lagan into Ormeau Park, then along the embankment and past the football pitches before exiting the park. On the Albert Bridge, I stop briefly to look at the tall twin Harland & Wolff cranes, standing sentinel over the bridge. I photographed them only this morning, but I've done so much today that it already seems like days ago.

I head back to the Europa Hotel where I get showered and dressed for dinner. I'm dozing on the bed when Mark arrives. He kisses me and gives me that boyish grin of his that splits his face in two.

'I think there's some beer in the minibar,' he says, throwing his jacket onto the bed. 'Help yourself while I get showered and changed. I've booked us a table at Stock Kitchen and Bar. I know how much you love seafood!'

I've never heard of the restaurant, but my tummy rumbles audibly at this news, which makes Mark chuckle as he disappears into the bathroom.

I don't feel like a beer after my run, but I find some peanuts and scoff them on the bed. I'll put on some make-up in a minute.

I'm flicking through the channels on the TV when I hear the ping of a text message. I'm about to get up and retrieve my phone from my handbag, but I realise it's Mark's phone. Glancing towards the bathroom door, I reach over to Mark's jacket and fish out his mobile from the pocket. The text notification has come up on the locked screen and my first thought is that if Mark had something to hide, he would have disabled the text preview function on his phone. My second thought – a passing one – is that I should stop my spying and start trusting my husband again. But before my conscience can kick in, I register the sender: Fiona Harris. The notification disappears and the screen goes blank. I saw her name for no more than a fraction of a second and I almost doubt myself. Almost.

I can still hear the faint noise of the shower. Five attempts. That's all I've got. I know this from experience. I've forgotten my own passcode a few times in the past. If I get it wrong on the sixth go, I'll lock Mark out of his phone for a minute. A minute isn't long. But it might be long enough for him to find out. I can't risk that.

Six digits, by the look of it. Perhaps it's a date: dd/mm/yy. I try his date of birth. My date of birth. The date of our wedding. I know his mother's date of birth, so I try that. Nothing works. I'll bet it's Fiona's date of birth, but I don't know it. One more go. I need to get it right this time.

Just then the door of the bathroom opens. Mark enters the bedroom, wearing a white hotel towel around his waist. I'm holding his phone in my hands, but he doesn't seem to notice. It's my stony expression he sees. His smile fades.

'Is something wrong?'

I can't win here. Mark probably deletes all the messages he receives from Fiona and any that he writes to her, if he writes to her. There will just be this one message from Fiona. And if I insist on reading it, I'll regret the words as soon as they're spoken. There will be no taking them back. They will shatter the fragile trust between Mark and me. Fiona's message might be innocent. Or at the very least, she might not have written anything incriminating. But I need to know what that text says.

'No, I'm hungry. That's all,' I say.

Mark puts on his boxers then sits on the end of the bed, his back to me, and pulls on his socks. He's talking to me, but I'm not taking in what he's saying. Water drips from his wavy hair. I watch the droplets trickle down the back of his neck. When he stands up to fetch his shirt, I slip the mobile back into his jacket pocket. Then I go into the bathroom to apply some mascara and lipstick.

When I come out, Mark is using his thumb to unlock his mobile with Touch ID. I observe him as he looks at the screen. He's reading her message, I'm sure of it. He scowls. I scowl, too. I still can't imagine what she has written.

I place my hands over his phone and he looks up from it into my eyes. 'How about we disconnect for this evening?' I suggest.

'Good idea,' he says. 'You look great. Good enough to eat.'

I give him what I hope is a seductive smile. He doesn't actually turn off his phone, flicking on silent mode and using the side button to turn off the screen instead. But he does put his mobile on the table next to the kettle, leaving it there when we leave the hotel room.

I have a plan now. I just need to keep up the act for a while longer. Mark kisses me and murmurs something about how much he wants me in my ear.

I push him away. 'Mark, I went for a run. I'm starving. Can you hold that thought until we've had dinner?'

*

I wait for at least an hour after he starts snoring. Early start, long day's work, big meal, alcohol and sex. He should be out for the count. Silently, I roll out of bed and tiptoe across the room to the table where he left his phone. My heart is pounding in my chest and my ears. I'm sure it will wake him up. But I glance at Mark in the bed. He hasn't moved. I walk slowly back towards him and pull back the covers to expose his right hand.

When I pick up his hand, he suddenly grips mine. I freeze.

But his breathing stays even. Gently, I press his thumb onto the sensor. As soon as I see his mobile light up, I drop his hand and scurry into the bathroom, locking the door behind me. Sitting on the closed lid of the toilet, I open his messages app.

I find what I'm looking for straight away. As I'd thought, there's only one message between Mark and his ex-wife. The one she sent earlier. All previous messages between them have been deleted.

My hands shake as I read her text. The anger rises inside of me like hot lava and I explode.

'What the fuck does that mean?' I shout, leaping to my feet.

The sight of myself in the mirror stuns me into silence. With my bedhead, pale skin and red eyes, I look like a Fury. The bright white LED lights no doubt accentuate the effect. My arm is raised – I was about to hurl the phone at the wall. I wait for a few seconds, immobile, as if someone has pressed pause. The only sound is the ventilation in the bathroom. My outburst hasn't roused Mark. I lower my arm and take a couple of deep breaths.

'What the fuck does that mean?' I repeat in a whisper.

I know what it means. It means I wasn't paranoid. I was right. It doesn't feel good. I would give anything to have been wrong. If I followed my instinct, I would go and shake Mark out of his slumber, thrust the phone in his face and demand to know what's going on. But I know what he'll say. He'll tell me it's not what I think. Even with his brain leaden with sleep, he'll proffer a plausible explanation and I'll fall for it. I don't want to hear it.

I look down at Mark's phone again, staring at the message until his screen times out and goes black. But even then, I can see Fiona's words. I can't seem to blink them away.

If you don't tell her soon, I will.

Chapter 17

On the drive home the following evening, I pretend to sleep so I don't have to talk to Mark and he doesn't talk to me. I need to sieve through the jumble of thoughts in my head and work out what to do. When I saw Fiona's message, I immediately assumed that she was giving Mark an ultimatum: if he didn't tell me about the baby, then she would tell me herself. But now I wonder if I could be wrong. Is there a chance Fiona is referring to something else entirely? Something that doesn't concern me? I don't know how she'd contact me anyway. It's not as if I ever gave her my phone number and Charlotte certainly wouldn't give it to her, even if she asked. I suppose, in this day and age, there would be a way for Fiona to get in touch with me if she really wanted to. Perhaps she wasn't even referring to me.

But I fail to come up with any other possible scenario and end up berating myself for refusing to face facts. I don't know how to deal with this. I've been asking myself the same questions since I left London. I feel as if I'm going round and round in circles at a vertiginous speed.

As soon as we get home, I pull my camera out of my overnight bag and make a hasty exit, muttering an excuse about the daylight fading. The conditions are actually quite good for taking photos, but that's not my intention. I walk to McCuaig's Bar, buy a lemonade and sit on the stone wall outside, away from the other customers sitting at the pub's frame picnic tables.

First, I ring my mum. I haven't spoken to her for a couple of weeks. I haven't seen her for a few months now. When we lived in London, more often than not, I would travel to Devon alone to visit. My mother and Mark have never argued or shown any animosity towards each other, but they don't like each other. On the rare occasions when Mark does come with me, they tend to dance around each other, eyeing each other warily like two boxers in the ring wondering who will throw the first punch. It's an unfortunate coincidence that both Mark and I failed to win over our mothers-in-law.

I've never understood what my mum holds against Mark. He has tried hard to ingratiate himself, but his charm hasn't rubbed off on her. Perhaps no one would be good enough for me in my mother's eyes. After spending so many years putting up with my father's philandering, she's distrustful of all men, although I've never told her Mark cheated on me once.

I make an effort to sound upbeat. I tell Mum about my visit to London, leaving out the part where Charlotte bumped into Fiona, as well as about my stay in Belfast, omitting the bit where my husband's ex-wife sent him a text message.

But I'm not fooling my mum. She must hear through my feigned cheerful tone, for at the end of the conversation, she says, 'If things don't work out, you know I'd love you to take over the B&B one day, don't you? This is a family home and I'd like it to stay in the family.'

I picture my mum, standing at the large window on the upstairs landing of the three-storey Victorian house in which I grew up in Ilfracombe, looking out to sea while she holds her mobile to her ear. I can see her constant worry about me scored across her face in wrinkles.

'Why wouldn't things work out? What do you mean?'

'You know what I mean, darling,' she says.

But I'm still pondering her remark several minutes after she has ended the call.

I fetch myself another drink from the bar – half a pint of lager this time – and resume my position on the wall. I look at my watch. Charlotte should be home by now, or at least on her way there by foot from the office.

She answers my call immediately. She dispenses with the formalities and niceties. It's as if she can sense something's up. She probably can because usually we text in the evenings or ring each other at weekends. I've never called her the moment she has left work before.

'What's wrong?' she says.

The whole story pours out then. I don't leave out anything. I tell her about my inconclusive snooping and Fiona's text. I tell her about my suspicions and my indecision. She listens without interrupting. When I've finished, instead of asking what I'm going to do, she asks what she can do. I love Charlotte for this. She's proactive and dependable. Even though I want to cry right now, I feel so much better for having confided in her.

'I'll do some digging,' she says when I don't answer. 'I could engineer another fortuitous meeting with Fiona and get her to open up to me.'

'She might not want to talk to you.' I'm stating the obvious, I know, but if Charlotte's chat with Fiona doesn't shed any light on the matter, I don't have many options.

'Then I'll spy on her,' Fiona says. 'Hopefully all this will turn out to be nothing.'

One thought in particular has been intruding on my mind since my last phone conversation with Charlotte. It bursts from me now. 'Didn't Fiona say her partner was moving to London?'

If Fiona's elusive partner and the father of her child does turn out to be Mark, that would mean he's planning to leave me for her. That would make sense. After all, they split up because she didn't want children. If she's pregnant with Mark's baby, that could change things completely. That might reverse the current situation. Since Fiona is more than eight months pregnant, Mark will have to make his move – in both senses of the term – very soon.

Charlotte doesn't need me to explain my reasoning. She has already grasped the implication. 'Yes, she did say that. But she also said I didn't know her partner.'

'Yes, but you said she was cagey when—'

'And why would Mark want a baby with you if he's planning to bring up a baby with Fiona?'

I don't admit to Charlotte that Mark has gone off sex a bit recently. We have made love a few times over the past few weeks and he was the one who initiated it at the hotel in Belfast last night, but he hasn't wanted to make love anywhere near as often as we used to. I'd put this down to grief after his mother's death, but what if Mark's backtracking and doesn't want to start a family with me anymore?

'Maybe Mark didn't know Fiona was pregnant when he left London,' I say.

'Try not to worry about it too much,' Charlotte says. 'There might be a simple explanation for all of this.' She's trying to be reassuring, but she sounds uncertain. She can't think of a credible alternative version, either. 'Try and act normal around Mark until I've managed to find out more.'

I look up to see Darragh and Tom striding towards the pub. They must have just finished work. I immediately lower my head and shift my position so my back is towards them. I feel as if a hole has been scraped out inside me and I don't have the strength to pretend everything is fine around Darragh right now. They pass within inches of me, but they're deep in discussion and they don't notice me. I say goodbye to Charlotte, leave my empty glass on the end of an outside table and head home.

I keep telling myself to act normal around Mark, as Charlotte

113

advised. But as soon as I enter the cottage and see him, the gossamer-thin thread that was holding me together snaps.

Mark is prepping the food for dinner and has his back to me, but he must sense my mood because he whirls round to face me when I storm into the kitchen. He backs away from me. His mouth opens to say something, but he closes it again and waits to hear what I have to say.

I decide to get straight to the point. 'I saw the text Fiona sent you when we were in Belfast.'

'What?'

'You had your phone in your hands. I was standing opposite you. In our hotel room. Just before we went out for dinner. I read the message upside down.'

I visualise us so clearly as I say this that I'm almost taken in by my own lie. I'm both amazed and ashamed at how many lies I've told recently. Falsehoods and half-truths seem to fire from my mouth like bullets. I don't like the person I'm becoming. Paranoid, suspicious, duplicitous. In this moment, I hate myself so much I'm tempted to turn around and leave it there.

'She wrote, "If you don't tell her soon, I will".'

'It's not what you think,' Mark says. I knew he would say this! It's as if he's playing a part in a play I scripted, reciting the lines I gave him to say. 'I can explain.'

I realise my hands are on my hips and I'm pouting, as if I'm overacting. Maybe I'm over*re*acting. I drop my hands to my sides. It's only now, as Mark waves his arms around, that I notice he's holding a knife. I feel as if I've walked onto the set of a mediocre melodrama.

'Fiona has found out ... er ... somehow ... that there are going to be some people laid off at Campbell & Coyle. One of them is a friend of hers and a colleague of mine. Fiona is putting pressure on me to let her know.'

'And you won't?'

Mark shrugs. 'There are official channels,' he mutters.

I look at him through slitted eyes. It's a plausible explanation, but he's a terrible liar.

'Why didn't you ask me about the message when you read it?' he asks. His eyes lock with mine. There's concern in his blue gaze, but I can't determine if he's genuinely worried about me or anxious that I might not swallow his story.

Now it's my turn to lie. Again. 'I didn't want to ruin our evening.'

He turns away from me and goes back to chopping vegetables. 'What did you think she meant?' he asks.

'I thought …' I hesitate, but only for a moment. I can tell Mark the truth. 'I thought you were leaving me for her.'

He snorts, puts down the knife and comes to me, taking me in his arms. 'You crazy thing. It's you I love. I don't tell you that enough. I love the life we're building for ourselves here.'

I bury my face into his chest and breathe in his familiar, comforting smell. He pulls his phone out of the back pocket of his jeans.

'I'll block her and delete her from my contacts,' he says and angles his phone so I can watch him do it. 'Kat, what happened with Fiona was over a year ago. It happened once and it was a mistake.' He strokes my hair. 'I won't ever do anything like that again,' he insists. 'You have to believe me.'

I nod into his chest. 'I do.'

'Then what made you think I was planning to leave you for her?'

I'm embarrassed to tell him now. I feel stupid. But I owe him the whole truth, especially after so many lies. 'Promise you won't get angry with me for jumping to the wrong conclusion.'

'Promise.'

'Charlotte bumped into Fiona. Fiona has a new partner, apparently, but she was secretive about him. She insisted Charlotte didn't know him, so Charlotte automatically assumed she did. Fiona said her partner was coming to live with her in London now that she was pregnant.'

Mark stiffens. I can feel the tautness in the muscles in his back as I hold him. His shoulders tense and he loosens his arms around my waist. I lean back and look up, into his eyes. They are wide open in disbelief. Gently, he pushes me away. Neither of us speaks. We're both frozen, standing close to each other, but not quite touching.

At length, Mark says, 'I'm surprised. She … er … I didn't know she was expecting a baby.'

I can tell from his expression that this is true. He didn't know Fiona was pregnant and he hadn't been planning to leave me for her. He's understandably shaken by this news. They split up because she didn't want children.

A voice pipes up in my head. Mark didn't know she was pregnant, but the baby could still be his. Fiona may have made up the bit about her partner coming to London to throw Charlotte off the scent.

I ignore the voice of reason. Its reasoning is flawed. I'm inclined to believe that Mark hasn't seen Fiona and has kept his promise to me. But I don't believe for a second the trumped-up explanation he gave me about Fiona's text – that an employee in the company was going to be made redundant. He was definitely being dishonest about that.

Chapter 18

At the weekend, Mark and I take *The Rathlin Express* to the mainland. More often than not, Mark parks in Ballycastle, as we don't need a vehicle on the island, and takes the faster foot passenger ferry home. Today, though, the boot is loaded up with tins of paint and groceries, so we'll sail home on the slower boat with the car.

Once we've finished the shopping, we stop off at a florist's, where Mark buys a huge bouquet of lilies to lay on his mother's grave. Then we head for St James's Parish Church. Despite the pungent smell the flowers release into the car, I can't help thinking they're wasted on my late mother-in-law, although I feel a tiny prick of remorse at having that thought.

The church is on a hillside and you can make out the sea, through the tall trees. My mother-in-law went to this church when she still lived in her bungalow. We stand side by side in silence looking at my mother-in-law's grave, its recent headstone, as yet undamaged by weather and age, the grass beginning to push up through the turf. I reach for Mark's hand and hold it, but say nothing to interrupt his thoughts.

We take the car ferry home and plan to spend the rest of the day painting the baby's room. Mark wanted to start by doing the bathroom – rip out the carpet and tile the floor – but we'll need to have that done professionally. Then Mark suggested we should paint the study first, saying he didn't want to jinx anything by touching the baby's room before the baby was at least on the way. He also argued that it would be hard to know what colour to choose without knowing the baby's sex. But the gaudy egg-yolk paint is peeling off the walls in the nursery and the room is in desperate need of a makeover, so I persuaded Mark to go for a neutral, pastel colour. We can decorate the room with brightly coloured pictures at a later date.

Mark spots Jenny and Tom before I do. They're walking down the hill, as we drive up it, towards the cottage. Mark stops the car and opens the car window.

I lean across him to talk to them.

'Were you looking for me?' I ask.

'No,' Tom replies at the same time as Jenny says, 'Er … yes.' She looks down, as if she's avoiding eye contact and then throws a glance behind her, in the direction of our house. She seems almost shifty.

'Have you come from the cottage?'

'Yes, um … I wanted to pop in to give you the money for the school photos or post the envelope through your letter box if you were out. Everyone was delighted with your photos, by the way. You did us a massive favour. I'm sorry – it's taken weeks to collect in all the money.'

It had slipped my mind that Jenny still owed me money for the school photos. I've taken photos for the end-of-year school play since then, for which Jenny paid me in cash on the evening of the performance. 'Oh, thank you. There was no hurry, though.'

Jenny makes a strange noise. I think she's choking, but then I catch her smile and realise it was a chuckle.

'I'm glad you're not in a hurry for the payment,' she says, looking at me now. 'I forgot the envelope.' She blushes and the red colour floods her white face from the neck upwards. 'I thought I had it with me.' She taps the handbag hanging off her shoulder. 'I'm such an eejit.'

Tom nods, clearly agreeing with her on that score.

'That's no problem at all,' I say. 'I'm sorry you both walked out here for nothing.'

'Do you want to come in for a cup of tea?' Mark asks.

'Oh, no,' Jenny says. 'We need to get back. We'll let you get on. I'll come round with the cheque tomorrow.'

Mark doesn't notice anything strange, so I don't voice my thoughts in case he thinks I'm going mad. What did Jenny and Tom really want? I can't help wondering if the envelope was just an excuse. She said they had to get back, but they live in Ballyconagan – uphill from us – and yet they're walking down the hill, towards Church Bay.

No sooner has this thought trespassed into my head than I dismiss it. Jenny and Tom may have an errand to run – something to buy from the local shop, for example – before they walk home. I'm far too mistrustful of everyone at the moment.

Mark parks in front of the house and grabs the two tins of paint from the boot, leaving me to lug all the shopping bags inside. He opens the front door and goes straight upstairs, but as I step inside, something stops me in my tracks. I can't place exactly what it is to begin with, but then I remember the first time I entered the house, Mark carrying me over the threshold like a bride, when the stale odour of the house hit me. It doesn't smell stale – on the contrary, it smells clean – but it doesn't smell like home. The scent is hard to identify, and I can't even decide if it's familiar or not. But a strange feeling scuttles over me.

Immediately, my imagination goes into overdrive. Has someone been inside the house while we were out? Stupidly, we keep a spare key in the most obvious place – on the kitchen windowsill, barely hidden behind that repulsive gnome my mother-in-law gave me. I know there's no way Jenny would have let herself in, even if she'd found the key. But maybe she and Tom noticed something odd or saw someone. I'll ask Jenny if I catch her when she pops round tomorrow. Then again, she might think I'm mad.

119

Setting down the bags of shopping at my feet, I sniff the air, but if there was a strange odour in here, it has gone. Mark came into the house before me. He must have brought the smell in with the tins of paint or perhaps it's an item in one of the shopping bags that came in with me.

Then it hits me. Pregnant women have a heightened sense of smell. That's one of the first signs. I was trying not to think about it, trying not to get my hopes up, but my period is six days late and this time I really believe I might be pregnant. I popped into the chemist in Ballycastle, while Mark was buying flowers, to buy a couple of pregnancy tests. I'll take one tomorrow as soon as I wake up – you're supposed to pee on the stick in the morning for a more accurate result. Picking up the shopping, I kick the front door closed behind me and go into the kitchen.

I put away the groceries, make some tea and then carry the mugs upstairs. Mark is in our bedroom, rummaging through the clothes in the wardrobe.

'Have you seen my football hoodie?' he asks.

'The one you discovered the other day? No. I haven't.' Mark's always losing his things, but I don't point that out. 'Why do you want it?'

'I need some old clothes to wear for painting the baby's room. I threw out most of the stuff I didn't wear anymore when we were packing up to move house.'

I expect Mark binned the football top the other day, too, and he's forgotten all about it. Unlike his mother, he's not a hoarder and there have been many occasions when he has chucked out something we then needed. Briefly, it comes to me that I'd thought someone had been in the house. But I'm sure now that I was mistaken and no one would steal an old football shirt, so I don't mention it.

'Mark, I think I might be pregnant,' I say. 'I'll take a pregnancy test tomorrow to make sure.'

He turns to face me. His mouth drops open. 'I don't believe it,' he says. My face falls. This isn't quite the reaction I was hoping for. But then he beams and I can tell he's as excited as I am. 'Finally!' he exclaims and I wonder how I could have doubted him, how I could have imagined, even for a moment, that he was the father of Fiona's baby. He comes over to hug me. It's an awkward embrace, around the mugs I'm still holding.

'Let's not get too carried away,' he says. 'We shouldn't get our hopes up.'

'You're right,' I concede. I try to adopt a serious look to mirror his, but my face breaks into a grin. 'Come on! We've got work to do, painting the baby's room!'

Mark trails behind me as I walk out of our bedroom and into the nursery, where we spend the rest of the afternoon. To begin with, we work in silence. Mark seems absorbed in his thoughts, and I leave him to sort them out in his head. He preps the walls while I stick tape around the doorframe and window edges as well as along the ceiling and skirting board. But one of the playlists on Mark's phone comes through the Bluetooth speaker while we work and before long, we're both singing along to Arctic Monkeys, Linkin Park and The Killers.

When we've almost finished applying the first coat of paint on every wall, Mark leaves me to finish up and goes to make us some dinner. I'm admiring our work and the colour we chose when my phone goes. Pulling my mobile out of the back pocket of my jeans, I see Charlotte's name come up on the caller ID.

I hesitate, my finger hovering over the screen. I'm excited about the idea that I might be expecting a baby and I feel reassured about Mark. Even though he seemed slightly taken aback when I told him I think I may be pregnant, he has spent the last couple of hours painting the nursery with me. I'm on a high and I'm worried Charlotte might be calling with news that will burst my bubble.

But Charlotte is my best friend. I can't ignore her. And she might actually have news that confirms Mark has nothing to do with Fiona's strange remarks or with her baby. She may even just be ringing for a chat. I decide to take her call.

Chapter 19

As usual, Charlotte gets straight to the point. 'Are you alone? Can you talk?' she asks.

'Yes. Mark's downstairs and I'm upstairs.'

'Right. Are you sure he can't hear you?'

I have my mobile in one hand and the paintbrush in the other, so I push the nursery door shut with my hip. 'Yes, I'm sure. What's going on?'

I picture her at home, sitting on her sofa, her legs tucked up underneath her, a glass of white wine on the coffee table in front of her. I have a sudden desire to be at her flat with her, chatting non-stop, a reality show or gameshow on TV providing background noise.

'I accidentally on purpose ran into Fucking Fiona,' she says.

'How did you manage to orchestrate that?'

'Well, I staked out her house—'

'You didn't!'

'No, not really. I loitered outside it.'

I'm about to ask what the difference is, but bite my tongue. Charlotte's a bit scary. I'm glad she's on my side. 'Go on,' I say.

I hear her slurp her wine. I roll my eyes and wait it out.

Charlotte is a born storyteller and loves to use pauses to create suspense.

'She's had the baby,' she says.

'Really? Did you see it?' I try – and fail – to work out the timings. When did Charlotte tell me about the baby? A week, ten days ago? 'Is it OK?' I ask. 'It wasn't born prematurely or anything?' *Please tell me it's not Mark's*, I think. Then: *It's not Mark's. I know it's not Mark's.*

'No, it's fine. Yes, I saw it. A bouncy baby boy—'

'OK. Did you find out any more about—?'

'—called Hashim.'

'Oh,' I say as that sinks in. 'Hashim?'

'Yup. Fiona's partner is of Pakistani origin. I met him, too.'

'Oh,' I repeat.

'Baby looks dead like him.'

'So, we made a mountain out of a molehill,' I say.

'Added two and two together and made eight,' Charlotte says. 'Sorry.'

'That's OK. Don't apologise. I'm glad it's all over.'

A wave of intense relief washes over me, followed by a pang of guilt. I didn't trust Mark, and yet he was telling the truth. I shouldn't have doubted him. What made me think he could possibly have fathered another woman's baby? I could laugh at myself if I didn't feel so ashamed.

'Well, I'm not sure about that,' Charlotte says.

I hear her sip her wine again and I wish I had a glass in my own hand. I realise I'm still holding the paintbrush and put it in the plastic tray. I sit down, cross-legged, on the floor, girding myself for the bombshell I sense Charlotte is about to drop.

'What do you mean?' I ask.

'Fiona desperately wants to get in touch with you. She practically begged me to give her your mobile number.'

I can't imagine what Fiona wants to talk to me about. I bet it has something to do with the text she sent Mark that I know he lied about. *If you don't tell her soon, I will.* But although my curiosity is piqued, I have no intention of talking to my husband's ex-wife. Ever.

'Oh, no, you didn't give it to her, did you?'

'Of course not. I lied. Pretended I didn't have my phone on me.'

Charlotte is very attached to her mobile phone. In fact, she's almost physically joined to it. It's permanently glued to her hand. Fiona doesn't know Charlotte well, but probably well enough not to fall for that one.

'Why would she want to call *me*?' I wonder out loud.

'Well, I think she meant you and Mark, actually. She said she'd been trying to get hold of Mark, but couldn't get through to him.'

'He blocked her from his phone,' I say.

'That would explain it.'

'It doesn't explain why she wants to get hold of him. Or me.'

'Maybe she simply wants to apologise,' Charlotte says.

'Isn't it a bit late for that?'

'Listen, it's unlikely I'll see her again, but if I do, should I give her your number?'

'No!' I take a deep breath. 'No,' I say, more calmly now. 'I don't want to talk to her. I want nothing to do with that woman.'

Charlotte snorts. I'll bet wine has come out of her nose.

'What?'

'She has probably asked Mark to be godfather or something like that.'

'That's not funny!'

Charlotte explodes with laughter. She's joking, but I find myself wondering if that could feasibly be what Fiona wants Mark to tell me. But then I remember Mark's reaction when I told him Fiona was pregnant. He definitely didn't know, so that can't be it.

'Sorry,' Charlotte says when she's finished her giggling fit. 'It's the wine.'

'Did Fiona say anything else?'

'Um … yes, she did, now you ask. She asked if I knew whether you and Mark were still trying for a baby.'

'Nosy cow! She just wants to gloat! I hope you told her to mind her own business.'

'Something like that.'

'What did you say?'

'I said as far as I knew, you were, yes. I couldn't very well tell her to ask you herself, could I? Next time I'll tell her you're up the duff. That'll shut her up!'

'Charlotte!'

'Anyway, Rupert's just come through the door. Better go. Haven't made the din-dins yet.'

'Thank you,' I say sincerely.

I feel ridiculous for thinking that Mark could have been the father of Fiona's baby and I'm grateful to Charlotte for going to so much trouble to put my mind at rest, even though she was the one who planted the idea there in the first place.

'No problem. Let's chat soon.'

I stay sitting on the floor for a few minutes, replaying our conversation in my head. What could Fiona possibly want to talk to me about? She has always struck me as a catty woman, the type who needs to knock down other women to feel tall, although I sometimes think that's catty of *me*. And a rather unfounded assumption, if I'm honest. I only hate her because she's Mark's ex. For all I know, she could be really nice. But she did sleep with Mark when he was *my* husband. So even if I have misjudged her, I don't want to hear anything she has to say. It would only cause trouble.

I'm about to get to my feet and go downstairs to clean the brushes and paint tray, but my mind shifts to something else. Someone else. I've been obsessing so much over Fiona this past week that I've almost managed to push Erin to the back of my mind. But now she's taking up all my headspace, screaming for my attention. Perhaps it's because I've been talking to Charlotte about Fiona and her baby. Or maybe it's because I think I might be pregnant and I'm standing here, in the baby's room, getting it ready for my own baby coming. Even though I couldn't recall it in detail when I woke up, the dream that I had during my nap the other day, in which a pregnant Fiona morphed into a pregnant Erin, comes rushing back to me now. And with it, Erin's penultimate letter.

I received Erin's letter about four months after that fateful August evening at the céilí and I read it more than any of her other letters. In fact, I reread it so many times back then that even though I haven't looked at it for years, I can still remember whole paragraphs word for word. I visualise one of those paragraphs effortlessly, as if I'm holding her letter in my hands. Erin's neat handwriting, the blue ink of her fountain pen, the flowery border of the stationery.

I'm pregnant, Katherine. I've known this for a couple of months. I wish I'd told you before. I wish I'd asked you for advice. By not telling you, I was able to deny it myself for a while. You're the only one who knows. I haven't told my parents yet, but it's showing now and I can't keep it a secret for much longer. My mam will go mental. She'll probably disown me. I'm so frightened, Katherine. If only you lived nearer and could help me.

I should have asked myself this before, when Darragh told me about the fatal car crash. I have no idea how to find out what I want to know. I can't possibly ask Darragh. But the question will be snaking around inside my head until I do know the answer.

What happened to Erin's baby?

Chapter 20

The next day, a Sunday, I come back from a few hours spent taking photos in the early morning light, expecting Mark to still be in bed, to find instead that he has turned the house upside down during my absence. He has tossed all his clothes – and mine – onto the floor and has apparently rummaged through every drawer and emptied every cupboard, upstairs and downstairs. It looks as though we've been burgled.

Mark is kneeling on the bedroom floor, surrounded by clothes, including my underwear.

'What's going on?' I ask.

'Where's my football sweater?' He throws me a look of reproof.

'I have no idea, Mark. Seriously? That's what all this is about?' I make an expansive gesture with my arms to encompass the mess.

'What have you done with it? Where have you hidden it?'

My eyebrows knit together in confusion. His behaviour is so bizarre I almost retort I'm glad he'll be away from home on business for most of the coming week and I can't wait to be shot of him. My mouth opens and closes, but the harshness in Mark's voice has taken my words away.

'Who have you been talking to? Did my mother say something before she died?'

He's not making any sense and he's scaring me. 'What are you talking about?' I manage.

'I think you know.' His aquamarine eyes are blazing and his face has gone puce.

I was annoyed when I came in and discovered this chaos, but I'm livid now. I take a deep breath. 'You hadn't set eyes on that bloody hoodie for about twenty years, much less worn the damn thing, and now you're acting like you've misplaced your most prized possession!'

Mark looks at me as if his eyes are about to pop out of his head. I don't often lose my temper and I hardly ever shout. But now I'm on a roll.

'If you want to throw your stuff around, be my guest,' I continue. 'If it's still there when you go to work tomorrow, though, I'll throw the whole lot out. Which, incidentally, is probably what you've done with your football sweater.' My voice has ratcheted up another couple of notches and I'm almost pleased to see Mark cowering slightly. 'I'm going out and when I get back, my clothes had better be tidied away *exactly* how they were.'

'Where? Where are you going?' Mark is subdued now, his voice several decibels – and pitches – lower than mine.

But I don't answer. I stomp down the stairs, grab my camera, book and purse and slam the front door as I leave. Although I'm still fuming at Mark, I get a strange sense of satisfaction as I storm out.

I get lunch at McCuaig's bar and sit outside. When I've finished eating, I call Jenny. I bumped into her earlier, on my way back from taking photos. She'd popped out to buy some milk. She asked me if Mark and I wanted to go for a walk this afternoon with her and Tom. I thought we'd be applying the second coat of paint to the baby's room today, so I said no. But now I decide to go, although there's no way I'm extending the invitation to Mark. I tell Jenny that Mark is busy, tidying the cottage. That makes me smile wryly to myself.

But deep down, I don't find it funny. It seems farcical to me, what just happened between Mark and me. I wish I hadn't lost my temper, but at the same time, Mark frightened me. He can be sulky at times and he's not always entirely truthful, but then again, neither am I. He's always been so supportive of me and affectionate towards me. I've never known him to be so accusatory. I have no idea what has got into him. I highly doubt this is about him thinking I deliberately hid his football shirt, but I can't work out what he's accusing me of.

I try to read my book, but I can't concentrate, even though I tell myself it was a trivial argument, some sort of misunderstanding. We'll kiss and make up later and it will all be forgotten. I give up on my novel for now, though, and put it back into my handbag.

I look out over the Sea of Moyle and am transported back to my home town and its esplanade. I feel a pang of homesickness mixed with guilt. When was the last time I went to Devon to see my mother? I'd hoped to spend a week or so there this summer, but summer is almost over. Next weekend is the last weekend in August. It's also the weekend of the Rathlin Run that Darragh told me about. I'd planned to enter, but the race organisers have asked me to be the official photographer, which I'm delighted about. I decide to spend the first two weeks of September at my mum's. Darragh has told me his girlfriend will be coming to visit him that fortnight. He wants me to meet Gloria, but it will have to be some other time. I miss my mum. I text her to check those dates suit her.

As I send the message, a sudden pain stabs my stomach and I rush inside the bar and to the toilet. When I pull down my underwear, there's blood. I have tampons and sanitary towels in my handbag. My pants are bloodstained but I haven't bled through to the outside of my jeans, luckily. I feel a little upset, but not devastated, as I usually do, although this time my period, usually as regular as clockwork, was nearly a week late.

Six days isn't long, but I don't think my period has ever been that late before. I read somewhere that many women miscarry very early in pregnancy and often don't even know they were pregnant. Perhaps it's just as well this happened before I took the pregnancy test. If I was pregnant, as I'd thought, I'd rather not know now. I shove these thoughts out of my head, resolving not to think about my period or Mark's behaviour while I'm out walking with Jenny and Tom.

As I leave the pub and head for the Manor House, where I'm meeting Jenny and Tom, I notice the wall of brooding clouds building up along the horizon. Northern Ireland really does have four seasons in one day, with the weather sometimes changing so rapidly that I can't always read the signs, if there are any to read. The forecast was good, and this morning it was clear and sunny, but I've got a feeling we're going to get caught out on our walk. It's hard to tell if we have minutes or hours; I can only tell that the rain is on its way. Probably.

'Hope you packed your waterproof in that,' Tom says by way of a greeting, nodding at my rucksack.

'Er … no. I've got my camera, book and money on me. That's all.'

Irrationally, I curse Mark for this, as if it's his fault I didn't think to bring an anorak.

'Let's go for a short walk,' Jenny suggests, 'and hope we make it back in time.'

'We were going to take you along the Roonivoolin Trail,' Tom says. I don't tell him I've already run along it. 'But, sure, we'll take a rain check, isn't that what they say?' He laughs at his own joke.

Jenny suggests walking as far as the coastguard's hut and back. My heart stops for a beat or two and then races to make up for it. That would take us up Church Brae, the steep hill that leads right past our cottage. Mark might see us and I don't want a scene in front of Jenny and Tom.

'It's too far,' Tom says. 'We'll not make it back before the rain.'

I breathe again.

In the end, we follow the coast path going west, past Station Pier. I'm disappointed that Darragh's not here. I thought he and Dexter might come with us. I enjoy Darragh's company so much, our chats about painting and photography and our runs together. I'm confident he can't possibly know who I am if he has confided in me about Erin's death and although he hasn't mentioned her since then, I feel a connection to her when I'm with Darragh.

We feel the first sprinkling of raindrops a few minutes into our walk, as we reach Mill Bay. In a few seconds, the sky turns a slate-grey so that it seems like night-time instead of the middle of the day. And then the rain falls more resolutely and noisily. Jenny and Tom hurriedly pull on their waterproofs and we run, back the way we've come.

We dash past the gift shop and the boathouse; their roofs have no overhang. We have to run all the way to McCuaig's Bar before we can take shelter.

'Stay here, ladies,' Tom says. 'I'll fetch the car. No point in us all getting wet.'

I'm already drenched, but Tom insists. I buy coffee for Jenny and me while we wait.

'It's good of Tom to do that,' I say.

'He's a good man,' Jenny says. 'Speaking of good men, where's yours?'

I'm not sure if Jenny has forgotten the excuse I gave her or is questioning it. Either way, I don't want to paint Mark in too bad a light. I adopt a flippant tone. 'Ah, well. Turns out he wasn't such a good man today. He made a mess looking for an item of clothing, so I got a bit mad with him and left him to tidy everything away.'

I feel bad, even saying that. I know Mark will be fretting at home, worrying about me being caught in the downpour. He'll have tidied everything away and will probably greet me at the door with a towel and an apology as soon as Tom drops me off at the cottage. He'll have boiled the kettle several times so he can make me a mug of tea the moment I walk through the front door. That's the sort of thoughtful thing he does, the sort of considerate man he is. That's part of why I love him so much.

Jenny breaks into my thoughts. 'Tom's always losing stuff. I know what you're going through.'

'How did you meet Tom?' I ask.

'Through Darragh,' she says. 'He introduced me to Tom when they started working together. They go way back. They've known each other since they were kids.' That surprises me. I would have thought Tom was nearer my age, quite a lot younger than Darragh.

'There's a few years' age difference, surely? They can't have been childhood friends.' I don't realise I've said that out loud until Jenny answers.

'They were next-door neighbours when they were kids in Ballycastle.'

'Ah, I see.'

Jenny looks at me, as if I don't see at all. She seems to hesitate, but then she adds, 'Tom was very close to Darragh's sister.' She looks down as if she has said too much.

How close? I wonder. I think I vaguely recall Erin mentioning her neighbour, who was also her classmate, but if she told me his name, I'd forgotten it. If Tom and Erin had been very close, surely Erin would have told me more about him? Then again, maybe not. I didn't know her for very long.

'Darragh told me a bit about his sister,' I say. 'Did you know her?'

'No.' She pauses, and for some reason I think she's going to ask me the same question. I get ready to lie. But she examines me through slitted eyes and says, 'What did Darragh tell you exactly?'

'Only that she died. He didn't say much more than that. He didn't even tell me when she died.'

'It was a long time ago,' Jenny says. 'Before I met Tom. She was sixteen, I think.'

I turn my head away so Jenny doesn't see I'm reeling in shock

132

at this information. Erin was fifteen on the night of the céilí, but I seem to remember her birthday was around Christmas time. If she died at the age of sixteen, it's possible her unborn baby died with her. When she didn't reply to my letters, I assumed she blamed me and didn't want to know me, that she was ghosting me, as we call it now. But now I realise she stopped writing because she was dead.

'Darragh said it was in a car accident,' I say, fishing for details. My throat is tight and my voice comes out strangled.

But Jenny doesn't seem to notice. She's distracted by her phone as it pings with a text. A car horn sounds faintly from outside. Our conversation is about to be cut short.

'Tom's here.' Getting to her feet, Jenny pulls up the hood of her waterproof jacket. She looks me in the eye. 'If that's what he told you, then it's not my story to tell,' she says cryptically.

I follow her to the door of the bar, and then, although we're already soaked, we sprint to the car.

Chapter 21

Thankfully, the weather is a lot better the following weekend for the Rathlin Run. Even though I'm not participating myself, I'm wearing my running kit. I plan to take photos at different stages of the race, so I will have to get from one spot to the next quickly. Darragh and I have run the ten-mile course together – with Dexter, of course – as training for Darragh and a recce for me. It is an out-and-back course and, although I prefer to run loops, the views are so stunning and varied that it seemed as if we'd taken a completely different route back.

Tom has entered the five-kilometre race, so Jenny has come along to support him. Tom, Jenny and Darragh are coming to the cottage when it's over as Mark has kindly offered to get some food ready for afterwards. He was very apologetic when I came home soaking wet from the rain after our row that day, and when I told him I'd got my period, he immediately found comforting and reassuring words. He has rung me every evening this week from the hotel to check I'm all right. Now he's home, he's still determined to make amends for his behaviour, hence the invitation to "afternoon tea", as Mark called it, which includes Darragh.

Both races start in Church Bay, the longer course heading to the westernmost point of the island, through Kinramer Wood and

Kebble Nature Reserve to the Seabird Centre, and the shorter race heading south, towards Ushet Lough. One of the race organisers has told me that he has another photographer to cover the finish line, so once both events are underway, I set off to take pictures of the runners doing the ten-mile race on their way back. I'll return to Church Bay in good time to take photos of the winners of both races on the podium. I've already picked the perfect place – at the brow of a hill with the sea in the background. I only just make it there and get set up before the first runner passes me on his way back. To my delight, the fourth man to come over the hill is Darragh. It gives me a spike of adrenaline and I cheer him on so enthusiastically I almost drop the camera. He flashes me a wide grin – or perhaps he's smiling for the camera. I wonder if he can catch the man in front of him and pip him to a podium position.

Only five minutes after Darragh, the first female competitor flies past me. She is in far better shape than I am, but she makes me wish I was competing today.

In the end, Darragh comes fifth, but he is the first male athlete from Rathlin Island, so he wins a prize anyway – a medal and a bottle of wine.

When it's all over, Darragh jogs off to get a shower at his place before joining us. Tom doesn't appear to feel the immediate need for any personal hygiene and pulls on a tracksuit top as he and Jenny walk back to the cottage with me.

Mark has gone to some trouble and has prepared an array of sandwiches and a homemade tomato and parmesan quiche along with a variety of nibbles and dips. Everything is on the kitchen table, ready to be taken through to the living room. I feel ravenous, as if I've run the entire ten-mile course. Jenny finds space among the plates on the table to put down her rucksack and unzips it.

'I've brought some snacks and stuff, but I expect it has all warmed up a bit by now,' she says to Mark.

'Pop it all in the fridge for a bit,' I hear Mark say as I head upstairs for a shower and to change my clothes.

I feel rude leaving Jenny and Tom with Mark, so I make it quick. I'm only gone a few minutes, but when I get back down, Darragh is pulling up in front of the house in his van and everyone else is carrying plates into the living room. For the first time since we've moved in, I regret not having a back garden. We could put a table and some chairs out at the front of the house, but as Mark said when I suggested it, it's never warm enough to sit outside in the mornings and we wouldn't get the sun in the afternoons.

Darragh has also brought a bag of food and so we've ended up with a full-on meal in the middle of the afternoon. Mark has served all our guests beer, but I'm sticking to non-alcoholic drinks. This house isn't really big enough for entertaining. There are plates of food on the floor because the coffee table is too small. Tom and Darragh are sitting in the armchairs, and Jenny is wedged between Mark and me on the two-seater sofa. I'm on the end nearest Darragh's chair.

'You didn't bring Dexter,' I say to him.

'No. He sends his love,' Darragh says. 'He didn't know he was invited. But he would have been a right pain in the arse, begging for titbits and drooling all over this delicious feast Mark has thrown together.' Mark smiles tightly at Darragh, apparently not sure if that was a genuine compliment. 'This is wonderful, Mark, thank you,' Darragh adds, as if to clear up any ambiguity.

Jenny chimes in with congratulatory comments and Tom, his mouth full, grunts appreciatively.

Jenny's staring at the painting above the fireplace. She looks from the painting to Darragh, and fixes on the picture again. It seems as though the scene unfolds in slow motion as she lifts her hand to point and opens her mouth to speak. I know what she's going to say. I grip my glass so hard I'm surprised it doesn't break. My shoulders tense and sweat prickles under my armpits, as I scrabble for a topic to throw her off course. But Jenny gets there first.

'Darragh, isn't that—?'

'Altacarry Head,' Darragh finishes. Somehow, he knew to step in and save me.

Jenny looks at Darragh, then at me. I shake my head at her.

'Altacarry Head. So it is,' Jenny says. 'I thought it looked … er … familiar.' I'm pretty sure she's trying not to smile.

'Yes, it's beautiful, isn't it?' Mark says. 'Kat bought it. The artist's local.'

'It's very good,' Jenny says.

My eyes meet Darragh's. The skin around his hazel eyes crinkle and I realise he finds this amusing. My face flames red. Great. I've dodged a bullet, but I've made a complete fool out of my husband. God knows what Jenny is thinking. Fortunately, Tom says nothing. I don't think he has followed the conversation, let alone its undercurrent.

I make an excuse about needing to nip to the toilet, mainly to calm myself down. Before going back into the living room, I fetch some more drinks from the fridge – bottles of beer and cans I don't recognise that look like fruit juice. I need a beer, but I bring the cans, too, in case anyone wants to switch to soft drinks.

Jenny takes a beer, but picks up a can from the table and waves it at me. 'Remember Bacardi Breezers?' she says to me.

For a moment, I think I've misheard. I do remember the first – and last – time I got drunk on Bacardi Breezers. Most of that night, anyway. The parts that haven't been obliterated by the Bacardi Breezers themselves. As the memory pounces on me, my stomach somersaults, making me feel as dizzy and nauseous now as I did that night.

'Is that what those are?' I say, hoping Jenny doesn't hear the tremble in my voice. 'I didn't know they still made them.'

'They don't. This is a new, revamped version. "Breezer", it's called.' Jenny turns the can and reads the writing on it. 'This one's "blood orange and ginger".'

'Sounds revolting.' I'm not sure who says that. Mark, Tom or Darragh.

I hear a can open. The conversation goes on around me. I catch snippets. *Different flavours ... disgusting ... strawberry ... elderflower.* But their words wash over me. I'm lost in the past.

Erin looked older than me and the make-up made her look older still. She was only fifteen, but she could easily pass for eighteen or nineteen. It was a hot summer's evening and we were young and foolish. I encouraged Erin to go up to the community hall bar and buy our drinks. She said the barman was a ride, and she didn't take much convincing. Erin had never drunk alcohol before and I'd never been drunk. I'd only ever tried alcohol on special occasions – champagne and wine at Christmas, a sip of my dad's whiskey when he wasn't looking – and I didn't like it. But the stuff in these bottles was so sweet and fruity you couldn't taste the rum. The orange-flavoured one tasted like Fanta.

We must have tried every flavour of Bacardi Breezer they had. I picture Erin and me, clumsily stepping on people's feet and staggering our way through the moves as we attempted to join in the dances. We couldn't walk straight and we couldn't think straight. Perhaps what happened next wouldn't have happened at all if we'd both been sober. Maybe Erin wouldn't have been raped.

My hand shakes as I reach for my glass and I try to turn my thoughts to something pleasant. I remind myself I'm going to visit my mum the following weekend and imagine us walking along the seafront together in my home town.

Someone changes the subject and I tune back in, although I don't trust myself to contribute to the discussion. Everyone will hear the quaver in my voice if I speak. I stare at the painting above the fireplace because if I so much as steal a glance at Darragh, I'll burst into tears. I nod and chuckle in all the right places, and eventually I feel as if I'm functioning normally again.

I do a good job of blocking the memory from my mind. But as we clear up after our guests have left, Mark brings it flooding back.

'Was it you who bought those Breezer things?' he asks.

'No,' I say. 'I assumed you did.' He shakes his head. 'They were in the fridge.' I shrug, feigning nonchalance, even as my heart rate rockets.

Until Mark brought this up, I'd assumed it was a coincidence. Now I'm not so sure. Who brought the cans of drink if Mark didn't buy them? All of a sudden, I don't know who I can trust. This feels less like a coincidence and more like a warning. Could this have something to do with Erin? I can't work out why, but I feel as if I'm being threatened.

Chapter 22

The fortnight at my mum's whizzes by and when it's over, I feel a twinge of homesickness, as I always do when I leave my home town. I know from experience it will last a week or two. But I also feel relaxed and revived. The summer season had ended for the bed and breakfast, so I spent a lot of quality time with my mum, who pampered me and cooked all my favourite meals for me. And she plans to come to Ireland, just before Christmas, so we can visit Dublin, Belfast and, of course, Rathlin Island together. I know Mum loves my visits and I'm already looking forward to hers. She feels lonely during the off-season when she's not nearly so busy. She has friends, but no boyfriend. After years of putting up with my father's sexual transgressions, she has sworn off men for the rest of her life.

Charlotte came down from London the weekend before I came back to Rathlin. It was lovely to catch up with her again. We met up with some of my old school friends for a pub dinner at the George & Dragon and had a great girlie night out.

I worked on my website when I was at my mum's, tweaking and adding to my online portfolio, and I've lined up some work in and around the county of Antrim – school photos, headshots, product photos and even a wedding for next summer. I've also sold some prints of my wildlife and landscape photos of Rathlin Island via my website, which I'm thrilled about. I'm putting together a calendar of top sights to see in Northern Ireland, which I hope to add to my online store well before Christmas.

While I was in Devon, Mark sent me text messages during the day – loving messages as well as funny ones. Several times we talked late into the night on the phone, as we did at the start of our relationship, when Mark was away and we were falling madly in love, unable to get enough of each other. Now I'm back, Mark has made it his mission to take over from my mum, pampering me and cooking for me. He has also got out of staying away overnight for work for the next three weeks to spend some quality time with me.

Mark banishes me from the kitchen while he makes the meal for my first evening back, so I come upstairs to unpack. Mum did my laundry when I was at her place, so it's mainly a question of taking my clothes out of my suitcase and putting them onto the shelves and hangers in the wardrobe.

When there's only one item left in my case, I hesitate, not knowing where to tidy it away. Or hide it away. I don't want Mark to see this. Or rather, what's inside it.

It's a jewellery box, a present from my father when I was a little girl. He bought it for me to say sorry for missing the school concert. I found out much later that he was with one of his mistresses, no doubt enjoying himself far more with her than he would have done listening to me playing a piece of music I was practising for my Grade 7 piano exam.

I went on to fail my exam and promptly gave up my music lessons. I haven't so much as touched a piano key since, but I've kept the jewellery box all these years. I lift it out of the suitcase and sit cross-legged on the bed. Opening the clasp of the pink and purple box, I lift the lid. Immediately a ballerina pirouettes in front of an oval mirror to the *Dance of the Sugar Plum Fairy*. Quickly, I take out what I'm after and snap the lid

141

shut, irrationally anxious that Mark will hear the tinny music from downstairs.

I'm not sure why I've brought the jewellery box back with me. I could have taken out the letters and read them at my mum's, or brought the letters back without the jewellery box. But when I was packing, almost on impulse, I picked up the jewellery box, with the letters in their envelopes inside, and wrapped it in a cloth bag, which I put in my suitcase, like a set of Russian dolls with my most shameful secrets concealed inside the smallest one.

I couldn't stop thinking about Erin the whole time I was at my mum's in Ilfracombe. I've put the incident with the cans of Breezer down to paranoia and coincidence, but that's not what has been preying on my mind. It's what Jenny said the afternoon we dived into the pub to get out of the rain. *If that's what Darragh told you, then it's not my story to tell.*

Her words have been on a grating loop in my head. It's as if they provide a cryptic crossword clue to the circumstances surrounding Erin's death, and if I can solve it, I'll find the answers to the questions I've been asking myself. When did she die? How did she really die? Because the more I think it over, the more I wonder if there ever was a car accident. Something about that story doesn't sit right with me. I'm convinced it's a lie Darragh concocted in order to shield the truth behind it, like some sort of cover-up.

Now I'm back, Erin is on my mind more than ever, as though I'm drawn to her by a magnetic force. I met her not far from here, in Ballycastle, the summer we were fourteen. When I came back to Ballycastle to visit my grandparents the following summer, I saw her again. In between, we wrote to each other, long letters in fountain pens on pretty stationery that we sent by post – snail mail, as we call it now, rather than email, as neither of us had a computer back then.

Just after my second summer in Ballycastle, my grandparents died within a month of each other. There would be no more visits to Northern Ireland, let alone holidays in Ballycastle. I didn't know when – or if – I would see Erin again. For a while, though, she and I kept up our correspondence.

I run my hands over Erin's penultimate letter, the one in which she told me she was pregnant and could no longer keep it a secret from her parents. But it's Erin's last letter I want to read again, although I still know huge chunks of it by heart. I slide the pages out of the envelope. When I received it, I didn't know it would be her final letter to me. But no more came after that, even though I replied.

I haven't read it for years, but I knew I would want to when I got home to Rathlin. I hear Erin's voice in my head, reading the words to me. She sounds like a younger version of Jenny. I used to think it was obvious, reading between the lines, that Erin blamed me for my part in what happened. But now I think I've remembered that wrong, or misinterpreted her meaning. Erin blamed herself.

I skim some of the sentences. *My mother is furious. I feel so alone and so ashamed.* Poor Erin. I can only imagine how scared she must have been. I pause when I reach a sentence near the end. *I have to go away for a while.* When I received no more letters, I took that to mean Erin wasn't going to write for a while, or wouldn't write to me anymore. A brush-off. Perhaps because in the previous letter she'd said she wished I could help, but I hadn't known what to do or say. But now I think I misinterpreted that. I've overlooked the next two sentences. *Strange to think I'll actually be closer to you. This is the only way.* Perhaps she wasn't giving me the cold shoulder after all. But what did she mean by that?

My thoughts are interrupted by Mark calling me for dinner. I hide the letters and the jewellery box behind some handbags on the top shelf of the wardrobe, paste a smile on my face and make my way downstairs.

*

After travelling today, I'm tired and can't wait to get into bed. When I came back to Rathlin after my weekend in London, it felt like I was going in the wrong direction. But this feels right. I'm home and I'm happy to be here. Mark and I have had a wonderful evening and I realise how much I've missed him.

I clean my teeth and wash my face in the bathroom. As I go to screw the cap onto the tube of toothpaste, I drop it on the floor. I bend down, but it has bounced somewhere or buried itself in the carpet and I can't see it, so I get down on my knees and grope around for it.

And that's when I see it. Not the toothpaste cap, but a ring. A silver ring with an oval blue-green gemstone. A woman's ring. Tucked almost behind the wash basin, but visible. I'm sure it wasn't here last time I did the housework, a couple of days before I left for my mum's – I would have spotted it. Which means the person it belongs to must have been in the house during my absence.

I straighten up, holding the ring between my thumb and forefinger. A fiery ball of anger pinwheels into my heart as I imagine Mark bringing a woman into our home. She takes off her ring as she washes her hands and she's so eager to jump into my bed with my husband that she doesn't notice the ring fall from the side of the washbasin onto the carpeted floor.

I won't put up with it. My mother turned a blind eye to my dad's infidelities and she should have thrown him out long before he died.

My legs feel heavy and shaky as I walk into the bedroom, holding out the ring in front of me. Mark is sitting up in bed. I'm bolstered slightly by my position, standing over him, looking down on him.

'Mark, how did this get into the bathroom?' To my dismay, my voice comes out whiny.

'What is it?'

'It's a ring. A woman's ring.' His question was a stupid one

144

and I regret answering it, knowing I've allowed him to play for time, time to think up a plausible explanation, as he usually does.

'I've never seen it before,' Mark says. His eyes are darting all over the place.

'It must have got in here somehow,' I say, waving the offending item of jewellery in his face. 'Someone left it here while I was away.'

'Kat, no one has been here while you were at your mum's, I promise.' He sounds defeated, as if he knows I won't believe him, no matter how many times he repeats himself and no matter how many times he promises not to cheat on me. I almost believe him. Almost. 'Where did you find it?' he asks.

'On the floor in the bathroom, by the washbasin.'

'Oh.' He sounds genuinely surprised. 'It's a … a mood ring, isn't it?' he says.

Now it's my turn to be surprised. 'A what?'

'A mood ring. You know, one of those rings that changes colour according to its wearer's body temperature. It's supposed to reflect your mood.'

I examine the ring more closely, sensing Mark studying me as I do so. The ring has turned a deep red colour, like blood. Mark's right. It's a mood ring. It's not a woman's ring at all. It's a girl's ring. I'm not sure what to make of that. Something is taunting me. A hazy memory that is hovering stubbornly out of my reach. I almost grasp it, but then it floats away.

'How did you know that?' I ask.

'Everyone knows what a mood ring is. You can buy them in all the gift and tourist shops. They've been around for years. Didn't you have one when you were younger?'

'Yes,' I say. 'Yes, I did.'

Mark leaps on this. 'Did you keep your ring? Did you bring any jewellery back from your mum's? Or could you have brought it back inadvertently?'

I look up sharply. Does Mark know about my jewellery box? No, I was on my own when I opened it earlier. I consider his suggestion. Maybe the ring was inside the jewellery box and somehow found its way into the bathroom. I can't see how, but it's the most likely explanation.

'I don't know what happened to my ring,' I say. 'I suppose this one could be mine.'

'There you go then,' Mark says, too triumphantly for my liking.

I narrow my eyes at him, wondering now if he found my jewellery box in my suitcase before I unpacked and took the ring out of it. Assuming it was in there in the first place. But why would he have done that? Another thought occurs to me and makes me feel cold all over. Did he read Erin's letter? I don't want him to know my deepest secret. I don't want him to know anything about Erin.

Mark must notice I'm shivering and he holds his arms out to me. I climb into bed. I resist the urge to turn my head away when he kisses me. It has been over two weeks since we last made love and we both need this.

I'm still obsessing about it long after Mark has fallen asleep. Whose ring is it? How did it get into my house, into my bathroom? *A girl's ring.*

It's not until sleep starts to overcome me that I realise what was niggling me earlier. A memory tugs at my tired mind, refusing to be ignored, and I know now I won't get to sleep at all. *A girl's ring.* When she was a teenager, Erin also used to wear a mood ring.

Chapter 23

The days have got considerably shorter and the weather has become colder and more capricious. It's only mid-October, but it's as if we've skipped autumn and hurtled into winter. I wonder what my first winter on Rathlin will be like. I imagine it can get lonely and I'm worried I'll feel cut off here, particularly when Mark's away.

As he promised, Mark didn't have to sleep over in Belfast for work for three whole weeks after my return. He's coming home this evening after two nights away. I'm glad. I've got used to having him around. The weather forecast can be wildly inaccurate here, but if it is to be believed, we're in for a huge storm later this evening or during the night. Already, a few noisy gusts of wind are blasting around outside. Mark's crossing will probably be a rough one, although he's not prone to seasickness. Unlike me, he has steady sea legs and a strong stomach.

I remember being stuck indoors for days after we first moved in and I open the front door and step outside, wondering if I can get out for a run before the stormy weather comes in. I look up at the sky. There are some low, threatening clouds, but some promising patches of blue still linger and for the moment the rain is barely falling, its fine spray hanging almost immobile in the air. The drizzle will cool me down once I get going. I decide to chance it and put on my running kit. I should have run earlier this morning, but I went out to take photos while the conditions were still favourable. I don't call Darragh. Even if he has finished work for the day, the weather might get worse by the time we meet up.

I select a playlist on my mobile, put in my earphones and set off, but I only get as far as the top of the hill before the wind picks up, a strong gust shoving me sideways and making me shiver. I look below me, at the harbour and out to sea, where the wind has whipped up white horses and a surging swell. The hostile, salty air stings my eyes.

The wind comes and goes, though, and it's still only spitting, so I carry on, heading west towards Kebble Nature Reserve. The storm isn't due for at least a couple of hours. I'll turn back before I get caught in it.

I get into my stride, enjoying the sensation of being exposed to the elements. I end up going much further than I intended and I'm running up the hill at Kinramer when the weather unleashes the full force of its fury on me. All of a sudden, the droplets of drizzle transform into pebbles, and I feel as if I'm being targeted, lapidated. The wind starts howling, so loudly I can no longer hear my music or even my own thoughts. The sky turns tar-black and I can't see more than a few metres in front of me.

My heart is pounding, far more from panic than from the exercise. There's nowhere to shelter. There's never any traffic on this island at the best of times – some days I go out running without seeing a car or, come to think of it, another living soul apart from cows or sheep. No one else will be out in this.

My body seems to know what to do before my head registers the idea. Instead of turning around and heading for home, I carry on running, up the hill and into the storm. It's not far away. It should take me only a few minutes to get there from here. If I can find it.

As I reach the brow of the hill, the storm delivers its fiercest onslaught. The wind almost knocks me over, somehow pushing me in the stomach and pulling my hair at the same time. The rain lashes my face and bare limbs. It's painful and terrifying. I brace myself against it and almost blindly, I keep going.

I can't make out anything in the fading light and the driving rain. I'm convinced I'm going the wrong way or I've gone past it when I finally spot it. I'm right next to where the gate would be if there was one. The lights are on in the big, isolated grey-stone house and his van is parked in the driveway. Relief rushes through me. Darragh's at home. Storms can abate as quickly as they arrive on this island. I'll ask him to drive me back to my place as soon as this one eases up.

I ring the bell, but if it works, I don't hear it, so I hammer on the front door with my fists, too. A dog barks faintly from inside the house. Dexter. Darragh opens the door and when he sees me dripping on his doorstep, he steps back to let me in.

'I was out running and got caught in the storm,' I explain needlessly. He gives me a lopsided grin and I feel stupid. 'Would you mind driving me home?'

'Not at all. Not yet, though. We're not going anywhere until this lets up a wee bit. Let's get you warmed up first, anyway.'

I kick off my sodden shoes at the door and follow him upstairs, through his bedroom to the en suite bathroom, where he hands me a surprisingly fluffy blue towel.

'Help yourself to whatever you need. My girlfriend forgot some clothes in the dryer when she was over last month.' I'd forgotten Gloria came to visit Darragh while I was at my mum's house in Devon. 'I'll leave them in there for you.' He gestures over his shoulder with his thumb towards the bedroom.

I take a long, scalding shower and use Darragh's minty shower gel, which I realise I've smelt on him. Darragh has left his girlfriend's clothes in a plastic bag on the bed. I tip the bag upside down and shake out a pair of jeans, socks, cotton pants, a T-shirt and a hooded sweatshirt. It all strikes me as strangely intimate. I've never been in Darragh's house before, but here I am, naked apart from the towel wrapped around me, standing in his bedroom.

It's a very minimalist, masculine room – a double bed with a dark grey and red quilt cover, light grey walls, a cream rug with a black symmetrical pattern. Over the bed hangs a large framed painting of a black and white collie. I walk around the bed so I can see the painting from up close and check for Darragh's monogram. Sure enough, the painting has been signed with the intertwined D and M in the bottom right-hand corner. This is a portrait of Dexter. Darragh has captured the mischievous look in the dog's blue eyes perfectly.

I pull on the clothes. The jeans are a bit loose and hang around my hips, but everything else is a good fit. I hang up the towel on the radiator in the bathroom and bundle my wet clothes into the carrier bag, then I go downstairs. I leave the bag with my running kit by the front door, then walk through the large living room, where Darragh has lit the log burner. It's a large room with terracotta tiles and two beige sofas. There's music on in here, Ludovico Einaudi, I think. The volume isn't up high enough to drown out the noise of the uncompromising rain, but it's beautifully soothing and I find myself wishing I still played the piano.

Two framed photos sit on the mantelpiece. One of them has been enlarged and even from several feet away, I easily make out Darragh, his arm around a tall woman about his age. They're standing on the distinctive hexagonal basalt columns at the Giant's Causeway, where I've been many times with my parents and grandparents. This must be Gloria. I approach the fireplace to examine the photo more closely. Darragh's girlfriend has shiny, chestnut hair, dark brown eyes and full, red lips stretched across very white teeth into a huge smile. She's striking. I feel a stab of jealousy, although I'm not sure why. Perhaps I envy her beauty.

I turn my attention to the other, smaller photo. It's a snapshot of Darragh and Erin and my heart pinches painfully. The colours have faded with age and in the sun into sepia. I pick it up to look at it more closely. Erin must be about a year younger in the picture than she was when I last saw her. She's gazing lovingly at her elder brother and they both look so happy, but a rush of sadness comes over me. I imagine Darragh must be infused with a sense of loss every time he looks at this photo.

I find Darragh in the kitchen. It's a country farmhouse kitchen with an Aga. It reminds me of the home of one of my uncles in Somerset and I feel inexplicably at home. Darragh is stirring something that is bubbling away in a cast-iron casserole on the hotplate. The smell is deliciously tantalising. Dexter leaps up from his cushion in the corner of the room and bounds up to me, wagging his tail so hard it's a wonder he doesn't put his back out.

'This is a beautiful house,' I say to Darragh.

'Thank you. How did you know where I lived? Or did you knock on the door of the first house you came to?'

'Dexter showed me. He ran up your drive the day he disgraced himself chasing sheep.'

'Ah, yes, I remember you telling me now.' At the kitchen island, Darragh pours a generous glass of white wine that he hands me without asking if I want a drink. 'Do you like chilli con carne?' he says.

'Yes. That smells sooooo good.' I sip the wine.

'Come here,' Darragh says, turning back to the Aga to stir the meal.

I obey. He holds out a wooden spoon for me to taste the dinner. It's spot on. Spicy, but not too fiery, not too garlicky. He has used chuck steak rather than minced beef.

'You didn't whip that up while I was in the shower?'

He chuckles. 'No. It had been simmering for a while when you gatecrashed my dinner party for one.'

I wince. 'Sorry about that.'

151

'Not at all. We're glad of the company. Aren't we, Dex?' Darragh's dog wags his tail in agreement. 'There's loads of it. I usually make huge meals and freeze some for another time.'

I remember Darragh saying he loved cooking, when he first met Mark and me. He gave us a token invitation to dinner that never came to anything.

'Come and help me choose some red wine.'

He also implied he was a wine buff, if my memory serves me well. He opens a door with an old-fashioned latch, flicks on the light switch and leads me down some stone steps. He has a wine cellar. At the bottom of the steps, an old, rusty key sticks out of a heavy wooden door.

'Do you lock your wine up?' I ask, surprised. Darragh lives in the middle of nowhere, on an island where nearly everyone leaves their front doors and cars unlocked. His house doesn't have a gate and he has a dog.

This makes Darragh smile. 'No. My father built this house for a famous musician. This basement room is completely sound-proofed. He used to lock himself inside, away from his family, when he wanted to compose. The door's unlocked. The key is just for decoration now.'

He leans across me to open the door and I see hundreds of bottles on shelves. The room is cool and smells slightly musty. I can't wait to get back upstairs to the warm kitchen with the aromas of Darragh's cooking.

'I know nothing about wine,' I say.

Darragh scans the shelves, his back to me. I shiver involuntarily. I'm a little cold, but I'm also a bit wary. I have no reason not to trust Darragh, and yet, now I'm here alone with him in the cellar of his house, I'm acutely aware that no one else knows I'm here.

I should text Mark. He might be home by now. I take my phone out of the pocket of the baggy jeans I'm wearing. There's no signal, not down here in the basement, anyway. Or perhaps it's due to the storm.

Darragh pulls out two bottles and turns to me. 'Argentina or France?'

'France.'

'Let's go for a *Châteauneuf-du-Pape* in that case.'

I follow Darragh back up the steps to the kitchen. Dexter is waiting for us by the cellar door.

'He's scared of the storm,' Darragh explains. 'He doesn't like to be left alone.'

I ask if I can help, but I'm instructed to sit at the kitchen table while Darragh puts on the rice. Dexter sits next to my chair and I fondle his ears. I take a few sips of the white wine Darragh has served me and he tops it up before I can protest.

As Darragh is serving the dinner, my phone pings with a text from Mark. There's reception up here, then. I read it and send a short reply.

'Sorry about that.' I say, switching my phone to silent mode. 'The ferries aren't running,' I tell Darragh. 'Mark's stuck on the mainland.'

His eyes, so similar to my own in colour, bore into mine. It's almost as if I'm looking into a mirror, and yet I can't decipher what I see in it. I'm conscious of my heart beating too fast and an ache low in my stomach. Then my face burns. Darragh looks away. I'm sure he has read me like a book, but I'm not sure if he's on the same page as me.

It's not sexual attraction. It's the alcohol. It has gone straight to my head after the run. I need to stop drinking. But Darragh has already poured me a glass of red wine to go with my meal. It would be rude to leave it. I make sure I drink some water, too.

As is so often the case between Darragh and me, the conversation flows easily at first, like the wine – Darragh seems to top up my glass when I'm not paying attention. I only realise how drunk I am when we leave the table. My head spins as I stand up and I stagger a little as I follow Darragh into the living room. He motions for me to take a seat next to him. I sink into the sofa and lean back, comfortably, enjoying the heat emanating from the fire. Darragh crosses his legs and stretches his arm across the back of the sofa, not quite touching my shoulder. I should sit forwards or perch on the end of the sofa, but I feel surprisingly relaxed despite the physical proximity and I don't move.

'The rain has eased off slightly. I think that's the worst of it over now,' Darragh says. 'I'll take you home shortly if you like.'

I want to ask if he's OK to drive, but either he's holding his drink much better than me or he hasn't drunk as much. Maybe both. I'm warm and sleepy. And undeniably aroused. I can't tear my eyes away from Darragh's lips as he talks, even though I've tuned out and don't take in a word he says. This is dangerous. I should go home. But I don't want to.

The wine hasn't only skewered my moral compass, it has also loosened my tongue. Catching sight of the photo of Darragh and Erin on the mantelpiece, the question is out before I can filter my thoughts.

'Darragh, what happened to your sister?'

He says nothing for a moment, then his words slice into me. 'Don't you know?' His voice is icy and he won't meet my eye. For a second or two I think perhaps he does know I was Erin's friend. A bad friend.

'No,' I say. 'How would I know?'

His tone softens. 'I thought maybe Jenny told you.'

'She said it wasn't her story to tell. Did she … did Erin really die in a road accident?'

He sighs. He looks at me then, through vacant eyes that are suddenly nothing like mine. 'No.'

I want to ask what happened, but I've already gone too far. 'I'm sorry, Darragh,' I say. 'It's none of my business. I didn't want to upset you, especially not this evening.'

He nods and I think that's the end of it. But he says, 'I've told you before that Erin and I had a very strict Catholic upbringing.' I nod. 'The car crash was my parents' official story because, in

154

their eyes, Erin brought shame on our family. They told no one the truth. Instead, they fabricated the story about the car crash. People didn't ask too many questions. That suited my parents. That way, it was a tragedy rather than a scandal.'

He pauses. I don't know what to say, so I wait. I resist the urge to take his hand in mine.

'Erin got pregnant,' Darragh continues. 'She was fifteen.'

I don't tell him that I knew that part, that Erin and I were pen friends and she confided in me in her letters. But I get the impression he's scrutinising me, measuring my reaction.

'The fecker who got her pregnant wanted nothing to do with her. Abortion was illegal in Northern Ireland at the time. It was illegal until quite recently, but it was impossible then.' A single tear runs down Darragh's face. He doesn't wipe it away.

I see the final sentences of Erin's last letter as if they're leaping off the page into my head. I hear her saying them as if she's sitting next to me. *I have to go away for a while. Strange to think I'll actually be closer to you. This is the only way.* I shudder. She meant closer to me geographically. I think I know what's coming now.

'My parents arranged for my sister to go to England to get a termination. Some distant cousin of my mum's took her in. By the time it was all organised, Erin was quite far on in her pregnancy. She died of a complication. A haemorrhage.' Darragh pauses, swallowing hard. My heart goes out to him. 'My father found solace in the whiskey bottle. He lives in Derry, still drowning his sorrows in the Bushmills. As for my mother, devout Catholic though she was, she killed herself a year or so after Erin died. She was ridden with guilt for not having been more supportive towards her daughter. My sister.'

'I'm so sorry, Darragh. Oh, God, that's terrible.' My words are inadequate and instinctively, I lean towards him and wrap my arms around him. He buries his head into my shoulder and we stay like that for a minute or so, with me rocking him very gently and stroking his hair, wishing I could ease his pain.

He lifts his head to look at me and we kiss. Tentatively at first, and then passionately. It's a good kiss, a really good kiss. I don't know who started it, but I do know I don't want it to stop. He smells incredible; he tastes incredible. He pulls my body against his, then pushes me back so he's lying on top of me. He holds my face in his hands; my hands work their way under his T-shirt, touching his skin, my lips still on his. My whole body is fizzing with longing. In this moment, I want Darragh more than I've ever wanted anyone.

But I can't do this. I can't do this to Mark. Reluctantly, I turn my head away and gently push Darragh off me. He sits up and looks at me. I can't quite read his expression. Is he disappointed? Annoyed?

'This isn't right,' I say. My words come out slightly slurred.

'It felt very right to me,' he says.

'It's not a good idea.' I don't sound convinced and I'm not. If Darragh kisses me again, I'll cave in. Mark cheated on me, at least once. Why shouldn't I sleep with Darragh? I almost reach for him.

But he stands up. I sit up, pulling down the hoodie I'm wearing that belongs to Darragh's girlfriend. Oh God. Darragh can no longer look at me, but his head is turned only slightly and I can see the sullen expression on his face.

'I thought you wanted this. I thought you wanted me. You led me …' His voice tails off, but not before I register its sulky tone.

I wonder what he was going to say and try to finish his sentence in my head. 'What were you going to say? Were you going to say I led you on?'

He does look at me then. 'No. Of course not. I was going to say that you led me to believe this was what you wanted.'

'I'm so sorry,' I say. And I am. Sorry about his sister, about what happened to her, about my role in it. Sorry, too, that I kissed Darragh, sorry that it has stopped.

'Don't be.' Still avoiding eye contact, he holds out his hand and when I take it, he pulls me to my feet. 'Come on. I'll take you home.'

The conversation we had about Erin should have sobered me up far more than it has, but my legs are wobbly as I follow Darragh outside. The rain is still coming down in torrents, but Darragh holds open the passenger door of his van for me before going round to the driver's side and getting in himself.

All the way to the cottage, we sit side by side in silence. Although the windscreen wipers are on full speed, they fail to keep up. They have a strangely hypnotic effect on me. My eyelids are heavy and I close my eyes for a few seconds. I snap them open again when a wave of nausea rushes over me as Darragh rounds a bend.

I try to think over what happened. Between Darragh and me just now. To Erin all those years ago. My brain is addled from the alcohol. Snippets of what Darragh told me about his sister's death replay in my head in the wrong order. Only one thing is clear. Darragh didn't tell me everything. He left an important part out. I glance at Darragh, wondering why he omitted that chapter of Erin's story. Doesn't he know she was raped?

Chapter 24

Embarrassed. Guilty. Confused. Relieved. Rejected. All these emotions churn and turn in my head, crashing into each other. Surprised, too, to find myself alone in my bed, wearing my pyjamas. I don't remember much of what happened at the end of the previous evening. It's all a bit hazy. I can't remember Darragh dropping me off, getting into my pyjamas or getting into bed. I groan, realising how drunk I was and what a fool I've made of myself.

There's no sound – no rain thrashing the windowpanes, no wailing wind. The storm has subsided, a thick silence descending in its wake. As I lie there, I can almost pretend I dreamt the whole thing, but then nebulous memories come back to me in fragments. I cringe as I remember practically throwing myself at Darragh on his sofa. He could have taken advantage of me; he could have taken me. I certainly wanted him to; my body was aching for him to kiss me again, even though I pushed him away. Instead, he brought me home.

It's just as well Darragh has more willpower and sense than me. Clearly, he wasn't as drunk as me. Maybe he isn't attracted to me. I don't like that thought much for some reason I don't want to explore, but I'm glad it stopped before it really started. Darragh and I would both have regretted it if we'd gone any further. He has a girlfriend and I'm married. It hurt when Mark cheated on me. It still hurts. I don't want to inflict that sort of pain and paranoia on my husband. Or on another woman. And what about Darragh and me? Who knows what would have happened if we'd had a one-night stand? Would it have ruined our friendship? Or would we have embarked on an affair?

I take my mobile from my bedside table and turn it on. When the screen appears, it's blurred. I must still be a bit tipsy. How much did I drink last night? So much for cutting down my alcohol intake. I blink and squint until the screen comes into focus. Then I send a text to Darragh.

Thank you for bringing me home safely.

And for behaving like a gentleman.

I'm sorry I overstepped the mark.

I grimace. Unfortunate choice of words given my husband's first name. But it's too late. I've sent it. Darragh's reply comes back immediately, making my heart skips a beat, much to my annoyance. I glance at his message, far more succinct than mine.

Not at all.

Next, I send a message to Mark to say good morning, realising as I do so that I've got this the wrong way round. I should have texted Mark first. He's my husband. I should be more concerned that he wasn't able to get home last night. I send him another text, hoping it won't come over as an afterthought, to ask where he is and when he's coming home. He doesn't reply and I don't know if he's put out or if he's not up yet. It's probably too early for the first ferry to Rathlin, even if they're sailing this morning.

I put my phone on the bedside table and roll onto my back,

159

my hands clasped behind my head. Staring at the ceiling, I sift through my thoughts, going over my vague recollections of last night. Darragh's account of Erin's death comes back to me, at first in pieces that I have to fit together, like doing a jigsaw puzzle, then in a rush, almost word for word. I'm overcome with an intense feeling of guilt, but I can't go there. Not yet. I don't want to ask myself if I could have prevented her death. I need a clear head to reassess my part in what happened to Erin.

I was right about one thing. The car accident was a lie, although it was fabricated by Darragh's parents, rather than by Darragh himself, to save face. But Darragh still hasn't told me the whole truth. Is it possible he doesn't know the rest? Maybe Erin kept it from Darragh because she was scared of how Darragh would react if he found out. Or perhaps she was ashamed.

Darragh would have been in his early twenties at the time. Erin spoke of him often. He was hot-headed and had a strong sense of justice, which he sometimes delivered with his fists, literally taking the law into his own hands. He was protective of his younger sister. Overprotective. He wasn't at home much anymore when I knew Erin – I never saw him. He might have left altogether by the time she died. He lost his sister, then his mother a year later. And he effectively lost his father in between.

Poor Darragh. I cover my face with my hands and groan again. I wish I'd consoled him instead of trying to seduce him. When he needed a friend, I failed him, and I've shown myself up in the process. This thought prompts unbidden images from last night to replay in my head. Darragh trying not to cry; me putting my arms around him; our kiss. Oh God, that kiss.

I was very turned on last night and I realise I've woken up aroused, too. Another image comes to me, like a still from a porn film. I had an erotic dream. I can't remember the details, but I do remember that Darragh and I played the leading roles. What is my problem? I love my husband. I want to have a baby with him. Surely, I don't fancy Darragh?

Miraculously, I don't have a headache, but I'm dehydrated. My mouth feels as if it's full of sand. I'm about to get out of bed, wondering if I can trust my legs this morning, but I register the glass of water on the bedside table, next to my mobile phone. It's the glass we keep our toothbrushes in. Seeing it reminds me I was thirsty in the night, too, and got up to go to the bathroom, where I guzzled water straight from the tap, then filled the glass in case I woke up thirsty again. I prop myself up on my elbows and gulp down the water.

As I set the glass back, I feel something. It's an ovulation test. I bulk-bought a stack of them on impulse in a chemist in Ilfracombe and brought them back in my suitcase. Yesterday, suspecting I was in the middle of my cycle and thinking Mark would be back later that evening, I peed on one of the sticks. I carried the stick into the bedroom while I was waiting for the result and then left it on the bedside table. I take the stick and look at it, although I already know the result. The smiley is still there. It hasn't faded. I've got today left if I'm going to conceive this month. I put the stick back, yawn and pull the covers up to my chin.

I'm nodding off when I hear a key in the front door. I thought I'd removed the spare key that we kept on the kitchen windowsill, although if I did, I can't remember where I put it. I don't truly believe anyone has been in our house, but that way, I thought Mark and I would both feel reassured.

But someone is in the house now. I hear quiet footfalls on the stairs and a rush of alarm zips down my body. Frantically, I look around for something to use as a weapon. Other than the lamp, there is nothing. I'm about to slip off the bed and crawl under it, even as I realise how ineffectual my hiding place will be, when Mark's head pokes round the bedroom door.

'Mark! You scared me!'

'Sorry.' He doesn't sound contrite. 'Who did you think it was?'

'I don't know.' Who else could it have been? Inwardly, I laugh at myself. I must still have been dazed from sleep. 'I didn't think you'd be home yet,' I say to Mark. I look from him to the alarm clock. It's gone nine. Later than I thought. 'You didn't reply to my text.'

'Phone battery's dead.' The sight of me cowering under the covers has made Mark grin. The look on his face reminds me of the smiley on the ovulation test. Perfect timing.

'I'm so glad you're home,' I say.

'Me too. I didn't want to wake you. I slept at Mum's, badly as it happens.'

'I'm not surprised. What did you sleep on?'

While I was in Devon, Mark told me over the phone that a sale had been agreed on his mother's bungalow. He has cleared everything out of the house. There are no beds or chairs anymore.

'On the floor.'

'Oh dear. At least the ferries are running again.'

'Yes. Got the first one back this morning. I'm shattered. I'm coming back to bed with you.'

I watch him take off his clothes. As he reaches under the pillow for the boxer shorts and T-shirt he wears to sleep in, I grab them and throw them on the floor on my side of the bed. Sitting up in bed, I take off my own pyjama top and wriggle out of the pyjama trousers, which I throw in Mark's direction. They fall short of their target, making us both laugh.

Mark's kiss is very different from Darragh's. I feel bad for comparing them, but I can't help it. I try not to think about Darragh, but it's his face I see when I close my eyes.

Mark kisses me and fondles my breasts tenderly, but I don't want foreplay. I pull him to me and wrap my legs around him. He needs no further stimulation, either. We move slowly and rhythmically at first, then it becomes urgent and animalistic. It's over quickly, both of us reaching climax at the same time. My body judders for several seconds afterwards, while Mark is still inside me. I hold him to me and he kisses me on the neck.

I smile to myself, a secret smiley of my own. Somehow, I know we've succeeded this time.

Chapter 25

According to the instruction leaflet inside my "early detection" pregnancy test, the levels of human chorionic gonadotropin – the pregnancy hormone – can vary from one woman to another, but it's possible that there will be enough hCG hormone only eight days after conception to give a positive result. Even though I've been through this before, I reread the instructions attentively and, as far as I can make out, a negative test at this stage wouldn't necessarily mean I'm not pregnant whereas a positive test would definitely mean I'm pregnant.

The best time to take the test is in the morning, so I barely sleep the night before. I end up peeing on the stick at five a.m., relieved that Mark's not here so I have time to absorb the result myself first. I've told myself I won't be disappointed if it's negative – it might be a false negative. But deep down I know if it isn't positive, I'll be gutted.

I'm fully expecting it to be negative, partly because that has been the result whenever I've taken a test, but also because I've never taken the test this soon before. I've always waited until at least the first day my period was due.

Three minutes I have to wait. I don't know why that seems interminable after waiting over a week to take the test in the first place, but it does. I leave the stick in the bathroom and go down-stairs to make myself a cup of tea. I make myself a piece of toast, too, and try not to keep glancing at the digital clock on the oven.

I wait a full five minutes. I've buttered the toast and made the tea, but I go back upstairs without touching either of them, resigning myself to the fact my body has failed me yet again.

I know what to look for. The first blue line shows the test has worked. If there's no second blue line, it means either I took the test too early or I'm not pregnant. I stare at the stick for several seconds, incredulous. The second line is very faint and I take the test over to the window to check. But there are two lines, not one. I take a photo with my phone, in case the second line fades away, so I don't doubt myself later.

Oh my God! I'm pregnant. Finally. I can't believe it. I squeal, do a little dance and an air punch, then go downstairs to eat my toast and drink my tea – both are cold, but I don't care.

After breakfast, I shower and get dressed, putting on lots of layers, a warm jacket and walking boots, then head out with my camera and binoculars. For a while now, I've been tracking some Irish golden hares in the field where I first glimpsed them shortly after arriving here. I'm fairly confident they'll be hanging out at their usual haunt this morning, despite the biting wind, the frost and the threat of showers. They seem to brave all the weather that gets thrown at them on this island.

Every time I come out here, I familiarise myself a little more with the hares' behaviours. I know that even if I stay downwind of them, they'll sense my presence. I've learnt to approach them slowly so as to gain their trust. I've worked out the best distance – a balance between getting close enough to get a decent shot, but not so close that I scare them off. If the hares twitch, it's a warning: one more step and they'll scarper. I think they're getting used to me, though.

At first, I think there are no hares around this morning. They tend to stay low and are hard to pick out. But then I spot them.

Once I've advanced as much as I dare on foot, to within fifty metres from them, I lie on my stomach and carefully prepare my equipment. I inch forwards with a commando crawl, holding my camera like a weapon in front of me. As soon as I see one of the hares straighten up and turn its head, I stop. This is far enough.

It might be a long wait before they come out into the open for me to photograph them. Lately my life has been all about waiting – eight days to take the pregnancy test, three minutes for the result. I'm usually impatient, but not when it comes to taking photos.

I rest the long telephoto lens on my backpack. I can't very well use a tripod while I'm lying prone on the ground and setting it up would startle the hares, but the light's not bad and I'm using a relatively fast shutter speed, so as long as I keep the camera steady, I should be able to get some good shots.

Almost two hours go by before I take any pictures I'm satisfied with, then I get several in a row. The first is of a hare standing on its hind legs and stretching, its fur a gingery gold in the faint sun. At full height, it's incredibly tall. Quickly, I change my focal length and only just manage to fit the whole of the hare into the frame. Then it sits, facing in my direction, its ears erect and I zoom back in and take more photos. I capture another hare sitting up with its back to me, its head turned to the side. The distinctive blue of its eye is very apparent in this shot. Finally, to my delight, two of the hares rise up to play-fight. At least, I think they're playing. It's almost as if I'm watching a boxing match.

Despite all the layers and gloves I'm wearing, I'm so cold I can hardly keep my hands from trembling for the last few photos I take. Glancing at my watch, I realise that I've spent three hours out here, lying on the ground. It's time to call it a day. I can't wait to see my photos on the computer.

I stand up slowly, trying not to alarm the hares, but they all flee immediately. I pack up my things and walk home. As

I pass the only two houses between here and my cottage, I notice both of them have decorations up. It's Hallowe'en in a few days' time. I make a mental note to buy some sweets for any trick or treaters.

When I get home, I make myself some lunch. I've had hours alone with my thoughts today and the fact I'm pregnant is sinking in. While I'm eating, I think about how to announce the news to Mark when he gets home this evening. I decide to wrap up the pregnancy test in the box my watch came in, which I've kept because it has the guarantee inside. I pack my plate and mug into the dishwasher and head upstairs.

In a cupboard in the room Mark and I share as a study, I dig out the little, rectangular box, some wrapping paper and some Sellotape. But there's no sign of the pregnancy test on my bedside table. I could have sworn I put it there after taking a photo of it with my phone, but I must be mistaken. I tip out the contents of the little pedal bin in the bathroom, in case it's skulking under the used tissues. But it's not there, either. I have no idea what I've done with it.

I go back into the bedroom, but by now I'm having second thoughts. A stick on which I've urinated might not be the sort of gift Mark will appreciate. I peer behind the table, on the floor, and finally I spot it under the bed. I get down on my hands and knees and reach for it. When I pick it up, I see it's cracked. I must have dropped it and walked on it without realising, then inadvertently kicked it under the bed. I put the pregnancy test on my bedside table, where I thought I'd put it in the first place. It doesn't matter now. I've decided not to give it to Mark, anyway.

I'm not sure I can wait until he comes home to tell him, though. Now I'm getting used to the idea that Mark and I are going to have a baby, I can barely contain my excitement. I need to tell someone and it wouldn't be right to ring my mum or Charlotte before telling Mark.

In the end, I send the photo of the positive pregnancy test to

Mark via text message. I wait for a few minutes, desperate to find out how he'll react. But although I can see from the read receipt notification that he has seen my message, he doesn't reply. He must be busy. Or perhaps, like me, he needs time to absorb this news.

Upstairs, I wander into the baby's room and scan it, working out how to decorate it and where to put the cot. Then I go across the landing into the office. Sitting at my desk, I transfer the photos I took of the hares to my computer. I'm delighted with them. I spend some time editing the best shots – cropping, enhancing the colours, adjusting the brightness and contrast, and so on. Cheating, as Mark would say. Then I post a few pictures to my social media pages and website.

When I've finished, I check my phone. Still no word from Mark.

I waste half an hour or so on the Internet, scrolling through Facebook and Instagram posts. Then I type "baby names" into the search engine. Mark wouldn't discuss names for our baby before it was conceived. He's not any more superstitious than I am, but he said he didn't want to tempt fate. I smile to myself, remembering how hard it was to talk him into painting the baby's room. I think he wanted to protect me from myself. I was so excited about starting a family and so devastated each time I got my period. Refusing to prepare for the baby's arrival was Mark's way of preventing me from getting my hopes up too much.

I take a pad and jot down some names to run by Mark.

Rose. Amy. Lily.

Oliver. Hugo. Ben.

Suddenly, a conversation with Darragh comes back to me. I remember him telling me that if he had a daughter one day, he would name her after his sister. I write down "Erin". Then I cross it out, tear the page out of the notebook, scrunch it up and throw it in the wastepaper bin.

*

Mark arrives home that evening armed with flowers and chocolates.

'I was in meetings all day. I couldn't get back to you. Pregnant, huh?' He looks at me with something like disbelief on his face.

'Yes! We're going to be parents!'

Mark picks me up and twirls me round. He looks a bit shocked. I can understand that. It's a big deal. And a little scary.

'Can we keep this a secret for now?' he asks, setting me down. 'You know, until we're past the three-month mark?'

I can't wait to tell my mum and Charlotte. If anything should happen and I don't make it past the first trimester, I'll need their support. But I expect Mark wants to get used to the idea he's going to be a dad. 'OK,' I say, deciding to make Charlotte and my mum swear to keep it to themselves when I tell them.

Mark takes off his shoes and follows me into the kitchen, where I fill a vase with water for the flowers.

'Kat, I've been thinking. We should put Causeway Cottage on the market,' he says. 'We're nowhere near a hospital here for when you go into labour. I'd feel happier if we moved somewhere less remote.'

'Where did this come from?' I ask. We discussed how we would cope with me being pregnant before we moved here and found solutions – or workarounds – for all our misgivings. I look at Mark suspiciously. 'What aren't you telling me?'

'I've been offered a promotion and a raise if I go back to Campbell & Coyle's head office in London.'

'Ah.'

'We could live somewhere outside London. Surrey or Berkshire, for example. I'll commute and you can continue your photography.'

'You've obviously thought this through.'

'We moved here because my mum was ill. She … isn't … we don't need to be here for her anymore. And we've got the money from the sale of her house. If we sell the cottage, too, we'll have enough for a deposit on a house in one of the Home Counties.'

'Do I get a say in this?'

'Of course,' Mark says, 'but you need to consider what's best for the baby now, too.'

I stare at Mark, open-mouthed. This isn't the reaction to my news that I was hoping for. I'd envisioned a romantic evening during which we'd make a shortlist of baby names. Instead, Mark has been thinking about moving back to England and now he's using the fact I'm expecting a baby to sway me.

A flicker of annoyance passes through me, but it quickly dies out. Mark has sprung this on me, but not long ago I had similar thoughts myself. After my mother-in-law's death, moving here became a pointless sacrifice. I felt lonely and longed to be nearer my friends and my mum. It's not as if I've made loads of friends here. Jenny and Darragh. That's all. And I'm not sure if Darragh's still my friend.

'OK,' I say. 'Let's put the house on the market.'

'Really? You don't want some time to think about it?'

'No. You're right. There's no reason for us to stay here anymore.'

If we move back to England, somewhere to the west of London – Guildford or Farnborough or Reading, say – Mark won't have too much of a commute and I'll be able to see a lot more of both my mum and Charlotte. One of the Home Counties. It might even feel like going home.

It also feels like running away. Building a future somewhere I can avoid the past. But maybe that's not such a bad thing.

Chapter 26

Mark wastes no time putting the house on the market. The estate agent who sold us the cottage only months ago arrives one morning the following week when Mark's at work. I open the door to find him standing on the doorstep, a huge "For Sale" sign under his arm. He asks me for permission to fix it to our gatepost and then comes inside to take some photos of the cottage, especially the rooms we've redecorated since our arrival.

Mark is displeased when he comes home. 'I didn't want anyone to know we were moving,' he says, bursting through the front door and thumbing over his shoulder in the direction of the gatepost.

'Why?' I ask. I can understand him not wanting anyone to know we're going to have a baby yet, but the cottage will be on the estate agency's website. And word travels fast on this island. I can't see what difference it makes if we have a "For Sale" sign out the front or not. 'Surely the more people who know, the sooner we'll attract a buyer?'

He grumbles something, but I don't catch it.

'Is everything all right, Mark?'

I was hoping, once Mark had had some time to process his mum's death, he would be less grouchy and back to his old self. Instead, his behaviour has been odd recently. There was that business with the football hoodie, which he more or less accused me of planting among his clothes and then hiding again. And now he's making a fuss about the "For Sale" sign. I don't know what has got into him.

'I don't want the sign there, that's all.'

'Take it down if you don't like it.' I follow him into the sitting room.

I put Mark's reactions and remarks down to him having to adjust to the idea that the two of us are going to become a family of three. I hope he snaps out of it and comes round soon.

'It's ugly,' he says, looking out of the window.

I follow his gaze. The sign isn't visible from here, but I don't contradict him. I notice our car parked in front of the house. Mark usually comes home on the foot ferry and leaves the car in Ballycastle.

'Is there something in the car we need to unload?' I ask, hoping to change the subject.

'No.'

'How come you've got it?'

'I want to go out for a drive this evening,' Mark says.

My eyebrows tent in confusion. The sun sets early now we're into November and it's already dark. I can't imagine why Mark would want to drive around the island without being able to admire the views or where he would want to go. The pub and the seafront are within walking distance and Mark is against drink-driving anyway. Not that he has ever gone to McCuaig's Bar without me.

'Do you want some company?' I ask.

'No.'

'Oh. Before I forget. A letter arrived for you this morning. I left it on the kitchen table.'

Mark insists on getting dinner ready and we eat it in silence – not a comfortable one, an awkward one. I keep trying to start a conversation, but my efforts are rewarded with only grunts and one-word answers. I'm about to give up, but then I remember the letter. We're sitting at the kitchen table and the letter is no longer propped up against the salt and pepper pots, where I left it. I scan the room, but I don't spot it anywhere else. Mark has moved it. Has he opened it?

'Who was the letter from?' I'm genuinely curious. It came in a thick, cream envelope with Mark's name and our address on it in neat handwriting. There was no sender's address. Neither of us receives letters anymore. Christmas or birthday cards, maybe. But no one sends letters these days. My mind drifts to Erin, who used to be my pen friend. There's a word that has fallen into disuse. Pen friends are a thing of the past. Nowadays, it's texts, WhatsApp messages or emails.

'What?'

'The letter. I left it here for you.' I tap my fingers on the table. 'Who was it from?'

His eyes flit from left to right and I can tell his brain is whirring to come up with something. 'The solicitor. About my mother's estate. Nothing you need to concern yourself with.'

Mark's lying. I know this with certainty, not only because he's a terrible liar, but also because the solicitor who dealt with his mother's will has his office in Belfast and the letter had a London postmark.

A London postmark. That's when it hits me. Of course. It's from Fiona. It has to be.

I should know better than to call him on it, even though I'm fed up with his behaviour and her hounding us. I try to bite my tongue, but it comes out. 'That's not true, Mark.'

'Are you calling me a liar?'

'I just … know that in this particular instance, you're not telling the truth. It's from your ex-wife, isn't it?'

'Well, you should know!' He gets abruptly to his feet, knocking over the chair. I flinch as he leans across the table, his face so close to mine I can smell his breath. 'You should know!' He actually shakes a fist at me. 'You steamed open the envelope and then stuck it down!' His voice has ratcheted up to top volume. He has never, ever shouted at me so loudly. 'God, Kat. You harp on about Fiona and think I'm hiding things from you and lying to you. And all along you're … You're such a fucking hypocrite!'

My anger rises inside me and threatens to boil over like lava erupting from a volcano. I almost slap Mark, even though I have never struck anyone in my life. Without another word, he storms out of the house. I don't know whether to run after him or if we should both calm down before we discuss this. Before I can make up my mind, I hear the car roar away.

I stay sitting at the table for several minutes, tears coursing down my cheeks. I can't make any sense of what just happened. Did he really call me a fucking hypocrite? Why? I cover my ears with my hands, as if by doing that I can unhear his words. What does he think I'm hiding from him? What lies has he caught me in? What does he know?

When I'm cried out, my thoughts turn to the letter. What on earth was in it? Who was it from? I'm upset that Mark could imagine I'd steam open his letter and read something that was written to him. But then I remember using his thumb while he was asleep to access his phone and read the text message from Fiona. It does sound like something the person I've become would be capable of doing.

My mum once sent a Christmas card that arrived partially opened. I think some dishonest person had got hold of it and checked to see if there was any money in it. Perhaps that's the case here. Mark has got wound up over nothing. But this only serves to wind *me* up more.

It's too late to steam open the letter now, but if I find it, I can read it. That way, I'll know why Mark lied and why he reacted the way he did. If I'd suspected earlier that the letter was from Fiona, I would have torn the damn envelope open, never mind bothering to steam it open and stick it back down. What has he done with it? I don't think he left the kitchen until he stomped out after our row. So it must be in here somewhere.

I open drawers and look in cupboards. The last place I look is the most obvious one. The bin. And sure enough, that's where it is. Torn into tiny pieces, some of which are peeking out from underneath some used teabags and uneaten leftovers Mark has also thrown out.

Minutes later, wearing surgical gloves and using a pair of tweezers, I'm sifting through the pieces of the letter I've retrieved from the bin, trying to reassemble them on a tray. I must look like an amateur forensic scientist and I feel ridiculous now as well as furious. My hands are shaking and I keep glancing towards the door and straining my ears for Mark's car, terrified he'll come back and catch me doing this.

After half an hour, I give up. The letter seems to have been quite short but the food stains and the tiny pieces have made it into an impossible puzzle. I can only make out a few words and some of them are incomplete: I … Kat … chi … abou … if … ance … will … fair … not … on … Mark … Other … can't. The most telling bit is a large letter "F" with a small "x" underneath, which, as far as I'm concerned, confirms my suspicions. This is from Fiona.

I assume the letter is in the same vein as "If you don't tell her soon, I will" and that Mark was definitely lying when he said his ex-wife was referring to a colleague in her text. What does she want Mark to tell me? And how dare she sign off with a kiss!

I know Fiona has just had someone else's baby. But although it seems unlikely, the only explanation I can think of is that she and Mark are having an affair. I gasp out loud as something dawns on me. Is that why Mark wants to move back to England? To be closer to Fiona?

At a loss for what to do or think, I scrape all the pieces of the letter back into the kitchen bin, cover them with food and then

174

discard my gloves, too, pushing them down the sides of the bin bag as best I can without getting my hands dirty.

I pace the ground floor of the house, forcing myself to take deep breaths. Then, when I think I can do it without sobbing and sniffing down the phone, I ring Charlotte.

Lately, Charlotte has listened to my troubles and she has a knack of asking the right questions, one after the other, until I can see things more clearly in my own head. Our relationship seems one-sided to me at the moment, but it hasn't always been that way. When Charlotte's mother was terminally ill, it was a horrible time for Charlotte and I provided a shoulder for her to cry on. When Rupert proposed and Charlotte decided she needed to lose weight before the wedding, I took on the role of sports coach and worked out with her several times a week for about six months until she reached her target weight.

It all pours out now, in the wrong order. The argument with Mark, my kiss with Darragh, putting the house on the market, Mark's mood swings, everything. Nearly everything. I can't tell Charlotte about Erin. I've never mentioned Erin to Charlotte. Charlotte has never judged me, but I'm afraid she might think less of me if I told her now. She might realise I'm not good friend material after all.

Charlotte doesn't interrupt my monologue. Nor does she spur me on when I pause. There's total silence on the other end of the phone and I know she has dropped whatever she was doing to sit down and give me her full attention.

When I've finally finished, she says, 'First of all, congratulations!'

'The baby, you mean?'

'Of course, the baby.'

She asks me about Darragh and if I'm in love with him.

'No,' I say. I'm fairly sure I'm being truthful. 'I'm having a baby with Mark, which I'm really excited about. I just got drunk and carried away. I'm glad nothing serious happened, although I think our kiss has made things awkward between Darragh and me.'

'Are you going to tell Mark?'

'No!' I feel like a hypocrite when I say that. Something cold pinches my heart. Perhaps Mark already knows I kissed Darragh. Is that what he meant when he called me a hypocrite? That would make sense. He was mad at me for harping on about Fiona. But I reject that idea. Mark can't possibly have found out that Darragh and I kissed on the night of the storm.

'For what it's worth, I don't think you should tell Mark,' Charlotte says. 'The two of you have had a row. It's no biggie. And you're selling up and leaving soon. No good can come of you fessing up to Mark that you snogged the local Irish hunk … What's his name again—?'

'Darragh.'

'—Darragh in a drunken lapse of reason. So, what are you going to do?'

'I'll send Darragh a message,' I say. 'See if we can meet up and put this behind us.' It occurs to me that Mark should have been foremost in my thoughts, not Darragh. But the problem with Darragh seems less complicated, easier to resolve.

As if reading my mind, Charlotte says, 'Yes, but what are you going to do about *Mark*? Are you going to confront him about the letter again?'

'I don't know. He'll only deny it's from her or come up with some rubbish about what she wrote to him.'

'Good pun.'

'What?'

'Rubbish. You know, seeing as you fished the letter out of the bin.' Charlotte manages to make me smile at that, although I know she can't see it. 'He owes you an explanation for his weird, inexcusable behaviour, Katherine,' she says. 'Plus, he clearly had something to hide and did hide it – in the bin. He's attacking you to defend himself. Which makes him the fucking hypocrite.'

'You're probably right,' I say.

'Of course I'm right,' she says. 'Can I do anything for you?'

'You've listened to me whining about all my problems. That's already … Hang on, now I think of it, you can do something. Can you give me Fiona's number? I don't have it and Mark has deleted it from his phone.'

'I don't have it, either,' Charlotte says, 'but I can easily get hold of it for you. I know people who know her.'

'Yes, do that. I didn't want to ring her, but at least that way, I can get to the bottom of this.'

'No problem. By the way, I'm really excited about you moving back to England.'

'Me, too.'

'I'll come and stay at weekends to help out with the baby and annoy Mark.'

'That's part of your contract if you accept to be godmother,' I say.

Charlotte squeals with delight. We talk some more, about Charlotte now, and when I end the call, I feel a lot better, even though the knotted dread in my stomach is still there, reminding me that things with Mark will have to be untangled and smoothed over, although I need to calm down a bit more first. And things with Darragh have to be sorted out, too.

I decide to go to bed. I'll pretend to be asleep when Mark comes home and keep up the pretence until he has left for work tomorrow. I have so many questions whirring around in my brain that my head hurts. What does Fiona want? Where is Mark? Why is he lying to me? But they will all have to wait because I can't deal with any of this tonight.

Chapter 27

Apart from that one text message in reply to mine the morning after the storm, I haven't heard from Darragh since the night we kissed. When I finally pluck up the courage and come up with an excuse to get in touch with him, he doesn't reply. I pace the sitting room. Even though I'm holding it in my hand, I keep checking my phone in case I don't hear the text notification sound. I sent him the message over an hour ago, asking if I should drop off his girlfriend's clothes somewhere or if he wants to stop by the cottage on his way home from work and pick them up. Darragh's probably at work and he'll hardly feel the need to get back to me urgently about his girlfriend's stuff. He might not be ignoring me. An hour's not long. I'm being impatient.

It's a long-winded text. A pretext. I waffled on about having washed the clothes and asked after Dexter. The real reason is I need to see him. I don't know if he's avoiding me, if he's mad at me or even if we can still be friends. Perhaps he's as embarrassed about that night as I am.

But I have to tell him what I've been trying to hide from him. My side of the story. If he hasn't mentioned that Erin was raped, then Erin can't have told him. And if Darragh doesn't know about the rape, then he doesn't know about me or about my role in it.

My secret is safe. But I think he should know what really happened to his sister. Which means I'll have to tell him the very secret I've been trying so hard to keep from him. I may lose Darragh's friendship, if I haven't already, but at least I'll have cleared my conscience and taken a step towards laying Erin's ghost to rest.

When my mobile finally pings with a text, it startles me. As usual, Darragh's reply to my wordy message is concise.

Lunch at McCuaig's? 1 pm?

I confirm that with an even shorter "OK", proud of myself for keeping the word count down for once.

I should have told him on the night of the storm. No, I should have told him way before that. When I realised who he was. The longer you keep something a secret, the harder it is to confess. And the easier it is to bury it under another layer of lies.

I don't know how to tell him. I replay the events of the night of the céilí in my head, trying to find the right words. But there are no right words to describe what I did. Or what I didn't do.

Erin and I were drunk. Far too drunk. And yet I encouraged her to keep going back to the bar and buy more Bacardi Breezers. Erin complied because she fancied the bartender. When she went up to the bar for what was to be the last time, she stayed there, chatting to the barman, or chatting him up, maybe. I got bored waiting for her – and for my drink. One of the boys we'd been dancing with came over to me, and he and I ended up in the empty cloakroom – no one had arrived wearing a coat on that warm summer evening. We'd been there for about twenty minutes, talking, giggling and kissing, when a girl around my age burst in on us, deliberately, to tell me my friend was in trouble. She said she'd seen her outside with a man and heard her screaming down by the river, and the man trying to get her to be quiet.

The boy I was with – to my shame I can't even remember his name – asked the girl what she'd been doing outside. She said she'd been smoking a cigarette. He retorted that she shouldn't be smoking at her age and that my friend was a big girl and could take care of herself. Then we carried on kissing.

I didn't go to look for Erin. She came and found me, pale and shaking, with mascara lining her face. She asked me to walk with her to a payphone to ring her brother. I did. She made me go before her brother arrived. She waited for Darragh outside the community hall and I watched her from inside it, peering through the round windows of the doors, until she got into her brother's car. I couldn't make out the driver. Then I threw up in the toilets and walked back to my grandparents' holiday rental, a few doors up the road from the community hall.

Tears stream silently down my face as I force myself to relive this now. Erin was raped and I could have prevented it. The rape set off a chain of events that I now know led ultimately to Erin's death. I've been trying hard to bridle that thought. It's too hard to process. Will Darragh tell me it wasn't my fault, that I was only fifteen? Will he blame me? I blame myself now, more than ever.

As I walk down the hill towards the pub, I rehearse my lines. When I get to McCuaig's, I know what to say. Keep it factual. Tell the truth. Apologise, both for not coming clean sooner and for not coming to Erin's aid at the céilí.

Entering the pub, I spot Tom before I see Darragh. My heart sinks. I can't talk to Darragh in front of Tom. But as I approach their table, Tom stands up, drains his pint and puts on his jacket, all rather hurriedly.

'Hi, Katherine. Lovely to see you,' he says. 'I'm dashing home for lunch, just stopped for a swift pint, so I won't be joining you, I'm afraid.' He seems keen to get away.

I hope my relief doesn't show on my face. I ask him to give Jenny my love. He practically sprints to the door, leaving me wondering if he's running late or if he can't wait to get away from me.

'Hey, you,' Darragh says to me as Tom leaves.

I hand him the bag of clothes, unwind my scarf and shrug off my coat, then sit opposite him in the seat Tom has vacated. My heart pounds, as much at the sound of Darragh's voice as at the prospect of telling him the awful truth. 'Hi.'

For a moment, neither of us speaks. Then both of us speak at the same time. That makes us laugh, albeit nervously, and breaks the ice.

'I was worried you wouldn't want to see me again,' he says, fixing his green-brown eyes on mine.

'I thought you were ignoring me. I'm sorry. I behaved terribly. I think the wine went to my head after the run, but that's no excuse. I'm so glad we stopped before we got too carried away.'

'No harm done,' he says.

He looks down, as if he's studying the menu, but I suspect it's to break eye contact. 'Shall we order?' he asks without looking up.

I tell him what I want and he goes to the bar. When he gets back, he says, 'So, how have you been?'

For some reason I can't fathom, I burst into tears. Something has tipped me over. Maybe it's relief because Darragh and I are on still on speaking terms. Or nerves because I've been psyching myself up to reveal my role in Erin's demise. It might simply be due to pregnancy hormones. Whatever the reason, I suspect the underlying cause is my row with Mark.

I wouldn't normally break down like this in front of someone, and I'm mortified I'm losing it in front of Darragh of all people. I bury my face in my hands, but he takes one of them and holds it in his own across the table.

'Do you want to tell me what's the matter?' he asks.

I should use this as my cue to confess. But if Darragh doesn't know Erin was raped, wouldn't it be better if he didn't find out? It would make him suffer even more if he knew how much she'd suffered herself. Do I want to tell him simply so I can offload my guilt and feel better about the whole thing even if it makes him feel worse? This hasn't occurred to me before and I need some time to consider it. Or is this an excuse to bottle out?

'It's OK. You can tell me.'

'Oh, it's nothing. A tiff with my husband.' I don't think I've ever used the word "tiff" before and it seems like an understatement. 'He's been behaving strangely ever since he found out …'

I break off, think through my next words. I don't want Darragh to know I'm pregnant. I promised Mark I wouldn't tell anyone, although obviously that didn't include Charlotte. But Darragh is … well, Darragh. I can't tell him. My mother doesn't know yet.

'Ever since when?'

'Since we put the cottage on the market.' I wince. I wasn't supposed to tell Darragh that, either. Mark asked me not to broadcast our plans to move away. But Darragh doesn't react. He must have already known. Gossip circulates rapidly on the grapevine on this island. 'No, since his mother's death, actually.'

'Oh?' He leans forwards. 'I thought she was ill. Or was her death unexpected?'

'No. She was ill. It just hit him really hard. We moved here to be closer to her and then … well, we hadn't even settled in when she died.'

As I say that, I wonder if I'd ever have settled in here. I've never felt completely at home. Despite Darragh's and Jenny's best efforts, I've always felt like an outsider. I'm glad we're not staying.

Our meals arrive and it's only now that I realise Darragh still has hold of one of my hands. I take it back and use the paper napkin to wipe my eyes and nose. I put salt, vinegar and ketchup on my chips and tuck in. I haven't eaten breakfast because I was still in a state after arguing with Mark last night. I'm starving now.

'You can't leave, Kat,' Darragh says, his mouth full of scampi.

I've lost the thread of the conversation, even though I was the one doing most of the talking and it was all about me. My mouth is full, so I tilt my head and frown at Darragh for him to clarify.

'You said you were selling your house,' he says. 'You can't leave

Rathlin. Not yet. Not now.' His voice has a strange undertone to it, like a strangled growl. It sounds almost threatening. Perhaps he didn't know we'd decided to sell. 'What I mean is, I'd like you to stay,' he adds, more softly, reaching across the table to put his hand on mine again. 'Kat, it's not my place to say this, but I think you should leave your husband.'

He's right. It's not his place to say that. I slide my hand out from under his, hoping the gesture will deter him from saying anything more. Is he suggesting I should leave Mark for him? Or does he think Mark's not right for me, not worthy of me? Either way, I don't want to know.

'Darragh, don't.' The intensity of his gaze is unnerving. 'Please don't.' I sigh. 'I'm not leaving Mark. I'm leaving this place with Mark.'

Chapter 28

Mark left this morning with his travel case, so I know he's not coming home tonight. We haven't said a word to each other since our argument yesterday evening. He was still very pissed off this morning, making a huge racket, stomping around and slamming doors. I'm sure he was doing it on purpose. He must have known I was only pretending to sleep through it.

As soon as I get home from the pub, I ring him, hoping to clear the air between us a little, but he doesn't take the call. I didn't really expect him to. He's usually busy during the day. I leave a message, saying I'm confused and upset about what happened between us and asking him to ring me back when he has time so we can talk.

At half past three on the dot, I hear the text notification sound on my mobile. I grab my phone and check the message but it's not from Mark. It's from Jenny. School must have finished for the day.

> Are you free for a cup of tea?
> I have cake.
> I need to talk to you.

I type out a reply.

I'd love to!
Your place or mine?!

We exchange a few more messages. I decide to walk to Jenny's house, which I've been to a few times. Jenny and Tom live in Ballyconagan, to the north of Church Quarter, about halfway between Causeway Cottage and the old coastguard hut at Cantruan. I could do with the walk, more to clear my head than for the exercise.

I need to talk to you. When I consider Jenny's message, it seems ominous. I wonder what she wants to tell me. I keep thinking about Tom leaving as soon as I walked through the door into the pub earlier. Was he avoiding me? I try to persuade myself I'm overthinking both Tom's hasty exit from the pub and Jenny's text. Tom said he had to rush home. And Jenny has invited me for a cup of tea and a slice of cake. There's nothing worrying about that. Lately, every thought that enters my head seems to shape itself into a question mark. I'm reading things that aren't there into innocuous situations.

It's a short, uphill walk, starting with the steep steps that lead from the church next door to the parochial house above it. A path continues the climb upwards from there. Shortly after some kissing gates, the path becomes a lane and weaves its way through a hamlet, or "clachan" as they call it here, offering terrific views of East Lighthouse. I've taken some beautiful photographs from up here. A small cluster of houses dominates the hilltop. Jenny and Tom's is the last of these, a former barn that they've done up beautifully.

A welcoming mixture of spices and fruit wafts towards me from Jenny's modern kitchen as I step inside the house. Jenny has baked a fruit cake. She must have made it as soon as she got home because the loaf is still warm from the oven. She cuts two slices and slathers them with butter and gestures for me to sit in one of the wooden chairs. She puts the plates and mugs of tea on the table and sits down opposite me.

'This is delicious, Jenny,' I say, biting into the cake.

'It's Irish barmbrack teacake,' she says. 'My grandmother's recipe. I can let you have it if you like. Traditionally, it's eaten around Hallowe'en, although kids prefer sweets these days. I'm rather late baking mine this year.'

We chat for a while, but Jenny picks at her cake nervously and then picks at the skin around her thumb. She obviously has something on her mind. I try to make it easier for her.

'What was it you needed to talk to me about?' I ask.

She takes a deep breath. 'This is difficult for me, Katherine,' she says. 'I wasn't sure whether I should tell you or not, but I think if it were the other way round, I'd like you to tell me.'

She pauses and I don't prompt her. I have no idea what she's about to reveal, but I don't think I want to hear it. Is this about Darragh?

'I bumped into Mark a little while ago, one Saturday morning, at the Co-op.' Ah, so it's about Mark. 'He insisted on carrying the shopping out to the car for me. At first, I thought he was being gallant, charming, you know. But he went too far.'

I'm sure she has worked out how to phrase what she wants to say, but she pauses again. I stay silent, allowing those words to sink in before she hits me with more. The ticking of the clock on the wall above the door reverberates around the room and I'm surprised I haven't noticed before how loud it is. I watch the second hand for a few beats as it makes its way round the dial.

'He came on a bit strong,' Jenny continues. 'Both Tom and I love you to bits, Katherine. I'm not looking to cause trouble. And I hope this won't affect our friendship. I'm sorry to be dumping this on you, but I thought you should know and I've discussed this with Tom and … well, we'd prefer it if we could see you without Mark from now on.'

I'm too stunned to say anything. I don't trust myself to speak, anyway. I shake my head in bewilderment and fight back tears of humiliation. I glance at Jenny, who is looking down at her hands.

Her thumb is bleeding where she has been scratching at it and she puts it to her mouth to suck at the blood.

This is probably the reason why Tom was so keen to get away from me earlier. It might even be why Darragh suggested I leave Mark. I don't want to rush to Mark's defence, but at the same time, this could be a case of he said / she said. There's a continuum with harmless flirting at one end and sexual harassment at the other extreme. The difficulty lies in determining where Mark is on that scale.

'Is there any way what my husband said to you might simply have been clumsy? Could he have been making a joke in poor taste? Or, I don't know, giving you a heavy-handed compliment?'

'No.' Jenny is categorical. I nod thoughtfully. I suppose that the point is, whatever it was Mark said, whether Jenny has misconstrued it or not, he made her uncomfortable. There's a fine line between charming and creepy, and Jenny feels that Mark has crossed that line.

Jenny breaks into my thoughts. 'It wasn't just what he said. He also … his hands … he groped—' She doesn't finish her sentence, but she makes a brief movement, lifting her right hand from her lap and splaying her fingers in front of her breasts.

'Oh. Right. I see.' I don't need her to elaborate. The word "grope" is unequivocal and her gesture says it all. My face burns and a wave of nausea surges inside me. I need to get out of this house, or I will throw up. 'I … I should go,' I stammer.

Jenny stands up. I haven't finished my cake and I've hardly touched my tea, but she's not going to stop me. 'I hope we can remain friends,' she says, 'and I'd like you to take the photos at the nativity play as we arranged, if you're still happy to do that,' she says as I pull on my coat and stumble outside.

I head home, feeling so shaky that I don't fully trust my legs to carry me. As I walk, I process Jenny's accusation in my mind. I want to confront Mark about this and he has the right to tell me his side of the story, but I know how he'll spin it. He'll claim he was being friendly. He wasn't coming on to her. His hand accidentally brushed her breast as he was putting her shopping in the car. He was mortified and apologised. She got the wrong impression. That's what he'll say, his face a picture of innocence as he protests.

Although I don't want to bury my head in the sand, I don't believe Mark is capable of sexual harassment. I'm inclined to think Jenny did get the wrong end of the stick, even though her words have nonetheless sown a tiny seed of doubt in my mind. In my head, I replay the scene she has depicted. She has given me her version of the truth, but I see it through a slightly different lens, although I'm not painting Mark in a much better light than Jenny did.

I imagine Mark flirting, Jenny being too polite to put him in his place and Mark taking that as encouragement to take it a step further. Could this be what really happened? If Jenny had been flattered and responsive to Mark's advances, would he have tried to seduce her? And if Mark did try it on with Jenny, is that any worse than me throwing myself at Darragh? Or is this different merely because Mark is a man?

As I arrive at the cottage, my mobile blares out from my back pocket. It's Mark. I don't answer the call, but once I'm inside the house, sitting on the sofa in the living room with my legs curled up, I listen to the message he left.

'Hi, Kat,' Mark's voice says. 'I'm sorry I missed your call earlier. I wanted to apologise for causing an argument. As you know, it has been a horribly stressful time at work. We're on tenterhooks waiting for the FDA approval for our new migraine medicine. But that's no excuse. I also wanted to remind you I'm not coming home until the weekend. Can we talk about all this then? I know we need to discuss what happened, but I don't want to do it over the phone. I love you.'

If Mark told me he was away until the weekend, I'd forgotten, but that suits me. It gives me time to think. I draft a quick reply.

OK.

See you on Friday.

Mark will expect me to add "I love you, too", but I can't do that right now. I contemplate apologising for my role in the row and decide against it. I don't think I did anything wrong. I accused him of lying about the letter, which he was. He's the one who resorted to name-calling. He called me a fucking hypocrite. I'm still fuming. I leave the text how it is and send it.

I put the phone on the coffee table, but it goes again. I pick it back up, intending to reject Mark's call, but then I see the caller ID. It's Charlotte. I sigh with relief. It will cheer me up to talk to my best friend. I don't have to tell her what Jenny told me. I tap the green button to accept the call.

We chat inconsequentially for about half an hour and I even surprise myself by laughing as Charlotte regales me with anecdotes from work. But Charlotte is perspicacious.

'Is something wrong?' she asks during a slight lull in the conversation.

'No,' I say. I almost leave it at that, but then I add, 'Can I ask you a question?'

'Fire away.'

'Has Mark ever hit on you? I mean, did he ever chat you up or … feel you up?'

'God, no!'

'And you've never known him to make sexual advances … unwelcome advances … towards anyone?'

'No. Never.'

Her answer would be convincing if it hadn't come two or three beats too late.

'Charlotte?'

'OK. Sorry. There was a rumour once. Rupert told me about it. It was a long time ago, when Rupert was still working for

Campbell & Coyle. But that's all it was. A rumour. It didn't amount to anything.'

'Was Mark married to me at the time? Or was he still married to Fiona?'

'He was engaged to you.'

'Why didn't you tell me? What happened?'

'I didn't want to upset you. Rupert didn't believe a word of this woman's story. He said she was a drama queen and had made up the whole thing. As soon as Mark's boss stepped in, she retracted what she'd said. I'd forgotten all about it until you asked just now.'

'What did she say? What did she accuse Mark of doing?'

'I honestly don't know, Katherine. I think everyone at Campbell & Coyle had been out celebrating. Someone's retirement or something.'

'Do you think he was drunk? Trying his luck?'

'Maybe. Listen, Katherine, you know me. Many women put up with lecherous men in the workplace instead of reporting them so they get their comeuppance. I wouldn't keep quiet about something like that or allow everyone to brush it under the carpet. But this is Mark we're talking about. I mean, it's not like he's got a rep for that sort of thing, is it?'

'He cheated on me with Fiona,' I remind her.

'That's not the same thing, is it? Fiona was his ex. She seduced him. Whatever this woman alleged Mark said or did, the point is, in her case, she made it out to be unwanted on her part. Rupert seemed to think she'd misread Mark's meaning.'

Charlotte has essentially drawn the same conclusions as I have. It sounds to me like Mark flirted ineptly with his colleague or maybe he went as far as making a pass at her, blurring the boundaries between acceptable and unacceptable behaviour. And now he has done it again. With my friend Jenny.

'Do you want me to ask Rupert for details?'

I think about that. Rupert will probably downplay whatever

Mark allegedly said or did out of loyalty to Mark. If he even remembers the details. 'No, there's no point,' I say.

'Has something happened?' Charlotte sounds concerned rather than curious and I love her for that. 'Do you want to talk about it?'

'Not yet.'

She doesn't push it. 'Well, you know I'm here for you when you do.'

'Thank you.'

'That's what best mates are for. Listen, Katherine, I actually called you because I've got Fucking Fiona's mobile number if you still want it. Do you?'

I ask Charlotte to text me Fiona's number, but with everything else going on – the argument between Mark and me, the cottage going up for sale, my pregnancy, Jenny's accusation and Charlotte's confirmation of a similar incident – the last thing I want to do is talk to my husband's ex-wife.

Chapter 29

Mark is a mess. His hair is dishevelled, he clearly hasn't shaved for a couple of days, and puffy bags droop underneath his bloodshot eyes. He looks terrible. He looks tired, too, as if he has hardly slept well while he was away. He can barely put one foot in front of the other – literally – and crosses the threshold into the house as if he's crossing the finish line of a marathon.

We haven't spoken a word to each other face to face since our row. We haven't seen each other since then. We need to talk. Urgently. I'm not sure exactly what to say, or how much. I can't decide if I should bring up my conversation with Jenny, too, or stick to the letter from Fiona.

But our discussion will have to wait as the estate agent is here, having scheduled a viewing of the cottage for a retired couple. The weather isn't great – it's rainy and misty, a dismal, grey day. The estate agent was keen for either Mark or me to be here when they came round, but I've let him get on with it.

Mark plops down into an armchair in the living room, a look of reproach on his haggard face, as the trio make their way up the cream-carpeted stairs with their wet shoes on. Sitting on the sofa, I remember admiring the views from the master bedroom the day I first set foot in our new home. They won't see far when they look out of the window today.

We hear the estate agent's voice from above us as he describes the different rooms and features. I imagine he used much the same spiel on Mark when he came for his first visit. We make out short, enthusiastic responses from the woman, but the man, although we can't discern every word he says, sounds more critical and fires ceaseless questions at the estate agent. I realise I'm staring at the ceiling, as if that might enable me to lip-read the exchange upstairs. Someone turns on the taps in the bathroom and a cupboard is closed noisily.

'Let's hope they don't check the roof,' Mark says sardonically. It's pretty much the only thing he has said apart from "hello" since he entered the house and I'm not sure what to make of his comment. 'Although, if they find out it's in need of repair, we could recommend an all-round handyman and painter named Darragh,' he concludes.

As I turn sharply to look at Mark, I notice his gaze fix on the painting of Altacarry Head. My heart clenches for a beat. Is it a coincidence he looked at it when he mentioned Darragh? But if Mark has worked who the artist is, he doesn't say anything. Either he still doesn't know or, like me, he finds it trivial now, compared with everything else that has happened recently.

He doesn't get up to see them out when the viewing is over. As I open the front door, I notice his company BMW parked behind the estate agent's sensible family Ford Focus. Is Mark planning on going for another nocturnal drive?

Once they've gone and I've rejoined Mark in the living room, he leans forwards in the armchair, his elbows resting on his knees, and clears his throat.

'I'm sorry, Kat,' he says, adopting his best hangdog expression. 'I behaved despicably. I'm still struggling to come to terms with my mum's death. I know I've already used that as an excuse and it's no excuse at all.'

He pauses and I know this is my cue to apologise, too, but I can't bring myself to do it. He's right. He can't keep using his mother's death to justify his moodiness. He has been lying to me for weeks now. Then again, I haven't been completely honest with him, either.

When I don't say anything, Mark continues, 'I don't want you to think I'm not delighted about the baby. I am. I'm rather shocked that I'm going to be a father, that's all.' He gives me a pointed look. Another cue to say something, but I'm not sure what this time. His lines sound contrived, rehearsed.

'Was the letter from Fiona?' I ask.

Judging from the look on Mark's face, I've deviated from the script. This wasn't what he expected me to say at all.

'No. I told you. It was from the solicitor.' He doesn't sound indignant. He's obviously too exhausted to fight. But he's sticking to the solicitor story. 'I went to see him at his office in Belfast yesterday and that's all sorted now.'

Wow. He's piling on the lies now. He's definitely getting better at lying. He maintained eye contact this time. Practice makes perfect, I suppose. Or perhaps he has learnt from the best. His hands are shaking noticeably and I assume it's because he's anxious.

'There was a London postmark on the letter. Isn't your solicitor based in Belfast?'

His face darkens. He doesn't answer the question. Instead, he says, more calmly, 'I didn't notice the postmark. Maybe you're mistaken.'

I'm not, but if I don't let it go, I'll cause another row before we resolve this one. I have another way of finding out what was in the letter if I really want to know.

'God, I could do with a drink,' Mark says.

I get up, walk over to the sideboard and pour him a generous measure of whiskey – two fat fingers of Black Bush. Like his father and my own, Mark has always drunk it neat. As I hand him the crystal glass, I remember Darragh telling me his father drowned his sorrow in whiskey. If I wasn't expecting a baby, I'd be tempted to drink myself to oblivion this evening, too. Not Irish whiskey, though. White wine. A huge quantity of wine would shrink my problems to a more solvable size.

For a while, neither of us speaks – Mark, I suspect, because he thinks the discussion is over and he's off the hook, and me because I'm having difficulty swallowing down the lump in my throat. I should be annoyed, but I'm unspeakably and inexplicably sad. Words can hurt people. But sometimes you can hurt someone more with what you don't say. Mark is hiding something and at this stage, I would rather he just came out with it.

I'd more or less decided not to mention my conversation with Jenny, but it sort of slips out when I find my tongue. 'I caught up with Jenny the other day,' I begin.

'Oh, yes?' Mark shows no sign of concern. On the contrary, he looks relieved, as if I'm changing the subject and about to tell him something unimportant.

'She said you …' Because I wasn't planning to tell Mark this yet, I haven't thought through what to say. Jenny's words come back to me: '… came on a bit strong.'

Mark's eyebrows shoot up. I have to hand it to him. He's a convincing actor as well as a compulsive liar. I could add Mark's colleague to the mix at this point, but I don't want to. It won't help to smooth over the problem. On the contrary, it will only stir up more trouble. All I want is for Mark to conduct himself correctly. I want him to stop hurling ludicrous accusations at me and I don't ever want to hear another accusation of sexual misbehaviour levelled against him.

'I bumped into her at the local shop and helped her carry her shopping to her car. I might have said something she misinterpreted. I don't remember what we were talking about.'

'According to Jenny, it wasn't just what you *said*. It had more to do with what you *did*. She said you groped her.' I make a similar gesture to the one Jenny made, placing my hand on my breast.

Mark is silent for several seconds. Too long. I wonder if he's ruminating on what I've said or if he's working out what to say. Is he going to admit Jenny's telling the truth? My pulse quickens at this thought. I hope not. I think it would be easier for both of us if Mark continued to deny doing anything intentionally wrong.

'Do you think you could possibly apologise to her?' I ask. 'Not in person,' I add hastily, remembering Jenny saying that she doesn't want to see Mark again. 'Perhaps you could write a card to say sorry for the misunderstanding?'

Another long silence stretches the short distance between us. I steal a sideways glance at Mark, but he doesn't look angry. Quite the opposite, in fact. He looks serene and controlled. He downs the rest of his whiskey and smacks his lips noisily.

'Don't you think you're being a wee bit hypocritical, Kat?' he says at length. There it is. He's accusing me again of being a hypocrite.

'What?' He spoke so quietly I genuinely think I might have misheard.

'Here you are, taking the moral high ground, telling me what I can and can't say, accusing me of … what? Trying to seduce your friend? When *you* … *You* should be apologising to *me*. In person. When were you going to come clean?'

'What?'

For a split second, I think Mark knows about Erin. I'm almost relieved he does. I desperately want to confide in someone about that night. I should have told Mark before. But the word "hypocritical" echoes in my head and I realise that can't be what he's referring to.

'Did you think I wouldn't find out?' Mark hasn't even raised his voice and I find myself wishing he would. It's somehow more frightening when he keeps his cool than when he loses his temper.

'Find out what?' It comes out as a whimper. I sound like someone who has something to hide. I sound guilty as charged. It comes to me in a rush and I know what he's going to say next.

'I know you're having an affair with Darragh.'

Now I understand why he called me a hypocrite and accused me of hiding things from him. My brain has gone into overdrive. Is this conjecture on Mark's part? Or does he know something? He can't know about our pub lunch. He was away on business. Even if someone had seen Darragh and me holding hands over the table, no one would have told Mark.

'You're wrong, Mark. Darragh's a friend. We're not having an affair.'

Not long ago I was the one asking Mark if he was cheating on me and he was the one denying my accusations. The tables have turned and the irony isn't lost on me.

'If that's true, it's only because it's over.' Mark is no longer cool and collected; he is cold. His face twitches with the effort of staying calm on the surface, but I can tell his anger is simmering underneath, ready to boil over at any moment. 'I know you've been sleeping with him.'

'I can assure you I haven't!'

I wonder if Darragh hinted that we'd kissed in order to cause trouble. He might even have implied we were sleeping together. I wouldn't put it past him. There's something about him I don't trust, even though he's my friend.

'What made you think that?'

Mark ignores me. Stony-faced, his eyes are locked on mine, but it's as if he's looking straight through me Setting his glass on the coffee table, he gets to his feet and extracts the digital car key from his back pocket.

'Where are you going?'

I expect him to ignore me again, but this time he answers. 'To Darragh's.'

Those two words send a chill through my body. I have it on the tip of my tongue to tell him that Darragh and I kissed and nothing more. How much would I have to admit in order to deny I've been having an affair?

'Why are you going to Darragh's?'

'To sort this out. To sort *him* out if I have to.'

'Mark, you're overreacting. There's nothing going on between Darragh and me.' I pull his arm, trying to restrain him as he strides purposefully towards the front door, practically dragging me in his wake. Feeling ridiculous, I let go of him and call after him as he marches down the driveway. 'Mark, come back! You don't even know where he lives.'

He turns around. Relief starts to ripple through me. But then he says, 'Yes, I do. I followed him home the other night. I kept my headlights off so he wouldn't notice. I know exactly where his house is.'

This isn't a spur-of-the-moment decision. Mark's not going to Darragh's on a whim. He has planned this. Whatever he's about to do, it is calculated. He deliberately came home with the car the other evening and followed Darragh home, probably from the pub. He must have worked out where Darragh would be in advance somehow. Or perhaps he took a lucky guess. He could have saved himself the trouble. Anyone on the island could have told him where Darragh's house was. And it's no coincidence that Mark has brought home the car this evening again.

'Mark! You can't drive! You've been drinking!'

I've never known Mark to take the wheel after consuming alcohol, but my last-ditch effort falls on deaf ears. As he drives away, I run back into the house. I need to ring Darragh and warn him.

But my mobile is not on the coffee table, where I'm sure I left it. Did Mark take it with him? Perhaps he slipped it into his pocket when he put down his glass and stood up? I stand in the middle of the living room, gripping tufts of my hair in my hands, growling like an animal and feeling helpless. Then I run from room to room to check.

I locate my mobile in the kitchen, almost drop it as I grab it and bring up Darragh's number with trembling hands. But he doesn't answer. I leave a frantic, garbled message.

'Darragh, Mark is on his way to your place. He's convinced you and I are having an affair. I think he's spoiling for a fight.'

I send a text message to say much the same thing. Then I check the volume of my mobile is turned right up. I slide my back down the wall and sink to the floor. Cradling my head in my hands and still clutching my mobile in one of them, I start to cry. Before long, my body is racked with uncontrollable sobs. I have no idea what to do next, but for the moment I can do nothing but wait.

Chapter 30

I end up falling asleep on the sofa, wrapped up in the throw, so I don't realise until the next morning that Mark hasn't come home. The first thing I do is check my mobile. I'm sure the ringtone would have woken me up if Mark – or Darragh – had called, but the text notification sound might not have roused me. But there are no missed calls and no texts. I try to get hold of Mark, but he doesn't answer the call and his phone rings out.

It's Saturday, so he can't be at work. It was quite late when he left for Darragh's place last night. Too late to book into a guest house or a B&B on the island. There would have been nowhere else for him to go but here. Maybe he slept in his car. I look out of the living room window, but his car isn't parked outside. If he did sleep in it, it wasn't in front of the cottage. Perhaps, wherever he is, he hasn't woken up yet. I look at the time on my mobile. Half past nine. I'm surprised I slept so late myself, but it must have been past three o'clock when exhaustion finally overcame me. He must be up by now, especially if he slept rough somewhere.

I try Darragh, but he doesn't take my call, either.

I pace up and down the living room, gnawing on my nails. What happened between Mark and Darragh last night? Why aren't they answering their phones? For a split second, I wonder if they've killed each other, but instantly I berate myself for being melodramatic.

An hour goes by – excruciatingly slowly. I make myself a light breakfast, more for the baby's sake than mine. Gradually, my worry becomes blotted out by anger. How dare Mark do this to me! How can he ignore my calls? I'm carrying his baby. He shouldn't cause me undue stress like this.

Half an hour later, I'm frantic with worry again. I've bitten all my nails down to the quick and have started to bite the skin around them. I know from Erin that Darragh used to have a reputation for using brute force to settle his disagreements. Darragh is muscular whereas Mark is, well, a bit weedy. Maybe Darragh is less handy with his fists than he once was, but if Mark throws the first punch, there's no doubt in my mind that Darragh could beat him to a pulp if he wanted to.

A memory comes to me from the day Mark knocked his beer over Darragh at the pub and a thunderous look came over Darragh's face as Mark fussed around him. I remember, too, when Mark and Darragh shook hands at the beach when we went for a picnic and Darragh flexed his hand afterwards as if Mark's grip had been too tight. Mark hated Darragh from the start. But recalling this scene, I see it slightly differently. I get the impression now that Darragh was itching to punch Mark then. I almost sympathise with Darragh. If Mark walked through the door this instant, I'd feel like hitting him, too.

I force myself to take deep breaths in an attempt to calm down. I've let my imagination go berserk. Darragh will have set Mark straight. They won't have come to blows. Mark will have been mortified at jumping to conclusions. Maybe Darragh smelt whiskey on Mark's breath and prevented him from driving home. The phone reception can be a bit dodgy at Darragh's house, if I remember correctly.

But I can't make myself believe this version of events. There was no phone network in the wine cellar, but it seemed to work elsewhere in the house. And Darragh could easily have driven Mark home.

An image appears in my mind: Mark bleeding profusely in his mangled BMW, upside down in a ditch. Could he have crashed his car on his way to Darragh's or on his way back? That might explain why Mark isn't answering his phone. But it doesn't explain why I can't get hold of Darragh. The most likely explanation is that Mark's phone is out of juice and Darragh is ignoring me after whatever happened between Mark and him last night.

I could jog out to Darragh's house and find out what's going on, but I don't want to leave the house in case Mark comes home. I don't know if he took his door key. Not long ago, I checked for the spare key and it was no longer behind the gnome so I must have removed it, although I still can't remember what I did with it. If Mark gets home, he'll be locked out. Oh well, it will serve him right. He can wait outside. I won't be that long.

I go upstairs and put on my running clothes. I take my phone and water bottle, as usual. I run without music and there's nothing to distract me or act as a buffer for my unruly thoughts. I picture Darragh opening his front door to me, looking decidedly the worse for wear with a split lip and a black eye. I imagine him joking weakly, something like, *you should see the other guy*, and then I do – I visualise Mark, lying on a hospital bed, machines bleeping all around him. I blink them both away and give myself a stern talking-to as I reach Darragh's house.

When I ring the bell, Dexter barks, but Darragh doesn't come to the door. I walk around the house, looking in through the windows. In the living room, Darragh has put up and decorated a Christmas tree, but the fairy lights aren't on. Dexter's in the kitchen and wags his tail at me, but there's no sign of Darragh. His van is in the driveway, though, which strikes me as odd. He won't have gone for a run without Dexter and he can't be working on a Saturday. He lives a bit far from the local shop to have walked there, especially if he's carrying back groceries, and

I think he would have taken the dog if he'd gone anywhere on foot. I ring the doorbell again and hammer on the door. But if Darragh is home, he's pretending he isn't.

I take my phone out of my belt and call him once more. For a second or two, I think I hear a tinny, ringing sound from inside the house, but when I strain to listen, there's nothing. Even if Darragh was in, I wouldn't hear his phone ringing from outside.

I run home, more slowly than I ran on the way out here, even though it's an easier, more downhill route back. My stomach is in knots; my mind is in turmoil. How can both Darragh and Mark have disappeared? This doesn't make sense. Although I'm trying hard to stay rational, there's a fear I can't contain. What if Darragh was home and wouldn't answer the door because he has hurt Mark, or maybe done something even worse to him? Maybe they fought and Darragh accidentally killed Mark. I keep telling myself I'm blowing this out of proportion, but however hard I try, I can't find any other logical explanation.

I reach my front gate, noting with a sinking feeling that Mark's car is not there. As I enter the house, I get the unsettling feeling I'm not alone.

'Mark?' I call out doubtfully. He'd hardly have driven off last night and then walked home today.

There's no answer. I can smell something familiar, a masculine smell. I remember arriving home that day with Mark, after seeing Jenny and Tom walking down the hill. I got the impression someone had been inside the house then, too. I ended up putting it down to my imagination, but now I'm not so sure. There was a faint odour I couldn't identify, I remember.

This time, it's different. I sniff the air again. I know the smell.

'Mark?' I call out again.

If he's not here, he definitely was.

I find his note on the kitchen table, pinched between the salt and pepper pots, exactly where I left the letter from Fiona for him. His handwriting is even messier than usual, almost illegible in places, and I imagine him scribbling his message furiously, his mind already elsewhere, in a place he is keen to get to himself.

Kat, I need to sort out a few things and also sort out my head.
When you get back, please text me to say you're OK.
Then stay indoors with the door locked.
I have something to tell you – we'll talk when I get back.

His message answers none of the questions that have been tormenting me. I still don't know what happened between Mark and Darragh or where Mark has been all night. On the contrary, it raises more questions: What does Mark need to sort out? What does he want to tell me? He says we'll talk when he gets back, but he doesn't say when that will be.

I read the note again. Mark seems to think I'm in danger. This puzzles me more than it alarms me, but I do as he asks. First, I lock the front door and pocket the key. Then I send Mark a text to say I am safely at home, hope he's OK and will see him later. I wait for a while, staring at the phone, willing it to beep with a text from Mark. I want him to reassure me, to tell me this will be all right, to say something – anything – that indicates he thinks we'll be all right because I'm no longer sure we will be. I try to envisage the next chapter of my life with Mark, but the pages are blank. I can't imagine a life without him, either. He's the father of my baby. But I don't know where we go from here. Can our marriage be fixed? Do I want to mend us?

Now that I know Mark is alive, a different scenario from the one I formed earlier builds in my mind. It's Mark who has killed Darragh and not the other way round. *I need to sort out a few things.* Even as I scold myself for being so morbid, I have this far-fetched notion that Mark has to get rid of Darragh's body, which he has put in the boot of his car. Is it typical human nature to always imagine the worst? Or is there something wrong with me for getting so carried away?

I have a headache, so I go upstairs to the bathroom and gulp down a paracetamol with a large glass of water. Then I take a shower, as if that might wash my troubles away along with my sweat. As I step into the bedroom afterwards, wrapped in a towel, my mobile rings. I race to it, hoping it's Mark, but it's a number I don't recognise. I don't want to talk to anyone except my husband, with the possible exception of Darragh, but thinking it might be important, I take the call.

I try not to groan in disappointment as the caller identifies himself, my hair dripping down my back as I sit on the bed. It's the estate agent. He's delighted to announce that the retired couple that visited the other day want to make an offer. It's nowhere near the asking price. In fact, the offer they're making is obscenely low, but after only a moment's hesitation, I accept it without negotiation and without waiting to consult Mark. It's not as if we'll have potential buyers queuing up in December and, to my mind, getting off this island has become synonymous with getting away from our problems. The quicker the better. A fresh start somewhere else. It occurs to me that the move to Rathlin was supposed to be exactly that – a new home and a new start – and now I'm desperate to move away.

I want to do something proactive rather than sit around and wait, but I have no idea what. I'd planned to work today, retouching some of my photos and working on my website. I'll soon be based in a different location, but that doesn't mean I need to start my growing business from scratch. I go into the study and sit down on the swivel chair, but I don't bother booting up my laptop. There's no way I'd be able to concentrate. I know Mark's all right – well, I know he's alive – but what about Darragh?

It dawns on me that there is something I can do; there is someone I can ask for an explanation: Fiona. It had completely slipped my mind that Charlotte had given me her number. I've had so much going on, what with Jenny's accusation about Mark's lecherous behaviour and the fight Mark and I have just had. In fact, since then, I've added to my list of woes.

I still have no desire to speak to Fiona. But whatever she wants to tell me, it might solve one of my seemingly insoluble problems or answer one of my unanswered questions.

Still sitting at my desk, I bring up Charlotte's text message with Fiona's number. Staring at the screen, I wonder if it's a good idea. There will be no going back after this, no unhearing whatever it is she tells me. This might make things worse. Do I really want to know what she has to say?

I decide not to do it, but it's as if some part of my brain is overriding that decision. Before I register I'm going to do it, I've pressed the digits in Charlotte's text to make the call to my husband's ex-wife.

Chapter 31

Fiona's phone rings and rings. I haven't hidden my number, but she won't recognise it. Maybe she doesn't accept calls when she doesn't know the caller's identity in case it's telemarketing or a robocall. I swivel, left to right and right to left, in my office chair, mentally preparing a message for when it goes to voicemail, but then she answers, which throws me.

'Hello?' Her voice is soft, conveying affability in that one word. A few minutes ago, when I answered the phone to the estate agent, whose number I didn't recognise, I know I sounded both gruff and unfriendly pronouncing that same, single word.

'Hello, Fiona? It's Katherine here. Katherine Fisher. I hope you don't mind me calling you out of the blue—'

'Katherine! Hold on a second.' Even now she knows it's me, she sounds nice. I find myself wondering again if I would have liked Fiona, had I known her in different circumstances. Perhaps we would have got on well.

I hear her talk to someone else in a muffled voice, her partner presumably, asking him to keep an eye on the baby for a few minutes. While I wait, I doodle on a Post-it with a black Biro, deeply scored squiggles, and circles that I trace over again and again, round and round.

'Sorry about that,' Fiona says as she comes back on the line again. 'I didn't want us to be disturbed.'

I'm not sure if I'm supposed to thank her or start over with the greetings. I decide to get straight to the point. I adopt a tone that, if not exactly friendly, at least won't sound frosty. 'A friend of mine – Charlotte, I think you know her – told me you were trying to get in touch with me.'

'Yes, I was. Well, initially I tried to get through to Mark, in both senses of the term. There's something I think he should have told you, but I don't think he has.'

If you don't tell her soon, I will. I was right. Fiona did mean me.

'Go on,' I say, when she hesitates.

'Can I ask you a question?' Before I can answer, she continues, 'You see, I heard from Charlotte that you and Mark were trying for a baby. Is that still the case?'

I have it on the tip of my tongue to say it's none of her bloody business, but I warn myself not to be prickly. If she has brought this up, she must have a good reason. I'm not about to drop my guard and confide in her, though. I don't want her to know I'm pregnant. Besides, I don't think Mark would appreciate me announcing to his ex-wife that we're going to have a baby.

'Yes, yes, it is. Why?'

But instead of answering my question, Fiona asks me another one. 'Has Mark ever mentioned to you that he was ill?'

'Ill? No. When was this?'

'When … um … he was married to me.' Fiona is clearly choosing her words carefully. Whatever it is she has to say, she's trying to break it to me gently. 'I've begged him to tell you. I called him and sent him text messages, but he appears to have blocked me from his contacts, so I wrote him a letter. I thought it was only fair you should know. I told him it would be better if you heard it from him, but that I would tell you if he didn't. I was going to contact you through your website.

You can't keep that sort of thing secret. I can't, anyway. It's not right.'

I hear her take a deep breath and I know she's about to chuck a metaphorical grenade at me after this lengthy introduction, something that will explode and upend my life completely. Perhaps Mark has some hereditary disease that he could pass on to our children. That might explain why he and Fiona split up. Mark told me Fiona didn't want kids, but maybe she just didn't want *his* kids. Instinctively, I put my free hand around my belly, even though there's no trace of a bump there yet.

'Look, Kat … Katherine. There's no easy way to say this, so here's the thing … Mark can't have children.'

'What?'

'Mark can't father any children. He's sterile.'

I burst out laughing. I think it's a nervous reaction as I certainly don't find this funny. I have physical evidence – I am the living proof – that this is not true. I nearly blurt out that I'm pregnant, but Fiona hasn't finished.

'He had testicular cancer. He could have had some sperm frozen before his treatment, but he refused to do it. He said he didn't want to tempt fate.'

That sounds like Mark, I think, but I don't say it. 'Are you sure?' My mind grapples for a rational explanation. 'Is it possible his treatment just reduced his chances of conceiving? You know, could it have lowered his … sperm count or something?' I can't believe I've asked Mark's ex-wife that. My face flames. She must think I'm desperately clutching at straws, and in a way, I am, although not for the reason she must imagine.

'I'm sorry, Katherine,' Fiona says. 'Mark had both radiation therapy and chemo. He had tests afterwards, when we …' She leaves her sentence unfinished. I can fill in the blanks myself. 'The doctors said that with the sort of treatment he'd had, for most men infertility was only temporary, but in Mark's case, the damage was extensive and irreversible.'

I should end the call, leave it there. 'Charlotte and Rupert knew Mark before I did. They'd know if he'd been ill. Charlotte would have told me.'

'Rupert was headhunted by RP Pharma, as I'm sure you know. He'd left Campbell & Coyle by then. Mark didn't tell Rupert. Mark was very secretive about the whole thing anyway, with both his colleagues and his mates. I think he was ashamed. There's a stigma attached to testicular cancer. He didn't even tell me immediately when he found the swelling, much less seek medical help. He left it too late.'

I'm still struggling to believe a word of this, but my disbelief is directed more at Mark than Fiona. How could he not have told me? Why did he keep me in the dark? But it's obvious. He lost one wife because he couldn't give her children. I might not have married him if I'd known. He didn't want to take that risk.

'I understand why you might think I'd want to stir up trouble,' Fiona continues, 'but I think I've caused enough trouble between you and Mark. I'd never make something like this up. I thought you might find it hard to believe what I wanted to tell you, so when Charlotte said you wanted my mobile number, I dug out some documents from the hospital.'

'What sort of documents?'

'Some emails and letters confirming Mark's appointments with both the urologist and the medical oncologist at the Royal Marsden in Chelsea. I've also got the results of some of Mark's blood tests. He has abnormal levels of … well, you can google. None of this will prove Mark's sterile, but it does show he had treatment for testicular cancer. I'll send all that through now, shall I?'

'Yes. Yes, please.'

'You can call me back if you need to. At any time.'

I can't bring myself to thank Fiona, but I do my best to end the call politely. I'm sure Fiona can tell that her news has hurled me into a state of shock and confusion, and although this is understandable, she won't guess the extent of my distress. I look down and see my hand still cradling my stomach. Does this mean I'm not pregnant?

A nasty, nauseating suspicion tries to voice itself in my muddled mind, something that has never made sense to me, but I'm not ready to listen to it yet. I need to start with something simpler, something that's more easily verifiable.

I bring up the photo of the pregnancy test on my phone. Although one of them is faint, there are definitely two lines. This is my physical evidence that I'm pregnant. Unless it was a false positive test. Is there any way the hormones from my recent ovulation might have affected the result of the test? I have a load more pregnancy tests in the bathroom. It will take me less than five minutes to check.

My hand shakes so much as I hold the stick under my urine flow that I end up peeing all over both the stick and my hand. I put the test beside the sink and close the lid of the loo so I can sit down while I wait. My hands aren't the only part of my body that's trembling and I don't trust my legs to hold me up.

I see myself in the ladies' toilets at McCuaig's Bar, the day I got my period, after an argument with Mark. My period was late and I wondered if it could have been an early miscarriage. If Mark's sterile, then it was just a late period. I was only about a week late. But how late am I now? My last period was due at the end of October, shortly after I took the positive pregnancy test. It's now December. Surely it can't be a late period at this stage?

Is Fiona telling the truth? I believe her, but I'm trying to force myself to think everything through methodically. Fiona has just had a baby with another man. She has no motive to make up something like this.

The text notification sounds on my phone, several times in a row. Fiona has sent me screenshots of all the documents. I glance at each one in turn. They all date back to when Mark was married to Fiona, before I met him. I don't understand the blood tests, but as Fiona said, I can check them on the Internet. But the confirmations of Mark's hospital appointments dispel any remaining doubt in my mind. Fiona was telling the truth.

How many minutes have passed? Four or five? I put down the phone and sneak a glance at the stick. I'm not sure what result I'm expecting – positive or negative. I don't know right now whether I want to be pregnant or not, but as I stare incredulously at the test, a huge wave of relief washes over me. There are two definite, blue lines. There's no doubt about it. I am pregnant.

Fiona's revelation reverberates in my head. *Mark can't father any children. He's sterile.* Her words are so clear it's as if she's here, in the bathroom, with me, which is a disconcerting thought. Mark isn't the father of my baby. And to think I was convinced he was the father of Fiona's baby!

Mark's face appears before me, shock painted all over it, the day I told him I was pregnant. I remember exactly what he said. *I'm rather shocked that I'm going to be a father, that's all.* I thought it was a normal reaction. I assumed he needed a little time to get his head round the fact that he was going to be responsible for a tiny human being. No wonder he was so shocked! He knew he couldn't possibly be the father.

This explains – partly, at least – Mark's odd behaviour. Now I know why he thought I was having an affair with Darragh. If Mark himself wasn't the father of my baby, there could be no other contender. That must have been Mark's logic.

Ironically, my earlier intuition, which I was doing my best to ignore, was along the same lines as Mark's reasoning. I thought I'd conceived this baby with Mark the morning after the storm, but, obviously, I was mistaken. I don't remember all the details of the night I ended up at Darragh's, but something about it doesn't sit right with me. I was trying to be careful not to drink too much wine, but I ended up far too drunk and unusually uninhibited. I woke up the next day still feeling sexually aroused. I thought

I'd had an erotic dream about Darragh, but perhaps the images in my head stemmed from something real.

Did I pass out when he got me home? Is that why my memories of the end of the evening are so sketchy? There's only one person who can answer these questions and there's no way I'm going to ask him. But there's another question I struggle to ask myself, although I already know the answer. It's hard to formulate, even in my head.

Did Darragh rape me?

Chapter 32

Sitting on the sofa in the living room, holding the pregnancy test in one hand and my phone in the other, I stare at the painting above the fireplace, as if there is a secret message hidden among Darragh's brushstrokes that will confirm my suspicions. In my mind, I comb through everything I remember from the night of the storm, wondering if there's any way I could be mistaken.

Wouldn't I have known if Darragh had raped me? Perhaps not. I was really out of it by the end of the evening. I don't even remember getting into bed or putting on my pyjamas, so I must have passed out. I got up during the night and drank some water. I probably went for a pee, too. I was still groggy and only remembered getting up at all when I saw the glass of water I'd fetched from the bathroom on my bedside table the following morning. When Mark came home, he and I had sex. Given all this, it's entirely feasible I wouldn't have realised if I'd been raped.

Why would Darragh rape me? I amend that in my head. I mustn't doubt myself. Why *did* Darragh rape me? I would have slept with him willingly. I would have had sex with him right there and then on his sofa. I was turned on. I wanted him. I'd pushed him away from me and put a stop to our kiss, but at the time, in my inebriated state, it was only a half-hearted effort to do the right thing. Deep down, I wanted him to resume our kiss.

Instead, he took advantage of me when I was unconscious. I didn't agree to that. I couldn't disagree, either. I didn't put up a fight. I didn't say no. I was in no state to defend myself; I was in no state to express myself. I didn't even remember it afterwards. I still don't recall any more than fragments of something I took to be a dream. But I'm sure of one thing. What happened at that stage was definitely not consensual. It was sexual assault. Rape.

Could Darragh have drugged me? I think back to that evening. At Darragh's house, my inhibitions and boundaries were lowered; I was dizzy, disorientated, sleepy and relaxed. I recall slurring my speech at one point. On the way home, I felt nauseous in the van. Once in my own home, or maybe even before we got there, I passed out. It's possible he spiked my drink, I suppose. But I don't think so. I doubt this was something he'd planned. I'm pretty sure that everything I felt that night was caused by my consuming far too much alcohol right after a strenuous run.

I continue to stare at the painting, but suddenly I can't see the lighthouse or the sunrise. It's Darragh's face I see. I close my eyes in an attempt to eclipse the vision, but not before I recapture the expression he had on his face that night. For a brief moment, when I rejected him, he looked like a petulant child, about to throw a tantrum because he didn't get his own way. He hid it quickly, but I saw it, even though he wouldn't look me in the eye.

His unfinished sentence comes back to me, too, as if he's standing next to me, whispering in my ear. *You led me …* I'm sure he was going to say that I'd led him on. Perhaps, in some twisted way, Darragh felt justified in doing what he did because I'd flirted with him, kissed him, in short, made sexual advances to him, but then failed to go through with it.

I look down to see I'm still holding the pregnancy test in one hand and my phone in the other. I realise that if I hadn't got pregnant and discovered my husband was sterile, I might never have found out what Darragh had done to me. I set the test on the coffee table and get up and pace the room. I feel hot, then cold. My breaths come in erratic gasps.

I tap 999 into my phone, but then I hesitate. If I tell the police Darragh raped me, he'll deny it. It will be my word against his. I have no proof. Even the fact I'm carrying his baby doesn't prove a rape took place. *I'm carrying his baby.* That thought causes a strong surge of nausea to rise inside me. I stop pacing and stand still, ready to bolt to the loo if I'm going to be sick. After a minute or two, the nausea abates slightly.

A text notification sounds from my mobile, which I'm still holding in my hand. I almost welcome the intrusion. Glancing at the screen, I see the text is from my mum. She booked a return flight from Bristol to Dublin back in September when I was in Devon. We'd planned to spend a couple of days in the run-up to Christmas, sightseeing in Dublin and then a day in Belfast, just the two of us, before I brought her to Rathlin for the rest of her stay. She's due to arrive tomorrow afternoon and wants to finalise arrangements. I'm suddenly overcome with such desperation to see her that tears spring to my eyes. But her visit couldn't come at a worse time. I decide to ask her to cancel her trip altogether. I can't do that by text message. Only after several minutes do I feel calm enough to ring her. But before I can do it, I hear Mark's key in the front door.

I resist the urge to run and bolt the door from the inside, to lock Mark out. I don't want to see him; I don't want to talk to him. I expect him to be beaten and bruised – a black eye, a broken nose or a bandaged hand. When he enters the house, he looks even more bedraggled and unshaven than the last time I saw him, but he has no apparent injuries. I'm tempted to pummel his face with my fists myself. I was already enraged because of the argument between Mark and me and the conversations I had with Jenny and Charlotte, but that practically pales into insignificance

216

compared with the lies I now know Mark has told. Something inside me has stretched until it has finally snapped.

Mark comes towards me. Although I flinch and keep my arms firmly by my sides, I don't push him away when he wraps me in his arms and holds me tight. Instead, I start crying into his chest. In seconds, I'm sobbing uncontrollably.

'I'm sorry I caused you so much upset. I'm so sorry,' he says. 'There's something I need to tell you.' I'm about to say that I've got something to tell him, too. I want to blurt out that Darragh raped me, but I can't catch my breath to speak. 'Something about Darragh,' Mark adds.

My jaw tightens at the mention of his name. I feel sick again at the thought that Darragh's baby is growing inside me. Mark leads me by the hand into the kitchen. I don't resist. He makes me sit at the table while he makes us both some tea. I can't even begin to find the words in my head that I need to say out loud. It's all I can do to hold it together. If I start talking, I'll lose it again.

Placing my mug in front of me, Mark sits down opposite me. 'So, I drove round to Darragh's place last night,' he says. Was it only last night? So much has happened since then. 'He corroborated what you said.' Corroborated? Mark's wording ruffles me. He makes it sound like I'm under investigation or on trial. He must notice the expression on my face because he rephrases what he said. 'He insisted you two weren't having an affair.'

Mark studies me as he says this, through bloodshot, turquoise eyes, as if trying to assess my reaction or read what's going through my mind. He pauses. I can tell he doesn't believe me. Or Darragh. I think he's waiting for me to tell him the truth. But the truth is not what he thinks.

It's easy to see this from Mark's point of view. He's convinced I've cheated on him, but he can't accuse me outright, partly because he once cheated on me, but mainly because he can't reveal his reasoning. The baby can't be his because he's sterile, so it must be Darragh's. It wouldn't occur to Mark that I was raped by someone I'd considered to be a friend. In fairness, it wouldn't have occurred to me either if I hadn't found out the baby couldn't be Mark's.

Even though Mark has reached a logical conclusion, it riles me that he has started with an accusation, albeit an implicit one, rather than an apology. He owes me an apology. Several, in fact. But they don't seem to be forthcoming.

The silence stretches between us. Mark fixes me with a penetrating stare. He expects me to admit I had an affair with Darragh. I hold his gaze. For me, he should have the next line. It's his cue to admit he can't have children. We're stuck in a stand-off, unspoken words hanging in the air between us.

I should tell Mark I know he can't have children. I should tell him Darragh raped me. But something tells me not to. Some sort of instinct is warning me to keep all of that to myself, to store that information until I've assimilated it and worked out what to do with it.

'I'm sorry I didn't come home and caused you to worry,' Marks says, dissolving the silence. He sounds genuinely contrite. 'When I left Darragh's, I had to go to the mainland to deal with something urgent. Something to do with Mum's death.' Mark is obviously going to use his mother's death and her estate as an excuse every time. 'Nothing you need to concern yourself with, though. I missed the last ferry back, so I slept in my car at the harbour.' Mark runs his hands through his thick hair. He needs a haircut, I notice, an incongruous thought.

'Where's Darragh?' I ask. It's the first thing I've said since Mark came home. Mark's eyes flash at the mention of his name, or perhaps it's because he thinks I'm concerned about his welfare. 'Did the two of you argue? Did you fight?'

'He was in one piece when I left his place last night,' Mark says. 'And no, I didn't beat him up, if that's what you're worried about.'

Mark knows as well as I do that he wouldn't have stood a chance in a fight against Darragh, although I find myself wishing that Mark had beaten Darragh to death and put the body in the boot of his car, as I'd imagined. 'So what happened?' I ask.

'He was … morose. Did you know he had a sister?'

My heart skips a beat. And then another one. What has Darragh told him? 'No,' I say. 'Did he?' I feel the blood drain from my face. I've used the past tense. But Mark doesn't seem to notice my mistake.

'Apparently, it would have been her birthday yesterday. Anyway, he was paralytic and not making a lot of sense when I got there. He didn't have any fight in him. He denied the two of you were having an affair when I asked. I had a whiskey with him and then left. It was all amicable and gentlemanly. More or less.'

So Darragh probably was at home earlier. He was probably sleeping off his hangover. Knowing what I do now, I'm glad he didn't answer the door.

I'm about to ask Mark to explain the note he left for me, asking me to stay in the cottage and lock myself in.

But Mark gets there first. 'Kat, listen.' His tone is suddenly very grave. 'We need to stay away from him. I think he might be dangerous. I think he might do something … bad.'

Mark studies the table, either lost in his thoughts or considering what to say next. This could be my last chance to tell him that Darragh must have raped me because I'm definitely pregnant and I know the baby can't be his. But I still can't get the words out. And shouldn't *Mark* tell *me* the baby can't be his? Shouldn't he have told me a long time ago that he can't have children? This is back to front. Right now, I'm nearly as angry with Mark as I am with Darragh.

'What makes you think Darragh is dangerous?' I ask. My voice quavers, although I'm not scared. Pronouncing his name almost makes me retch.

'He said things. He was so drunk that I don't think he even knew who I was, but I think he might have meant what he said.'

'What did he say?'

'Nothing specific. He was ranting.' I get the feeling Mark is backpedalling now.

'Don't you think if he'd wanted to hurt you, he would have done it when you showed up on his doorstep?'

'He was talking about *you*, Kat. Not me. Like I said, he wasn't making much sense. But I got the impression you might be in danger.' Mark sighs and stands up. He walks round to my chair and wraps his arms around me from behind. 'I don't know why,' he says, burying his face in my hair.

'I don't either.'

But I think I do. Darragh must know about Erin and me. I've been backwards and forwards on this so many times, and I still can't see how he could have found out. But it's the only reason he would have to harm me. Is that what he's up to? Does he want to avenge his sister's death?

I reason with myself. I have nothing to fear. I won't let Mark spook me with his talk about me being in danger. His warning has come too late. If Darragh had wanted to harm me, more than he already has done, he could have done it last time I saw him, when we were together in McCuaig's Bar.

Mark puts his hands either side of my belly. I feel my shoulders tense and Mark must feel it, too, because he releases me from his embrace and straightens up.

'You're the one not making much sense,' I say, turning to face Mark. 'You had a friendly chat with Darragh over a whiskey and then you warn me to stay away from him because you think he wants to hurt me.' It's an effort not to raise my voice. 'Is that about the gist of it?'

If Mark thought Darragh was somehow out to get me, why did he leave me here on the island, cut off from the mainland and the rest of the world, with Darragh supposedly at home, only a few miles away? How could Mark have left me stranded like that if he thought I was in danger? I don't think I've ever felt so mad in my life. Everything Mark says and does seems to make my blood boil a little more. But I'm exhausted and upset, and I don't have the energy for another row.

'I just think we should stay away from him.' Mark isn't telling me everything. But I know if he's bent on withholding something from me, there's no point in me trying to worm it out of him. 'The sooner we sell up and leave this place the better,' he adds.

I haven't had the chance yet to tell Mark I've accepted an offer on the cottage. I'll save that conversation for later. Now's not the time. I get to my feet and tip my tea, undrunk and cold, down the sink.

'In the meantime,' Mark continues, 'it might be a good idea if you went somewhere, you know, until we officially move. Perhaps you could stay with Charlotte or your mum.'

Mark's suggestion reminds me of my mum's text. I was about to call her when Mark came through the front door. I make a quick decision. I'm not frightened of Darragh and I won't allow him to drive me off the island. But there's no reason for my mum to cancel her trip. I want to see her. I need to talk to her about all of this. Urgently. I won't bring her to Rathlin, though. She was looking forward to seeing my new home, but it's not that new anymore and it won't be my home for much longer. Anyway, I need to get away for a while. Mum and I can stay in Dublin for the week instead.

I bring Mark up to speed with my newly revised programme. By the look on his face, he'd forgotten all about Mum's visit and feigns disappointment when I tell him she won't be coming to stay in Causeway Cottage.

Mark offers to take me all the way to Dublin airport. In the end, we agree he'll drive me as far as Belfast in the morning when he goes to work. I'll get the bus from there. It feels like I'm running away from my problems, but I'll use the time away to get my ideas straight before coming back to sort out this mess. One way or the other.

Chapter 33

The flight is a little late and the wait seems interminable. I feel like a child. I so badly want my mum. When she comes through the automatic doors, I rush towards her and hold her a bit too tightly and for a bit too long.

When I let her go, I catch her furrowed brow. But the airport is not the place to go into what's been going on or what's on my mind.

We get a bus to the city centre and check into our hotel in Stephen's Green. On the way there, I tell my mum there has been a change of plan and at the reception desk, I change the booking so we can stay for longer.

We have a spacious twin room. As soon as Mum has freshened up and hung up her tops and trousers, we head out to look for somewhere to have lunch. We walk slowly along Grafton Street and I relax a little for the first time in weeks, drinking in the atmosphere and admiring the Christmas decorations. It's a bustling, colourful pedestrianised street and we thread our way through the crowds – tourists like us, no doubt, as well as Christmas shoppers – past pubs, coffee houses, boutiques and buskers. Live music spills out from the pubs, mixing and clashing with buskers' songs here and there.

We make a detour to see the Molly Malone statue in Suffolk Street. Just as she does in the song, the fishwife is wheeling her barrow through the streets, plying her wares – cockles and mussels.

'I remember Dad singing that song to me when I was little,' I say to my mum. 'I used to join in for the chorus. Alive, alive-O!'

'Your father could certainly carry a tune,' my mum says, smiling.

Memories of my dad come flooding back to me. Music was part of our lives. He sang, played the tin whistle, the guitar and the harmonica. A pang of regret at giving up the piano pierces me and I vow to take it up again one day. I used to listen to music in the house all the time. Mark prefers the silence. The last time I recall listening to music with him was when we were painting the baby's room, both of us singing along happily to a playlist coming through the speaker. Anger bubbles inside me at the thought that Mark would agree – albeit reluctantly – to decorate the baby's room with me when he knew there was no way he could father a baby genetically. How could he do that?

I'm distracted by the loud laughter of two tourists in front of us, one of whom is taking a photograph of his friend fondling Molly's bronze breasts. Judging from her worn, smooth cleavage, it's far from the first time Molly has had to put up with unwelcome, wandering hands, taking advantage of her immobility and inability to defend herself. The two men are roaring with laughter. I take Mum's arm, steering her away from the tourists and the statue.

We find a quiet café in a side road off Grafton Street. It's only when we've ordered – jacket potatoes with baked beans and cheese – that my mum asks what is going on.

'Don't get me wrong,' she says, 'I'm quite happy to spend more time in Dublin and not see your new home, as long as I'm with you, but I can see something's up and it might help you to share it.'

My mum is probably relieved she's not going to see Mark on this trip. If she never sees him again, there will be no love lost. I can understand now why she has never liked him or trusted him. I no longer trust him myself and I don't know if I still love him.

I'm not sure where to begin. Mum doesn't even know I'm pregnant. I suppose that's as good a place to start as any.

'I'm pregnant,' I say. Her instant smile practically splits her face in two. 'It's not Mark's.' Her face falls. I wish I'd thought out beforehand the order in which I should tell her all this. 'He can't have children, but he kept me in the dark about that. He still hasn't told me, in fact. He knows I'm pregnant, he knows it's not his, but he hasn't admitted to me that he's sterile.'

'And you haven't confronted him about it?'

I sigh and shrug. I tend to shy away from confrontation. I rarely win arguments. Either I lose my temper or I'm stunned into silence. But this isn't something inconsequential that can be swept under the carpet. I do want to confront Mark about this. But I desperately want him to be the one to bring up the matter. If he still won't come clean, even now I'm carrying a baby that can't be his, how can I ever trust him again?

'Not yet,' I reply.

'Have you been to see a doctor?'

'Not yet,' I echo. My mum frowns. 'I'll make an appointment,' I promise.

I pause as the waiter arrives with our meals.

There are some glaring gaps in my account that need to be filled in, so I explain Darragh's role in all this, watching my mother's face become more and more horrified with every detail I add.

'He raped you?'

'He must have done.' I lower my head – and my voice. 'I drank too much and passed out.'

She reaches across the table for my hands, but stays silent for a while, as if digesting what I've said or weighing up her next words. 'Darling, you do know it's not your fault,' she says at length, 'don't you? A woman is never to blame for an assault, no matter what she's wearing or how drunk she is.'

It occurs to me that my mum could be talking about Erin as much as about me and tears well up in my eyes, threatening to spill over. I grab a paper napkin and dab at my eyes. Erin was so young. She must have been so scared. And, if Darragh is to be believed, their mother was more concerned about the shame Erin could bring on the family than the emotional support she should have been providing for her daughter.

'Have you been to the police?' my own mother asks now, snapping me back to the present.

'No. It will be a case of he said / she said. He'll claim it was consensual. He'll probably even say I initiated it. I was the one who turned up at his house. I kissed him. He could certainly spin it that way. For all I know, that's what he truly believes.'

My mum nods. She's not going to push me on this. If I'd told Charlotte about this, she wouldn't have given in until I'd reported it. She'd say that men get away with this sort of thing when their victims don't report them. She'd argue that if I let Darragh get away with it, then he could do it again. To someone else. She'd be absolutely right, of course. But there are two major reasons why I'm reluctant to go to the police. Firstly, I have no proof. None whatsoever. And, more importantly, I'm pregnant. That complicates things.

'How did Mark react when you told him you were raped?' Mum asks, keeping her voice low so as not to be overheard by the other diners.

'He doesn't know.'

'What? Don't you think you should tell him, darling?'

'Hmm,' I say noncommittally.

I've decided against telling Mark about the rape. I know Mark thinks I've been having an affair with Darragh and lying to him about it. But I'm not going to set him straight. Not yet. I know the rape is not my fault, as my mum has said. But I feel dirty and violated in a way that I wouldn't have done if I had cheated on Mark. It's not something I want to talk about to my husband.

Nor can I confide in my best friend. I've opened up to my mum. And, for now at least, I don't want anyone else to know.

But there's another reason I'm loath to tell Mark I was raped. Some sort of instinct is warning me not to. Mark's infertility is not the only thing he has been hiding from me. I'm sure of that. And until I find out what else he's keeping from me, I don't feel under any obligation to tell him what has happened to me. On the contrary, I think I should be keeping as much from him as possible.

'And what about Darragh?' my mum says. 'Does he know you're pregnant?'

'No. And …'

'And what?'

I shake my head, look down and push my baked beans around my plate. I told Darragh that Mark and I were trying for a baby, but Darragh can't possibly know I'm pregnant. Mark certainly wouldn't have said anything; he's the one who wanted it kept a secret and Darragh is the last person Mark would have told.

I get the disconcerting feeling that I'm missing something important, but I can't work out what it is. I'm not thinking things through logically. I need to put a few more pieces of the jigsaw puzzle into place to make out the full picture.

'No,' I repeat. 'Darragh doesn't know.' I don't tell my mum that Mark says Darragh is dangerous and that he has threatened to hurt me. I certainly don't want my mum to worry any more than she's already worrying. So I keep to myself what I was going to say: *and he mustn't find out*. Instead, I say, 'I'm leaving Rathlin soon. That way, he'll never know about the baby.'

All of this is a lot for my mum to take in and she hasn't touched her lunch, either. We ask the waiter to heat up our meals and I force myself to swallow some of mine, but I have no appetite and it makes me feel sick.

Neither of us has been to Dublin before and we'd originally planned to kick off our sightseeing with the Book of Kells at

Trinity College. Although Mum asks if I'd rather do something else, I know how much she wanted to see the famous illuminated manuscript, so we wander back up Grafton Street towards College Green.

There's a long line of people waiting to get into the university's Old Library and we take our place in the queue. I'm not dressed up warmly enough, and the cold seeps in through my coat, chilling me, but bringing with it a welcome numbing sensation so that I can almost pretend that what happened over a hundred and fifty miles away in Rathlin Island happened to someone else.

The lavishly decorated Gospel script is magnificent and the exhibition is fascinating. To begin with, I struggle to concentrate, but after a while, I become immersed in the history and beauty of it all, absorbing the information avidly and welcoming the diversion from my trials and tribulations.

But as I stand, mesmerised, in the library's Long Room, inhaling the leathery, musty smell of the thousands of old books, I glance at my mother next to me and see how pale and shaken she looks. I know she's thinking about what I told her earlier. None of this has taken her mind off my shocking revelations. She must sense my concern because she turns to me and forces a smile.

It's not until we're back at the hotel that she asks the question she must have been itching to put to me all day. 'Are you going to keep the baby?'

This isn't something I've had to reflect on. It seemed obvious to me. It's not that I'm anti-abortion. In fact, I consider myself to be pro-choice. But this is me. And my baby. Even though I'm horrified beyond words that Darragh raped me and I was sickened to realise I was carrying his baby, having a termination or giving up my baby for adoption never entered my head. Anyway, I loved this baby before I found out I was raped and that hasn't changed. 'Yes, of course,' I say.

'Will you leave Mark?'

'I don't know. Maybe.'

Even if Mark was willing to bring up a baby that isn't his, which I'm beginning to think might actually be his intention, would I want to stay with him, knowing how deceitful he has been? I don't think I'll ever forgive Mark for not telling me he can't have children. It's bad enough that he kept such a monumental secret from me, but he has made it far worse by pretending to go along with our plans to start a family and consoling me every month I got my period. Fury flushes through my body every time I think about it.

'I used to tell myself I put up with your father's infidelity for your sake,' my mum says, sitting next to me on my hotel bed and placing her hand over mine. 'He was a lousy husband, but he was a good father. But the real reason I didn't throw him out sooner was simply because I loved him. I forgave him time and time again because I loved him.'

I don't know if I still love Mark, but I don't say this out loud.

'Women bring up babies themselves these days all the time,' my mum continues. 'If that's what you decide to do, or have to do, you won't be on your own, darling. I'm here.'

And with that, she gives my hand a pat, gets up and goes to the bathroom to take a shower before bed. I wonder if my mother would leave my father sooner if she could go back in time. Is that what I should do? Leave my husband? Or would Mark be a good father even though he hasn't been the best husband and even if the baby isn't genetically his?

Maybe my mum didn't mean for her experience of marital life to have any bearing on mine. But I think there are more parallels than she knows. Mark cheated on me, too, even if it was only once. With his ex-wife.

My thoughts turn to Fiona. And then it comes to me, the feeling I had earlier that I was overlooking something. I think I know now what it is I should have grasped.

I take my phone out of my handbag and, sitting cross-legged on my single bed, I type a text to Fiona, asking her what she wrote in her letter to Mark. I only managed to fish stained pieces out of the bin and I couldn't put any of them together to make isolated words, let alone complete sentences. I need to know exactly what she said. Did she send a cryptic message like the text I intercepted or did she go into more detail? It takes her a few minutes to get back to me.

> Hi Katherine,
> I can't remember the exact words. Something like: "Dear Mark, you have to tell Kat about your cancer. She needs to know you can't have children. It's not fair on her. This is your last chance to tell her. Otherwise, I will."
> Hope that helps.
> Fiona

It's what I expected, but her words have the effect of a sudden icy draught billowing into the hotel room and I shiver. Images unravel, unbidden, before my eyes, even as I try to shut them out. The spare key I used to keep on the kitchen windowsill; the positive pregnancy test that I found, smashed, under the bed; Fiona's letter that Mark accused me of steaming open and reading. I can almost smell the odour I detected the day Mark and I came home with the paint cans that made me think someone had been in the house. It was a clean smell. A minty smell, I realise now. Minty like the shower gel in Darragh's bathroom.

Darragh. He has been in my house, several times, probably, invading my privacy. Another violation. He must have broken in the day I found out I was pregnant, when I went out to photograph the hares. I picture him rummaging through my things before picking up the pregnancy test from my bedside table and examining it. Did he wonder then if the baby might be his? Did that upset him? Did he feel any remorse? Perhaps he threw the test to the floor and stamped on it, crushing it before kicking it under the bed, as if destroying a positive pregnancy test could erase what he'd done.

He must have come into my house the day Fiona's letter arrived, too. I imagine him looking though the post, boiling the kettle in my kitchen and using the steam to peel open the envelope. How did he react when he read the letter and found out Mark was sterile? Darragh would have known then without a shadow of a doubt that the baby was his.

I desperately needed to keep all this from Darragh – the fact I'm pregnant, the fact he's the baby's father. But he has found out everything. He has found me out.

Chapter 34

His text arrives the day I leave Dublin. My mum has taken a taxi to the airport and I'm in the bus on the way to Belfast. There's less than an hour of the journey left if we arrive at Europa Bus Station in Belfast on schedule. I realise we must have crossed the British-Irish border because the distances on the motorway signs are now in miles instead of kilometres and the lane markings look familiar again. There was no sign to say we were leaving the Republic of Ireland and were now in the United Kingdom.

When my phone sounds with the notification, I assume it's Mark, texting to confirm he'll be there to pick me up or to say he's running late. But then I see the sender. Darragh. My heart pounds in trepidation and I remember with shame that my heart used to beat faster for him for a different reason. For a second or two, I wonder if Darragh somehow knows I've been away and that I'm coming back today. If he has driven or run by the cottage, he might have realised I'm away. But he can't possibly know when – or even *if* – I'm coming back. And I'm sure he has better things to do than surveil my house.

This last thought resuscitates a memory. One night shortly after Mark and I first moved in to Causeway Cottage, when I was having difficulty getting to sleep, I got up to open the window.

I thought I saw someone outside, looking up at our bedroom window. At the time, I put it down to a trick of the light and my imagination, but now I'm not so sure. Has Darragh been watching the cottage all along? If, as I believe, he has let himself into the house on occasion, he'd hardly balk at staking it out.

I hesitate before opening his message. It would be better if I simply deleted it and ignored him. I should do what Mark advised and stay well away from him. But curiosity gets the better of me and I read it.

Xmas dinner at mine?
Dex would love to see you. Bring Mark too.

That's not what I anticipated. As far as Darragh's concerned, he and I are still friends and since he and Mark have bonded over a whiskey, whatever Darragh may have intimated, they're best buddies now, too. But I get the impression Darragh is up to something and I don't want to play his game. I have no idea what his next move will be. He will cheat and I can't win. I put my phone back into my handbag without replying.

I intend to tell Mark about Darragh's text on our way back to the cottage. But when he meets me off the bus, Mark refuses to take me home.

'It's not safe, Kat,' he says. 'You should have gone to Devon with your mum. I want you as far away as possible from that man.'

'I won't be pushed around, Mark. I won't be scared into exile. By Darragh, or you. We're leaving soon enough, anyway.' I told Mark I'd accepted the offer on the house on the journey to the bus station last week. If he was shocked by how low the offer was, he didn't say anything. On the contrary, he seemed very relieved that we'd had an offer so quickly and after only one visit.

'And you say he's dangerous, but seriously, Mark, what's he going to do?' I continue. 'He's hardly going to kill me, is he?'

Mark's face darkens. 'There's no reason for you to come back to the cottage,' he continues as if I haven't spoken. 'I've made headway with packing everything up while you were away. I can finish up and come and join you in England.'

I get that feeling again. The one I seem to have all the time around Mark these days. That he's keeping something from me. It's infuriating.

He sighs and looks at me as if he has read my thoughts. 'Listen, there's something you should know. Something important. Can I take you for a coffee? And then, when you've heard what I have to say, if you still want to, I'll take you home.'

This is it! This is where he's finally going to confess he can't have kids. I nod mutely.

We walk to a quiet café, around the corner from the bus station, in Glengall Street, where Mark has parked his car. I order a large coffee and regret my choice when it's served. I'm wired enough today without an extra caffeine hit.

Mark leans forwards across the table and takes both of my hands in his. I flinch involuntarily at the touch of his cold hands. His voice almost inaudible, he says, 'Kat, I think Darragh might have killed my mother.'

'What?' I think I've misheard. Either that or Mark has misinterpreted something Darragh said. 'Did Darragh admit that when you went to his place?'

'Not in so many words, no. To be honest, he was rambling. He was so drunk I doubt he even remembers what he implied. He probably doesn't even remember I was there at all. He called me Tom a couple of times. But I'm certain he had a hand in my mum's death. In fact, I'm sure he killed her with his own bare hands. That's what I was doing when I didn't come home. Like I told you, after I'd been to Darragh's, I got the ferry to Ballycastle. I went to Marconi Care Home.'

When Mark said he had to sort out a matter concerning his mother's death, I thought it was an excuse. But now he's talking murder.

'It must have been late when you got there. Weren't visiting hours over at that time of evening?'

'Yes, but there's always someone there. I rang the emergency bell. That's probably how he got in the night he killed Mum. As it happens, Nadine was there, which was a stroke of luck.'

'The one Mrs Gillespie introduced us to? The one who found—?'

'Yes. Do you remember? She was under the impression I'd visited Mum the night she died.'

'Yes, I remember. Go on.'

'Well, Nadine said when she found my mother dead that morning, she clearly recalled seeing someone coming out of my mother's bedroom the previous evening. A man. A tall man. She called after him, but he didn't turn around. She ran after him, but he left the building before she could catch him up. She assumed it was me.'

'And from her description – a tall man that she saw from behind – you assume it was Darragh?' My voice comes out sounding both incredulous and sarcastic.

Mark looks nothing like Darragh. He has thick, salt and pepper hair whereas Darragh's hair is fine and blond. Admittedly, they're both tall, although Darragh dwarfs Mark when they stand side by side.

'Mark, don't you think you're jumping to conclusions?'

'No.'

'What exactly did Darragh say?'

But Mark shakes his head. Perhaps he won't say anything more because I don't believe him. Or perhaps he has another reason for not telling me the whole story. Again.

'Mark, if you really believe that Darragh killed your mother, we have to call the police,' I say. I don't add what I'm thinking, that if Mark's right, then Darragh is a murderer as well as a rapist.

'I don't want to, Kat,' Mark says. 'It would be a serious allegation. It will never stick. We didn't have a post-mortem, there's

234

nothing to suggest Mum's death was suspicious and it could just as easily have been me coming out of my mum's bedroom. In the end, it would come down to his word against mine.'

It strikes me as ironic that Mark is reluctant to involve the police for the same reason as me. *It would be his word against mine.*

'If I report Darragh, it could backfire on me,' Mark continues. 'The best thing we can do is to get off the island and get away.' Here, too, we have the same reasoning.

Mark sips at his coffee. He scans the room, apparently checking no one has eavesdropped on our conversation, but the café is almost empty. I observe Mark as he studiously avoids meeting my eye. If Mark really suspects Darragh murdered his mother, why does he want to run away from Rathlin without doing anything about it?

'What possible motive could Darragh have for murdering your mother?' I ask. 'I don't get it.' Mark looks at me now through panicky, blue eyes and I know I've pinpointed the crux of the matter.

'No, I don't get it, either,' Mark says. He's still skittish. 'It was something Darragh suggested rather than said explicitly. A passing remark that made me think—'

'Mark, when you're ready to tell me what's going on, then we'll talk,' I say sternly. I resist the temptation to slam my hand on the table for emphasis. 'I'd like you to take me home now.'

On the way to Ballycastle to get the ferry, an awkward silence descends over us and Mark steals glances at me from time to time, as if trying to read what I'm thinking, but I don't know what to think myself.

I'd more or less come to the conclusion that Darragh was trying to make me pay for Erin's death, but it makes no sense for him to have killed Mark's mum. What possible motive could he have? I didn't even like my mother-in-law. Oh, God. Unless Darragh intends to hurt everyone I'm close to. My mother-in-law could be some sort of prelude or warning. Is my own mum in danger? But I dismiss that idea. I'm being ridiculous, letting my imagination go berserk.

Could Mark have concocted the whole story? I wouldn't put it past him. He's been so deceitful I no longer trust anything he says. This seems a far more likely explanation to me, but why would he make up something like that?

Mark makes an attempt to strike up a conversation. He asks me about my trip to Dublin. His questions and voice sound over-formal, as if he's addressing someone he barely knows. I respond as briefly as possible. I resent the intrusion on my thoughts and I don't want to talk to him. I feel a twinge of nostalgia for a simpler time, when we would tell each other everything, or so I believed, and stay awake, talking long into the night about our plans for the future. Those plans are scuppered now.

I switch on the radio to deter Mark from talking any more. Radio Ulster, a station I've never listened to before. I don't listen to it now, not attentively. I just welcome the background noise of the presenter's voice with his broad Northern Irish accent – rising intonations at the ends of sentences and the distinctive vowel sounds. The first thing I fell in love with when I met Mark was his accent – the same as my father's.

I think about what my mum said. She stayed with my father because she loved him, even though he hurt her by cheating on her. Some music comes on and I recognise the opening bars. But before I can identify the song, Mark turns off the radio. I glare at him and then turn away and look out of the car window. I don't love him anymore. In fact, I feel an aversion to him. Mark knows I'm not carrying his baby, and although he can't possibly be sure that *I* am aware of that, I don't think he intends to set me straight. In fact, I think he wants me to believe this baby is his. Perhaps that explains why he's making Darragh out to be so dangerous and why he's so keen to sell up and move away. Mark has his own motives for keeping my pregnancy a secret from Darragh.

If Mark had told me about his cancer treatment and offered

to be a father to this baby even though it's not his, things might have been different and perhaps there would have been a way forwards for us. But now it's too late. I can't trust my husband anymore. I'll think this through some more before I ask Mark for a divorce, but it's clear to me that our marriage is over and we won't be leaving this island together to start a new life somewhere else, as Mark has planned.

*

It's not until I'm at home, unpacking my suitcase in the bedroom, paradoxically surrounded by packed boxes, that I remember. My phone pings with a message from my mum to say she has got home safely and that's what reminds me: Darragh's text.

'Mark!' I go down the stairs to the living room, where Mark is packing books into a cardboard box. 'Mark! I got a text from Darragh this morning. I'd forgotten all about it until now. He's invited us to dinner at his place!' I watch his eyes widen, in anger or disbelief, I can't tell which.

'Can you make up some excuse?' he says. 'Or ignore it?'

I have every intention of avoiding Darragh until we leave and absolutely no desire to see him ever again. I regret coming back to Rathlin now and wish I'd listened to Mark and gone to stay with my mum or Charlotte. I only came back here out of stubbornness, out of some misguided notion that I shouldn't allow myself to be driven off the island. That and the need to settle things with Mark before we move away.

But I suddenly wonder if I can use this invitation to find out what Mark is being so deceitful about.

'I've already accepted it,' I lie. 'I sent him a text in the bus on our behalf. It was before I knew you thought he was responsible for your mother's death.'

'I can't believe you accepted an invitation without consulting me! Well, *I'm* not going. And you can't go on your own. You can either cancel or we won't show up. We'll steer clear of him until we leave this place.'

'I *can* go by myself, and I will if you refuse to accompany me,' I say. I strive to stay poker-faced as I call Mark's bluff. The last thing I want to do before leaving this island is spend an evening with the man who raped me and the very thought of being in that man's presence, let alone of eating Christmas dinner with him, makes my stomach churn.

'Kat, sit down.' Mark waves the tape dispenser gun at me. I do as I'm told and perch on the end of the sofa. Mark has turned pale. 'You have to believe me, Kat. Darragh killed my mum. I can't prove it, but I know he did it.'

'Mark, Darragh has been a true friend to me.' I almost choke on my own lie. 'Darragh, Jenny and Tom are the only people who have made us welcome here and you have … upset Jenny and Tom, and been hostile to Darragh. And now you're lying about him. I don't believe a word of your cock-and-bull story about him killing your mother. I can't see what possible motive he could have.'

'Kat, you have to trust me on this.'

I snort. 'With the way you've been behaving and all the lies you've told recently, how can you ask me to trust you? How can I believe a word you say?'

I've gone too far. I expect Mark to throw my supposed affair in my face at this point. I know he thinks *I've* been lying to *him*. I'm not at all prepared for what he does say.

'I know. I'm sorry. But you have to believe me, Kat. Darragh killed my mum. And if we don't keep away from him, he'll kill you, too.'

My blood freezes as Mark says that. It takes me a while to recover. Beads of sweat have broken out on Mark's forehead and he looks as if he might faint, but I fix him with a stern, compassionless expression.

'If you want me to believe you, you'll have to tell me everything,'

I say, rising to my feet. 'Right now.' I take deliberate steps towards him and poke him in the chest with my index finger. 'No more omitting details or telling bare-faced lies. The whole truth.'

'OK.' Mark looks both sheepish and scared. 'OK.' He sighs. 'I don't know where to start.'

I want to know why Mark thinks Darragh might kill me. But it might be better to go through things in order. 'Start at the beginning,' I say. 'Tell me why you think he killed your mother.'

Chapter 35

It's not late, but it's pitch-black outside. It gets dark here horribly early in the winter; there's no daylight left at all by the middle of the afternoon. The wind roars, although it's nowhere near as strong as the gale that swept the island on the night of the storm. My hair is blowing all over the place, so I take the elastic band I often wear around my wrist to tie it back. I didn't want to come out in these conditions, but Mark wanted some fresh air and suggested we should "walk while we talk". His face is still a ghastly white.

Walking down the hill, I look out to sea. The moonlight picks out the white caps of the waves; the water is dark and wild.

'Did Darragh ever tell you how his sister died?' Mark says as we reach the harbour.

A shiver crawls up and down my back. Mark must assume I'm cold because he takes off his own coat and wraps it around me, over mine. He's only wearing thin layers underneath, but I don't protest. It's cold out here. Sometimes, Mark does things like this for me and I remember why I fell in love with him.

I don't know how to answer. 'No,' I hear myself say. 'He didn't even tell me he had a sister. I didn't know until you mentioned it the other day.' I feel hypocritical. I insisted Mark tell me the whole truth and here I am, lying through my teeth. I can't tell Mark about Erin, though. I can't. I don't know why Mark has brought up Erin or what he knows, but I need to get him off this subject. 'But I wanted to know why you thought Darragh was involved in your mother's death,' I say to get him back on track.

'I'm coming to that,' Mark says. 'It's a long story.'

'OK. Take your time. Tell me everything.'

'A long time ago, when I was still a kid, I was working as a barman one night at a dance and I met Darragh's sister.' My heart stops for what seems like several seconds. When it starts up again, it beats too fast and too violently. 'We … we were both drunk and … um … we ended up having sex. It was little more than a teenage fumble, really, and it was the only time I saw her or had sex with her, but, well … unfortunately, she got pregnant.'

I try to stifle my scream, but it emerges as a feral growl from my throat and is instantly drowned out by the whistling wind. I want to thump Mark, scratch him, gouge his eyes out. I want to yell at him that he was not "still a kid" and what happened was not "a teenage fumble". Erin was a teenager – in fact, she was a minor at the time – but Mark would have been in his early twenties. My legs feel unsteady and threaten to let me fall, so I stop walking and sit on the stone wall. Mark sits beside me, looking at me, a mixture of worry and confusion etched on his face.

'It only happened once,' he says, an echo of his words when I found out he'd cheated on me with Fiona.

'Sometimes, Mark, once is enough.'

He turns away and hangs his head. He doesn't see me clench my teeth and my fists.

'Go on,' I say, although I'm not sure I want to hear any more.

'We were outside, in front of the community hall, where they were holding the céilí – the dance. Afterwards, she was cold, so I gave her my football sweater.'

'That old hoodie that showed up and then disappeared?'

'Yes. I think that was Darragh's way of threatening me. Along

241

with the Breezers – I served her Bacardi Breezers that night – and the mood ring. She had one just like it. She tried to give it to me, as a gift, when we were talking at the bar. Anyway, she was still wearing my top when she left that night. That's how Darragh found me. The football club logo on the sweatshirt. He turned up one night, a few months later, at a training session, throwing his fists around.'

A wave slams into the wall we're sitting on and icy-cold water sprays over us, making me gasp. I shrug out of Mark's coat and hand it back to him. It's wet, and also seems soiled to me, now I know he bundled a shivering Erin up in his hoodie that night after getting from her what he wanted. What I'd perceived as a sweet, gallant gesture a few minutes ago has become sour and gauche.

'What did he want?'

'He told me she was pregnant. He wanted me to man up and be a father and, I think, ultimately, a husband for his sister.'

I notice the word "ultimately". Erin would have needed her parents' consent at the age of sixteen to get married. She was only fifteen when she got pregnant. I notice, too, a vital word Mark can't seem to bring himself to say. Her name. Erin. He hasn't used her name once so far in his account of that night.

'I didn't know what to do,' he says. 'Darragh followed me home after football practice and spoke to my mum, well, shouted at her really, but she wasn't having it. She said I was only a kid and had my whole life ahead of me. She told Darragh no one could prove it was my baby, which was true. There were no prenatal paternity tests back then and his sister could have slept with someone else for all I know, maybe even lots of other blokes.'

I can't bear to look at Mark. Erin only ever had sex once in her short life – with Mark – and it wasn't by choice.

'Are you saying Darragh killed your mother because she wouldn't make you marry his sister?' I ask incredulously.

'No! No. There's more.'

I inhale deeply through my nose, breathing in the salty air. I'm not sure how much more of this I can listen to, how much more I can take. Without consulting each other, we both get up and resume walking, slowly, past McCuaig's Bar and towards Mill Bay. It requires physical and mental effort for me to put one foot in front of the other. Gradually, the buildings become scattered and the houselights and Christmas lights run out, leaving the moon and stars to light the coastal path. The moon is almost full and has a strange reddish tinge to it, like a blood moon.

While Mark no doubt drafts the rest of his monologue in his head, I try to digest the first part of it in mine. But it's impossible to take in. Mark raped Erin. My husband raped my friend. I can hardly breathe.

'A few months later, I heard she'd died in a car crash,' Mark says, continuing from where he left off. 'No one mentioned a baby, so I assumed it had died, too. I didn't know how far along she was when the car crash was meant to have happened, how soon after … you know.'

I bet Mark hoped the car crash took place shortly after his encounter with Darragh. He must have been relieved. In effect, his dirty secret would have been buried with Erin. Rage smoulders within me and I try not to let it consume me.

'It wasn't until the other night, at Darragh's place, that I found out the truth,' Mark says.

I know this part, but I can't interrupt. I can hardly breathe. I'm compelled to listen as Mark tells me that Erin was sent to England for an abortion and died there due to a massive haemorrhage. I turn my face slightly, away from Mark and into the wind, letting the cool air dry my silent tears for Erin.

Mark has glossed over the most important part of what happened that night. He has camouflaged his rape of Erin, reducing it to a "teenage fumble" and giving me a scaled-down version of his crime. I feel sick to my core. I am furious on Erin's behalf as well as my own. My breathing is still ragged, but I catch it enough to speak.

'Her name was Erin.' My voice is strangulated and I don't recognise it. Mark stops dead in his tracks and turns to me. 'And you raped her, Mark.'

'You said Darragh never mentioned his sister. I don't know what he told you, but—'

'I knew Erin! She was my friend.' My arms flail wildly. I pound my fists on Mark's chest and claw at his face. Mark grabs my wrists and immobilises my arms at my sides. The wind has picked up and I can barely make out my sobs above its howling.

'How? What?' Mark says.

'I was there that night, Mark, at the céilí. I didn't see you.' Even if I had glimpsed Mark that night, I wouldn't have recognised him so many years later when I met him in London. 'But I was with Erin. What you did, it was rape!'

'She changed her mind at the last minute,' he says. 'She only cried rape when she realised she was pregnant.'

'She said no, Mark. It doesn't matter at what point she said it. She didn't consent to have sex with you. It doesn't matter if she wanted to have sex with you to begin with and then changed her mind. You raped her.'

Darragh's face swims briefly into focus and it seems as if part of my fury is directed at him. I could be spitting more or less the same words into his face about what he did to me.

'Darragh used that word, too. But it wasn't like that.' Mark says this so quietly I can barely hear him above the noise of the wind and sea. 'I was ... gentle. I wasn't violent.'

He's still gripping my wrists. He's hurting me. He's also preventing me from hurting him.

'Let go of me,' I hiss.

When he does, I turn around and head back the way we came. I walk fast, but Mark stays by my side. I don't want him there. Neither of us says another word all the way home, but I'm screaming inside. *Her name was Erin! It was rape!* Over and over in my head.

It's not until we reach the cottage that I realise Mark hasn't told me why he thinks Darragh is capable of murder.

'I still don't see what this has to do with your mother,' I say. I can't look at him.

'It's part of Darragh's revenge,' Mark says, opening the front door and standing back to let me in first. 'He wasn't very coherent that night. He was so drunk he could hardly stand up. He talked about his sister. Darragh said what happened caused not only his sister's death, but also his mother's death.'

Mark still can't say her name. He bends down to take off his shoes. When he straightens up, he says, 'That's why you're in danger, Kat. Darragh said he would avenge his sister's death. Tit for tat. He lost the two women he cared about most. He said he'd do the same thing to the person he held responsible. He said he'd get the fecker who killed his sister and mother back. Tit for tat. That's how he phrased it.'

'You.'

'Yes. He didn't directly accuse me. As I said, I'm pretty sure he didn't even realise he was talking to *me* – the fact he included me in that bloody invitation seems to prove that. But yes, he intends to do the same to me. The two women who matter most to me, well … my mother and my wife. That's how I know he killed my mother. And he means to harm you next, I'm certain of that.'

I kick off my own shoes and take off my jacket. Darragh wasn't out to get revenge on me. He was taking revenge on Mark. Have I been collateral damage all along? I trusted Mark and I trusted Darragh and they've both lied to me and let me down. They've both used me and betrayed me. I feel absolutely murderous towards the pair of them.

'Tit for tat?'

'Yes, that's what he said.' Mark runs his hands through his hair as he walks away from me into the living room.

I remain standing in the doorway, feeling numb and shocked to the core. There are parallels between what happened to Erin and what happened to me and it's only now I consider these similarities that I realise that I'm not responsible for Erin's rape. I'm no more accountable for what happened to Erin than Erin herself. She wasn't raped because I encouraged her to put on make-up and wear a short skirt. Nor was she raped because I allowed her to get drunk. It didn't happen because I left Erin to flirt with the barman while I kissed a boy in the cloakroom. Erin was raped because Mark didn't stop when she said no. I've been blaming myself for years, harbouring a guilty secret that has festered inside me, but Mark is the only guilty party here.

Does Darragh blame me, though? Darragh knew his sister was raped – Mark has confirmed that – and yet he raped me. How could he? Did he think it was somehow fitting to do to me what he believed I allowed to happen to his sister? If so, he has two reasons to kill me. Two motives. To get revenge on Mark. And to get revenge on me.

But Darragh has had ample opportunity to kill me. So why hasn't he? I'm not so arrogant as to believe it might be because he likes me. He befriended me with an agenda. If he hasn't killed me yet, it can only be because the baby wasn't part of his plan. What will he do now I'm expecting his baby? Somehow, I think Darragh is probably asking himself the same question.

Chapter 36

This is a bad idea. I don't know what we're doing here. I should have thought this through. I should have talked this through with Mark. I'm convinced we're walking – maybe even running headlong – into a trap.

'Mark, it's not too late,' I say, grabbing his hand and pulling him back towards the car, which Mark has parked in the driveway. 'Let's go home.'

He throws me a look I can't read, a mixture of sadness and regret, perhaps. It might be because I've barely spoken to him since the other night, when I found out he was Erin's rapist, and I certainly haven't physically touched him until now. Or maybe it's because I used the word "home". Causeway Cottage will only be our home for a few more days. I've made Mark sleep on the sofa and I'm sure he knows our marriage is over. I haven't told him in so many words, but I've packed my stuff separately from his and I'll be going home to Devon – without Mark – when we leave this place.

'I don't know why Darragh has invited us tonight,' I insist. 'I know he thinks everything is fine between us and doesn't know we've found him out. But he must have an agenda, Mark, and you said yourself that he's dangerous.'

'Trust me,' Mark says. 'I have a plan. It's foolproof. It will work out for the best – for both of us and the baby.'

Mark has already told me he has a plan. He tried to talk me into scheming with him to beat Darragh at his own game, but I wouldn't discuss it with him. I regret that now. I thought I knew what he was up to, though. I'm sure he's motivated more by what is at stake for him than by protecting me or the baby. I assumed he would warn Darragh to stay away from us, perhaps relying on some form of blackmail or intimidation: if you come near us, we'll go to the police, that sort of thing.

But Darragh will realise as well as I do that had Mark wanted to go to the police, he would already have done so. There was no post-mortem and there's nothing to prove Mark's mother died of anything other than natural causes. Mark can't prove Darragh killed his mum. Darragh can't prove Mark raped Erin, either. But if he accused Mark of rape even without evidence, it would damage Mark's reputation irrevocably. Especially if women like Jenny and Mark's colleague came forward to say that they were sexually assaulted by him, too. Mark would lose his job. As well as his wife. Not to mention the baby he's pretending is his.

It wasn't until just before we set out for Darragh's house that I began to suspect that Mark's plan extended beyond blackmail. I saw him slip a little packet of pills into his coat pocket. Mark's a registered pharmacist – he used to work as a chemist, before he got his PhD and pursued a career with Campbell & Coyle – and he has easy access to drugs, maybe even poison. Now my imagination is oscillating between two scenarios: either Mark will slip a drug into Darragh's drink and throw him unconscious into the Atlantic Ocean or he'll poison him and leave his body for someone else to discover. Of course, this is all conjecture on my part, and it's entirely possible that my imagination has run wild, but I'm sure Mark will do something – anything – to silence Darragh as well as avenge my mother-in-law's death.

I have my own reasons for accepting Darragh's invitation.

I'm hoping to find proof of what Darragh did to me, although I can't imagine what form that evidence would take. I don't think Darragh drugged me, so I'm unlikely to find a date-rape drug and even if I did, it would have long since left my system, so that won't prove anything. And Darragh will hardly have written down what he did in a diary. But if I can at least get him to confess or allude to what he did, maybe even record what he says on my phone, perhaps I can get him to pay for what he did to me; perhaps I can get justice.

If I'm honest with myself, I'm not optimistic I'll find any proof of what Darragh did or that I'll be able to make him confess. So perhaps if Mark manages to pull off whatever he's planning, that will indeed work out for the best, for Mark, me and the baby. I don't care what Mark plans to do. I can't find the words to express how livid I am with Mark and horrified I am at what he did. And I feel exactly the same way towards Darragh.

But no matter what happens tonight, I want to be able to leave this island, knowing I'll never see or hear from Darragh again. Otherwise, I'll spend the rest of my life looking over my shoulder. Above all, I want to know with certitude that I'm not in any danger. I need to protect myself if I'm to protect my baby.

Mark and I stand side by side on Darragh's doorstep. I can sense the tension coming off my husband in waves. It matches my own frame of mind. Mark rings the bell insistently, even though Darragh comes to the door almost immediately. The smell of cooking hits me as soon as we enter the house, making my mouth water in a way that seems treacherous. As we cross the threshold and step into the warm hallway, it feels as if we're passing the point of no return.

'I'm so glad the two of you could come,' Darragh says, a bright smile stretched taut across his face. 'Let me take your coats.'

Mark mumbles something indiscernible, then points to a suit-case in the hallway. 'Going somewhere, are you?'

'Aye, as a matter of fact, I am. I'm leaving tomorrow for the States. I'm spending Christmas with my girlfriend in America.'

'Oh, how lovely,' I say, aiming for courteous small talk. 'Where exactly did you say she lives?' I continue in the same forced jovial tone, despite the scowl on Mark's face.

'I don't think I told you. She lives near Boston. Massachusetts.'

Darragh hangs our coats on pegs inside the cupboard under the stairs. Then he leads the way along the corridor and through the living room, where a log fire is burning, jolting me back, for a brief moment, to the night of the storm. The Christmas tree lights are on, too, and there are Christmas carols playing over a Bluetooth speaker. Cards adorn the mantelpiece, although I notice Darragh has been careful not to cover the photo of Erin and him that must have been taken mere months before she died.

In the kitchen, Dexter jumps up from his bed by the Aga to greet me, licks my hands and face when I bend down to him, and wags his tail vigorously.

'What's your poison, Mark?' Darragh asks.

Mark freezes and I wonder if my imagination didn't get carried away after all. Does Mark really plan to poison Darragh? *What's your poison?* I remember Darragh asking me that question at the pub quiz. I found it sinister even then, long before I knew how malevolent Darragh was.

'I'll have a whiskey, please,' Mark says, recovering quickly.

'I'll join you.' Darragh turns to me and hesitates. He knows my "poison" would be white wine, but he also knows I'm pregnant. 'What would you like to drink, Kat?' he asks, efficiently digging himself out of that little hole.

'I'll have a lemonade, please.' I have no intention of taking any more than a few sips. Just in case.

He doesn't comment. I keep an eye on him as he gets the pre-dinner drinks ready to make sure he doesn't add anything to my lemonade or Mark's whiskey. Darragh's fingers brush mine as he hands me the glass. I recoil from his touch, almost dropping the glass.

'Are you all right, Kat?' he asks.

'Yes, fine.' It doesn't sound convincing. I clear my throat. 'The glass is cold, that's all.'

Darragh grabs a bowl of nuts and another of green olives and we take everything into the living room. Mark and I sit on the sofa, leaving the armchair for Darragh. I try to evict from my mind images of Darragh and me kissing on this sofa last time I was here.

The atmosphere is unsurprisingly tense as we all size each other up. I can hardly look at Darragh and it's an effort to act normally around him – and Mark. Conversation is stilted, fraught with undercurrents and overtones and punctuated with awkward pauses. It's all a complete farce and no one knows what to say. Mark's contribution to any discussion amounts to grunts and snorts, and Darragh and I soon exhaust most of the safe subjects I can come up with, such as the weather and Dexter.

'So, how long are you going away for?' I ask.

'Four whole weeks,' Darragh says. 'Tom will have to manage without me for a month!'

'Mark is taking some time off work, too.' Mark shoots me a meaningful glance, a warning no doubt not to mention we're moving away over Christmas, but I'm sure Darragh knows. Everyone knows everyone else's business on this island, as old Billy Duffy said when we met him at the artisan market. 'What about Dexter?'

'He's going to the kennels.' Darragh jumps to his feet. 'I need to baste the turkey quickly.'

'Turkey?' Mark echoes.

'Yes. I thought I'd have my traditional Christmas dinner this evening, with you folks. Didn't Kat tell you? I'm sure I mentioned it in my text message.'

'I may have just said dinner,' I reply.

'Many Americans don't eat turkey on Christmas Day,' Darragh explains. 'My girlfriend's family prefer roast beef because they have turkey for Thanksgiving in November. Won't be a sec.'

'What do you think he's up to?' Mark asks as soon as Darragh is out of earshot.

'Shh. He'll hear you,' I whisper. 'I could ask you the same thing.'

'Yes, you could,' Mark hisses. 'I wanted to tell you. I wanted you on board.'

I turn to look at him. He reaches for my hand and I let him hold it. It's the two of us against Darragh. We need to be united, this evening at least.

'Do what's best for the three of us,' I say. 'You, me and the baby.'

Mark's eyes glisten and I realise I've probably given him false hope. Before either of us can say anything else, Darragh comes back, armed with more snacks and the whiskey bottle. I haven't touched the nibbles or my drink, as a precaution, even though I feel peckish.

As Darragh sinks into the armchair, I rack my brains, searching for harmless opening gambits: *Are you looking forward to your trip? Have you been to the States before?* But I sound like a bad journalist, conducting a disastrous off-the-cuff interview, asking closed-ended questions, requiring laconic yes or no or one-word answers. Darragh doesn't seem inclined to help me out by elaborating. Perhaps he's ready to drop the charade. He hasn't drunk much. I've rehearsed in my head what to say to try and tease some sort of confession out of him, but I was counting on the alcohol loosening his tongue. I'll have to wait a bit.

Mark's leg jiggles up and down and I can tell he's refraining from asking Darragh what we're really doing here.

Darragh changes position slightly on the armchair and leans forwards, his elbows on his knees and his chin resting in his hands. 'Gloria is hoping to move here one day.'

I remember him telling me this before and I open my mouth to say that, but something in Darragh's expression keeps me silent.

He has a strange glint in his hazel eyes, although it could be the reflection of the flames from the fire.

'She and I are hoping to have a baby one day. If it's a girl, we'll name her Erin, after my sister.' Darragh has already shocked me with these same lines, so I don't react, but I feel Mark tense next to me and his leg stops twitching. 'Did Kat tell you I had a sister?' Darragh asks Mark.

Darragh's convincing, but I can see through him. This is all an act. Darragh picks up a bowl of crisps and reaches it across to Mark, an innocent peace offering. Then he tops up Mark's glass again. Mark is being less vigilant than I am. He has already had two large whiskeys. I know, exceptionally, he'll expect me to drive home tonight.

'I need the toilet,' I say, putting down my glass, which is still full, and getting to my feet.

'The first door on your right along the hallway,' Darragh says, even though I used the downstairs bathroom last time I had dinner in this house. Mark doesn't know I've been here before, though, and perhaps for his benefit rather than mine, Darragh points towards the living room door.

When I get back into the living room, Mark and Darragh have both disappeared. Their glasses of whiskey are on the coffee table, half-full. Shit! Where are they? What if Mark's in danger? The music is still on; a carol is blaring out of the speaker. I race into the kitchen, where Dexter is lying on his bed. Darragh and Mark aren't in here.

The door to the cellar is ajar. I breathe a sigh of relief. Darragh must have taken Mark to choose some wine to go with the meal. I open the door wider and their voices float up to me. I can't make out what they're saying, but judging from the tone, the pretence at camaraderie is slipping. Mark sounds whiny, as if he's pleading. And Darragh's voice has a hard edge to it.

I tiptoe down the stone steps. The wooden door to the cellar is wide open. Darragh has his back to me. I can see Mark's face, but he hasn't noticed me. I stand back, against the wall and keep still, as I eavesdrop on their conversation, thankful that the light in the stairway is dim.

'I told you earlier about my girlfriend Gloria,' Darragh is saying. 'Poor thing, she suffered for years from uterine fibroids.'

I can tell from the look on Mark's face that he has no idea what Darragh is talking about. 'Why are you telling me this?' he asks.

'Do you know what uterine fibroids are?'

Darragh proceeds to explain his girlfriend's condition in some detail to Mark. *Non-cancerous growths.* My head starts to spin. *Pain and heavy bleeding.* I am rooted to the spot, scarcely breathing, not only because I don't want to attract attention to myself, but also because his words have taken my breath away. I know what's coming. *Hysterectomy.* Darragh's girlfriend can't have children.

A tiny sound escapes me, but neither Mark nor Darragh seems to hear it. I feel sick and swallow to try and keep myself from vomiting. I know what Darragh is after. And I know why he hasn't killed me. Yet. Because there's no doubt in my mind now that he'll kill me. I've just been granted a stay of execution until he gets what he wants. The words he said to me over our pub lunch echo in my head, taking on a far more sinister meaning. *You can't leave Rathlin. Not yet. Not now.*

'You don't seem very moved by this, Mark,' Darragh says. 'I thought you of all people would show some empathy. I mean, Gloria's tumours weren't cancerous, but you should be able to relate to the fact her operation left her sterile.'

I need to run, but it's as if cement has set around my feet. My brain is screaming at my body to move, but my body is staying put.

'What do you mean, me of all people?' Mark growls.

I may have joined the dots, but Mark needs Darragh to spell it out. He doesn't realise that Darragh knows I'm pregnant. And he doesn't know that Darragh read Fiona's letter and knows he's sterile.

'You still haven't told your wife you've been shooting blanks, have you? You don't want her to know the baby's mine, do you? I can't believe you're hoping to pass it off as yours.' Darragh laughs maniacally.

Mark takes a swing at Darragh and I hear a cracking sound. Mark must have broken Darragh's nose. But Darragh doesn't go down. In one swift movement, he twists Mark's arm behind his back, making Mark cry out in pain. Now they are both facing in my direction, Darragh behind Mark, towering several inches above him. If I move even a muscle, they will notice me.

'How did you know she was pregnant? You bastard! I'll—'

'What a topsy-turvy world,' Darragh continues, in an annoying sing-song voice, as if nothing has happened and Mark hasn't spoken. 'Ooh, the irony! I've heard of women who don't let on to their husbands that the baby is the result of an affair, but this is the other way round. It's the first time I've ever heard of a *man* pretending to his wife that he's the father of her baby when he's not.'

There's no mention of rape. Darragh seems to be implying we had an affair. Mark clenches his fist and tries to take another swing at him, but because Darragh is restraining him, Mark can hardly lift his arm, let alone throw a punch. I only realise I've been clenching my own fists when I feel my nails digging into my palms.

'You made your point,' Mark growls. 'What is it you want from me?'

'Isn't it obvious?' Darragh says. He's enjoying this. 'To begin with, as you know, I wanted revenge. Tit for tat. You killed my sister and my mother. Two deaths. The two women I loved most in the whole world. That's what I owed you. Payback. But circumstances have changed. Now I want what's mine. And you're going to help me get it.' I watch as Darragh's lips brush Mark's ear. 'I want the baby.'

For a second or two, they're both silent and still while Darragh waits for Mark to say something. My mouth drops open. Will

Mark agree to this? Will he give Darragh my baby to save his own skin? Mark cranes his neck to the side, twisting away from Darragh's face, and that's when he spots me.

'Kat!' Mark has given me away. Darragh looks up sharply, an expression of surprise mingled with disdain on his bloody face.

My instinct is to turn and run back up the steps and as far away from here as possible, but I know without taking the time to think it through that I wouldn't get far. Instead, I take a step towards the cellar. My hands shake as I reach for the door. Darragh seems to sense my intentions before I register them myself. He drops Mark's arm and bolts for the door. I scream as he runs towards me. It's as if everything is happening at an accelerated pace, as if I've accidentally pressed the fast forward button on the remote control while watching a film. And yet, I can only move painfully slowly. My arms feel heavy; my hands are sweaty and slip on the key. Despite that, Darragh is not fast enough. I close the door a split second before he reaches it and turn the key in the lock.

I picture the two of them suddenly united in their fear and desperation, on the other side of the heavy wooden door, pounding on it and screaming for mercy, or maybe for help, but if that's what they're doing in there, I can't hear them. Just as Darragh told me, the cellar is completely soundproofed. I strain my ears, but there's no noise at all. Pocketing the old, rusty key, I turn and walk back up towards the light emanating from the kitchen at the top of the stone steps. As I step into the kitchen, I can make out the lyrics of the Christmas carol playing over the speaker in the living room.

All is calm. All is bright.

Chapter 37

Something is ringing as I step into the kitchen and I panic. What is it? Some sort of alarm? A siren? It seems to get louder, and I want to cover my ears and scream. I'm so disorientated it takes me a while to identify the sound. The timer on the shelf next to the Aga is signalling the dinner is ready. Dexter seems unperturbed and remains curled up on his mat, barely raising his head as I fumble around, trying to work out how to turn off the timer and the Aga. Without thinking about what I'm doing, I take the baking dishes out of the oven and set them on metal trivet stands, then drain the vegetables, tipping them back into the saucepans.

I'm in a daze, almost incapable of making a conscious decision. I feel an urgent need to get out of here, to run away from this place, but at the same time I'm aware that I need to carefully map out my next moves in my head.

I sit down at Darragh's kitchen table, visualising Mark and Darragh downstairs – my husband and the father of my baby, locked in the cellar beneath me. I imagine their fear at being trapped. I recall my own claustrophobia at the escape game on Charlotte's hen night. I'd wondered how long the seven of us could survive if we were left forgotten in that confined space with only the bottle of tequila we'd sneaked in as sustenance. How long can Mark and Darragh survive with wine as their only nourishment? Or will they kill each other before they starve to death?

Guilt engulfs me and getting to my feet, I slide the key out of my pocket and head for the door leading to the cellar. I can't leave them in there to die. But this isn't like time out on a naughty step. If I let them out, they won't be contrite and docile. They won't have come to their senses. They'll be enraged. Bloodthirsty. Homicidal.

Maybe I can ring Jenny in a few days' time and have Tom let them out. I could leave the key for him somewhere. But even as I contemplate that, I know I won't do it. Even if Mark forgives me, Darragh will find me, take my baby and then kill me.

All right. I can't let them out. As I reach this conclusion, the hairs on the back of my neck prickle. There's someone behind me. They've escaped! I whirl round, expecting to find myself face to face with Mark and Darragh. But it's Dexter. I'm sure he can sense something is wrong. I caress his soft ears and it seems to soothe him. He trots back to his bed and plops down with a sigh. Stroking him has calmed me down a little, too, enough to start thinking straight.

I'm on the brink of committing a crime. I have to cover my tracks. I need to make it look – at least on the surface – as though Darragh has left for America. I need to check there's nothing in the house that incriminates me if anyone should report Darragh missing. I decide to do this methodically, room by room.

I go into the living room and turn off the Christmas tree lights and music. I see Darragh's phone on his armchair. To my surprise, it's unlocked. I delete all the text messages he and I have exchanged since I've known him and then delete myself from his contacts. Then I scroll through his photos, starting with the most recent and working backwards. He has mainly taken photos of his dog and the sea.

One photo stands out from the rest and a wave of nausea

rushes over me. I stare in disbelief at the screen. It's a photo of me, lying on my own bed, unconscious and naked. Darragh must have taken it on the night of the storm, on the night he raped me. Judging from the angle, he was kneeling between my legs when he took this shot. My hands fly to my mouth and I drop the phone. I race to the bathroom and throw up in the toilet. When there's nothing left to come up, I flush the loo and rinse my mouth at the tap.

Dexter is waiting for me when I open the bathroom door. He licks my hand.

'Good dog,' I say. 'It's OK. I'm OK.'

I'm not and I think the dog knows that. He follows me back into the living room. I pick up Darragh's phone, but can't bring myself to look at the picture again. Would this be enough proof that Darragh raped me? I could call the police and have him arrested now. My hand closes around my own phone in my back pocket, but then I hesitate.

If I have Darragh arrested, I'll have to face a trial. I'll have to face him. I heave a long sigh. I can do it. I'm strong enough. I take my mobile out of my pocket. But then another thought occurs to me. What if the photo isn't enough? What if Darragh says the sex was consensual and the jury believes him? If he's found not guilty, he might even be able to claim custody of my baby. And even if I win, one day my child will find out its father is a rapist. I can't allow that to happen. I can't report Darragh to the police. I have to protect my baby, no matter what. I put my mobile back into my pocket and delete the picture from Darragh's phone.

My hands shake as I continue to look through his mobile – photos, messages, contacts. I find nothing else of note except for the numerous texts that Darragh and his girlfriend Gloria exchanged. Until now, they've written to each other nearly every day, sometimes several times a day. I suppose they phone on the days when they don't send each other messages. I contemplate sending her a text message, purportedly from Darragh, saying that he can't find his passport or that it's expired and promising he'll get back to her as soon as he sorts out the problem, but I decide against it. I don't want to lie to Gloria, but I can't tell her the truth, so I'd rather say nothing at all.

I turn off the phone and carry it out to the hallway. In a dish on the console in the hall, I locate the keys to Darragh's van and his house keys. His passport and the print-out of the boarding pass are under the dish. There's a pair of leather driving gloves in the console drawer and I pull them on as a precaution. My fingerprints will be all over Darragh's house, and while in some rooms that is perfectly normal, it would be harder to explain on things like his passport, suitcase and van.

I wheel his suitcase outside and hoist it into the back of the van, then I open the garage door and park the van inside. Now, not only is the suitcase out of sight if anyone should peer inside through the frosted glass of the front door, but the van is also invisible. I leave Darragh's passport, boarding pass and mobile phone in the glove box, lock the van, and close and lock the garage door.

I still have work to do in the kitchen. I can't leave food lying around. I wrap the turkey in tinfoil and find empty ice-cream tubs and Tupperware dishes with lids to put the potatoes and vegetables in. I remember Darragh telling me he always made big meals and froze some of it for another day, so I leave out enough for me to heat up and eat tonight when I get home and tomorrow before I leave. I put the rest of it into Darragh's freezer.

I fetch the glasses and bowls from the living room and do all the washing up, then tidy everything away. I don't know where it all goes, but that doesn't matter. Looking for space for the glasses, I open various cupboards, but they're all full.

I carry the glasses to the living room, remembering a sideboard in there, and tidy them away in one of its cupboards. On impulse, I open the sideboard drawers to see what Darragh keeps in there.

I'm not expecting to find anything out of the ordinary, so

260

when I stumble on the letter, it comes as a complete shock. I recognise the stationery. It's the last letter I ever wrote to Erin. I know without opening it the gist of what I wrote. I apologised – profusely – for not coming to Erin's aid on the night of the céilí. I told her that if I'd been less selfish, I could have prevented what happened to her.

I clutch the letter to my chest. As I'd suspected, Darragh has known about my role in his sister's rape all along. In his warped mind, would he have felt justified in raping me, stealing my baby and killing me? He was wreaking vengeance on Mark, but I wasn't merely collateral damage. Darragh clearly planned to serve me my just desserts, too. He has been toying with me from the start and has treated me with unspeakable cruelty.

I walk over to the log burner and throw my last letter to Erin onto the fire. I watch, mesmerised, as the edges of the envelope turn yellow and curl upwards before a flame flares up and consumes the whole letter. Gone in a puff of smoke.

'I'm so sorry, Erin,' I whisper.

Half-blinded by tears, I take one last look around the ground floor of Darragh's house. I'm nearly finished. I take the rubbish out to the big wheelie bin, which I leave at the end of the drive. It's rubbish collection day tomorrow.

In the cupboard under the stairs, I find Mark's coat and go through the pockets. His phone isn't there, so he must have it on him. My heart thuds for a couple of beats until I remind myself that there's no reception in the cellar. If Mark and Darragh had the means to escape – a phone with a signal, a spare key to the cellar – surely, they would have got out by now. I realise, too, that the pills I saw Mark put into his coat pocket earlier are also missing. I can't help wondering if he'll think about using them for Darragh, or even for himself, given their current predicament. Thankfully, the digital key to Mark's BMW is in his jacket pocket. I take Mark's coat out to the car, then I load my Christmas dinner into the boot. I also load up the huge bag of dog food I found in one of the cupboards and Dexter's bowls and bed.

I turn off all the lights and check I haven't forgotten anything. I don't know if I can get away with this. But Darragh is due to go on holiday tomorrow, so no one will miss him for a few weeks, if I'm lucky. His suitcase isn't in the hallway; his van's not in the driveway. It's not immediately obvious that something is wrong.

His girlfriend Gloria will think it's weird when he doesn't come, but she probably doesn't have phone numbers for his friends in Rathlin or his father in Derry. She might end up thinking he has dumped her and is ghosting her. Or she may call the police, but they might not bother over Christmas about a grown man not taking the plane to see his girlfriend in the States.

Perhaps Tom will report him missing when he doesn't show up at work in the New Year. If Tom doesn't have a spare key to Darragh's house, he'll have to break in to search it. And even if he finds the van in the garage and realises something is up, he probably won't think of breaking down the cellar door straight away. I doubt it can easily be broken down anyway. But I expect someone will eventually find Darragh. Then they'll come for me. Because they'll find him in the cellar with my husband. The game will be up. Or the rules will change. I'll still play to win.

'Come on, Dex,' I say to the dog, who follows me out of the house. I turn off the light in the hallway and lock the front door, then Dexter and I get into Mark's car. Thinking Mark would be horrified if he knew Darragh's dog was sitting in the passenger seat of his prized BMW, I make a half-hearted effort to get Dexter to sit in the footwell. But Dex is having none of it, so I lower the window for him to stick his head out, as he used to do in Darragh's van.

We make a detour on the way home and drive out to Altacarry Head, the point where I first met Darragh. I park the car as close as I can get. Dexter and I walk the rest of the way, using the torch on my phone and the dim light from the moon and stars to see the way. Standing on the edge of the sheer cliff, I throw the rusty cellar key as well as the keys to Darragh's house and van as far as I can. The cliffs rise several metres above sea level and it's a little windy tonight, but, despite that, I think I hear two soft splashes as the keys land in the sea.

*

I get up long before daybreak. I start by packing Mark's clothes into bin bags. One of his shirts smells so strongly of him it nearly breaks me, and I have to force myself to keep going and forbid myself to cry. But then, at the bottom of a pile of clothes on the shelf in the wardrobe, I find the football hoodie he lent to Erin the night he raped her, the one that Darragh planted in the house to taunt and threaten him. I put it, too, into one of the bin bags and I continue my task with renewed determination.

'We've got a lot to do today,' I say out loud to my baby, stroking my tummy, 'and I'll have to carry some heavy things. It's not good for you. I'm sorry. Bear with me and hold on tight, OK? I promise it won't happen again.'

I load up the car in time for the first ferry of the morning. It takes me three round trips to take over everything I need to recycle or get rid of – Mark's clothes, mainly, which I take to a clothing bank, but also our tableware, pots and pans, and some of the smaller pieces of furniture, which I take to a charity shop in Ballycastle. Fortunately, Mark has done most of the packing for me, so it's a question of lifting it into the car and getting rid of it.

A couple of the ferry operator crew recognise me on the second crossing and for once I don't have to lie – I tell them I'm moving house. While I wait for the ferry to set off on each crossing, I make my phone calls.

Firstly, I ring my mum. I tell her I'm leaving Mark. It's the truth, in more ways than one. She's not surprised and tries to adopt a solemn tone when she commiserates with me, but she

263

can barely contain her excitement that I'll be spending Christmas with her in Devon.

Secondly, I call Jenny. I was going to tell her I have a tummy bug and won't be able to take the photos at this evening's school nativity play, as I was supposed to. But I come up with a better idea. I tell her I'm leaving Mark and going to spend Christmas with my mum in England. Although I'm letting her down, like the old codger who used to take the school photos, I feel pleased with myself, as the excuse I've given her is quite close to the truth. But Jenny makes me promise to send her my new address when I have one and I have no intention of doing that. I feel bad about doubting her when she told me Mark had groped her. I should have known she was telling the truth. After all, there's no smoke without fire. But I can't stay in touch. I'm leaving this island and need to leave everyone on it behind.

And finally, I ring the estate agent. I tell him we're moving sooner than we thought because of my husband. I'm deliberately vague, hoping he'll think it's because of the demands of Mark's job. I ask him to organise the removal of any furniture we leave behind that the new owners don't want and tell him to bill me for it or deduct it from the asking price.

I load up the car with my stuff for the final crossing of the day. I have time to take a shower and feed Dexter before leaving. I wolf down a turkey and cranberry sauce sandwich.

I lock the house and leave my key and Mark's key, which was in his coat pocket, behind the gnome on the kitchen window ledge, as I told the estate agent I would. He'll come round first thing tomorrow morning. I walk up the drive, Dexter at my heels, and close the front gate behind me. With my fingers, I trace the lettering on the rotting wooden sign that we never did get round to replacing. *Causeway Cottage.* I take one last look at the cottage, the bare canes of the climbing rose bush clinging to the white walls, the upstairs windows like eyes glaring at me and the ugly, ceramic gnome leering at me from the kitchen windowsill, where it occupies pride of place.

I open the passenger door of Mark's car for Dexter before going round to the driver's side.

'You'll have to hide on the boat,' I say to the dog, who has jumped onto the passenger seat again. 'Someone might recognise you.'

I pat Dexter's head as I drive away, down the hill, towards the harbour to take *The Spirit of Rathlin* to the mainland. The last ferry of the day and the first leg of my journey to a new life.

Epilogue

Dexter gets up and comes over to my armchair, wagging his tail. He knows it's time for his last walkies of the day. It's part of our routine. After Erin is born – she's due any day now – I'll be able to take up running again. In the meantime, Dexter and I walk miles every morning, along the South West Coast Path or the Tarka Trail. And every evening, our route takes us down the steep hill from the bed and breakfast towards Tunnels Beaches, then along Ilfracombe seafront as far as the pier and back.

I say goodnight to my mum, who will be in bed by the time we get back, and promise to help her with the breakfasts in the morning. Then I put on my trainers in the hallway and grab Dexter's lead and my keys from the hooks behind the front door.

This week, the first in July, the weather has been wonderful. Even though it's getting late, it's still light outside. In the summer months, tourists flock to this seaside town in their droves and mill around late into the evening, strolling along the promenade, spilling into the parks and gardens or onto the beaches. Schools don't break up for another fortnight, but already the town is filling up with people.

I can't believe I've been here for seven months. Every time my phone rings or the doorbell goes, I expect to be interrogated or arrested, but no one has come for me. Some days, I wonder if I've got away with my crime. Other days, I live with the sword of Damocles hanging over my head, thinking it's a question of time before it descends on me and I'm caught.

The only time I've had to deal with the police was when Mark's BMW, which I'd deliberately left near Lower Slade housing estate with the digital key in view on the dashboard, turned up near the Itchen Bridge in Southampton. I told the officer who called me the same story I'd concocted for Mark's boss at Campbell & Coyle when he contacted me – that my husband and I had split up and I hadn't heard from him since before Christmas. The officer informed me that the Itchen Bridge was a notorious suicide bridge and after heavy rains, the river was unusually high. I thought I'd let the police draw their own conclusions, although I did mention my husband had been so devastated by the breakdown of our marriage that he'd threatened to take his own life.

I saw once, months ago, a short online article in the *Ballycastle Chronicle* about a missing local man. Police were asking anyone with information regarding Darragh Moore's whereabouts to contact them. There was never any follow-up story. Missing middle-aged men don't seem to make headlines.

I'm brought out of my reverie by someone shouting. Dex and I are at the top of the zigzagged path leading up Capstone Hill when I hear it. Someone is calling my name. I stop dead in my tracks. Kat, not Katherine. Dexter's ears prick up – he has heard it, too. I look around me, my heart skipping a beat or two, but I realise it must be the wind and think nothing more of it. I stand still for a moment, admiring the panoramic view, taking in the truncated cones of the Landmark Theatre behind me to my left, the harbour to my right and the sea in front of me. The light is fading and I can't make out Lundy Island, but I can see lights glimmering along the Welsh coastline across the Bristol Channel.

As we near The Quay restaurant, the tantalising smell of fish and chips wafts towards me. My tummy rumbles, but I ate a huge dinner and can't possibly be hungry. I can hear my mum's voice in my head, insisting I'm eating for two, but I ignore it. I glance at a couple sitting on a bench. The man is holding a bag of Roly's fudge; the woman is eating the flake from her ice-cream cone. This time my mouth waters, but I've come out without my handbag, which prevents me from giving in to temptation. I'm not sure if it's the sea air or the pregnancy that has fuelled my appetite in the seven months since I've come back to my home town.

At the end of the pier, we pass Verity, Damien Hirst's controversial twenty-metre-high statue of a pregnant woman. She stands on a pile of law books, holding aloft the Sword of Justice in one hand. She's naked and on one side of her belly the skin is peeled away, as on an anatomical model, revealing the foetus. As a few people surround her, snapping photos with their cameras, I cradle my own rounded tummy protectively.

I don't look up at Verity as I walk past her, thinking not for the first time that I could avoid coming out to the pier and head back at the harbour instead. I used to love this statue, but Verity stands for the truth and she makes me feel uncomfortable now. But she also serves as a necessary reminder of all the lies I've told and all the stories I've concocted – to Mark, to Darragh, to Jenny, to my mum, to Charlotte, even to myself.

We invariably stop at Wildersmouth Beach on the way home for Dexter to have a swim, but he takes a nightly dip here, too, bolting down the slipway from the pier and throwing himself into the water with gusto. This evening is no exception. As I watch Dexter swimming around, the hairs on the back of my neck bristle, as if, in turn, someone is watching me. I whirl round, but there's no one I recognise and no one looking my way.

When Dexter finally gets out, he shakes himself all over me, as usual. Gently, he takes his lead from my hand to carry it in his mouth. I never go on walks without the lead, but I hardly ever clip it onto his collar. Except if we're near sheep. I haven't forgotten the stunt he pulled just over a year ago.

Dexter and I walk round to the other side of the harbour. This is the last part of our walk before we turn back. Standing by the low stone wall, I look out across the harbour, at the moored boats, some of them sitting on the sandy beach waiting for the tide to come in. I feel the weak warmth of the rays of the setting sun on my face. Beside me, Dexter lifts his head and sniffs, as if he's taking in the salty air. But then he turns to me and gives a little whine.

'What is it, Dex?' I say, patting him on the head. 'What did you smell?'

The man next to me points something out to his friends and they all turn to look. I follow their gazes. At first, I'm distracted by the people paddling in the sea, kicking water over each other and squealing. Then I see what everyone else is staring at.

It's a sand sculpture, right at the water's edge. The artist has carved a dramatic coastline into a large, upright semi-circle of sand. Perhaps it depicts Ilfracombe's rugged coast, but it could be anywhere. It's clever and beautiful. I wonder how long it took to make. It won't be there for much longer – the tide is coming in and the water is already lapping at the base of the sculpture.

As I stare at it, a realisation hits me and panic stretches its cold hands around my throat and squeezes so tightly that I can't catch my breath. I look all around me and then back at the sculpture, my eyes widening in disbelief. The most eye-catching element is to the right of the sculpture and I focus on it, squinting in a useless attempt to zoom in. The artist has coloured the sand to create a tall black and white lighthouse with red railings around its gallery.

This isn't some random seaside scene. And it's definitely not Ilfracombe. This is Altacarry Head, where I first met Darragh and Dexter, the view Darragh painted for me just after my arrival on Rathlin Island. He left the painting as a gift for me, wrapped in brown paper and leaning against the wall of Causeway Cottage. It's now propped up against my bedroom wall, still bubble-wrapped from the move. I was unable to throw it out, but, at the same time, I didn't want to be reminded of that place.

I watch, both shocked and mesmerised, as the water comes in. The lighthouse topples into the sea and a few minutes later, there is nothing left of the artwork at all. Even though around the harbour walls and on the beach itself people were taking photos, it didn't occur to me to whip out my phone and capture it. I could tell myself I imagined it, but I know I didn't. The sand sculpture is still vivid in my mind.

But as Dexter and I start to walk back the way we came, doubt tiptoes into my mind and eases it. I no longer feel so sure that the scene was familiar. Perhaps the sculpture only bore a passing resemblance to Altacarry Head. The artist probably conjured up the scene from his – or her – own imagination. I convince myself that the black and white lighthouse was merely a coincidence.

A Letter from Diane Jeffrey

Thank you so much for choosing to read *The Couple at Causeway Cottage*. I hope you enjoyed it!

Sometimes the ideas for my novels spring from the setting. That was the case with *The Couple at Causeway Cottage*.

I visited Rathlin Island several times when I was little, and went back with my family more recently

Photo credit: Nathalie Gatineau

in August 2019. Although the weather was wonderful, the crossing, on the *Rathlin Express*, was really rough. My children, husband, parents and dog were on the ferry with me, and I was terrified for their safety, as well as for my own. Despite having spent a lot of time growing up actually *in* the Atlantic Ocean (I was a lifeguard and did Surf Life Saving competitively), I don't have sea legs. This crossing is echoed in a scene in my book, where Kat feels both seasick and scared.

My family and I hiked around the island that day and I knew then that I would set a novel there. I've always been fascinated by island life and sometimes imagine living on an island, perhaps when I retire. But while that's all very well in the spring and summer, when the sun is shining, I couldn't help wondering what it must be like for islanders on Rathlin in the winter when the weather is stormy and they're cut off from the mainland. This sowed the seed for the plot of *The Couple at Causeway Cottage*, in which my main character, Kat, is stranded on Rathlin Island with a dishonest – potentially dangerous – neighbour.

The Couple at Causeway Cottage was my lockdown book. Initially, I was teaching full-time from home, but was soon back in the classroom. I had more free time than usual during that rather stressful period. Writing this book provided me with essential escapism and I loved writing it!

I hope you enjoyed reading *The Couple at Causeway Cottage* as much as I enjoyed creating it. If you did, I'd be very grateful if you could leave a review. I always love to hear what readers think, and it helps new readers discover my books too.

If you'd like to be the first to know about my new releases, follow me on Instagram, Twitter or on Facebook, or find out more about my books on my website.

Thank you,

Diane

xxx

https://www.instagram.com/dianefjeffrey/

https://twitter.com/dianefjeffrey

https://facebook.com/dianejeffreyauthor

https://www.dianejeffrey.com

The Guilty Mother

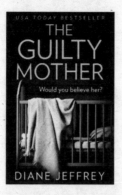

She says she's innocent.
DO YOU BELIEVE HER?

2013

Melissa Slade had it all: beauty, money, a successful husband and beautiful twin babies. But, in the blink of an eye, her perfect life became a nightmare – when she found herself on trial for the murder of her little girls.

PRESENT DAY

Jonathan Hunt covered the original Slade Babies case for the local newspaper. Now that new evidence has come to light, Jon's boss wants him back on the story to uncover the truth.

With Melissa's appeal date looming, time is running out. And, as Jon gets drawn deeper into a case he'd wanted to forget, he starts to question Melissa's guilt.

Is Melissa manipulating Jon or telling him the truth? Is she a murderer, or the victim of a miscarriage of justice?

**And if Melissa Slade is innocent,
what really happened to Ellie and Amber Slade?**

The Silent Friend

Tragedy brought them together.
The truth will tear them apart.

It's supposed to be Laura's dream holiday: a trip to France with a group of friends to see their favourite band play live. But the holiday quickly turns to disaster, and Laura is left haunted by terrifying images from the worst night of her life.

When Laura finds an online support group for victims like her, she's not convinced it will help. But then Sandrine replies to her message, and she seems to understand what Laura's going through, in a way that no one else can.

Soon, Laura and Sandrine are sharing their deepest thoughts and feelings with each other. But one of them has a terrible secret – she isn't who she says she is. And once the twisted truth is revealed, there's no going back . . .

Those Who Lie

**Emily Klein doesn't know she has killed her
husband until the day of his funeral.**

At first, signs point to a tragic accident. Yet, as Emily pieces
together the events leading up to the accident and her own
memory loss, she begins to suspect that her husband's death
may have been the result of more than a terrible twist of
fate . . .

But the accident is only the beginning. Because while
Emily's physical scars will heal, the trauma of the accident has
awakened old ghosts. She hears strange sounds, catches things
that can't possibly be there in the corner of her eye . . . Before
long, everywhere she looks, she seems to see her husband.

Emily doesn't know who to believe or who she can
turn to. And suddenly, she finds herself asking the
most dangerous question of all:

Can she really trust herself?

Acknowledgements

Although writing feels like a solitary occupation at times, the first draft is only the beginning and the publication process requires considerable team effort. MASSIVE thanks to the following people, whose invaluable work and support has helped craft *The Couple at Causeway Cottage* into my fifth psychological thriller.

Abigail Fenton, my amazing editor. Thank you for your insightful editorial feedback and for pushing me to make this story into the best version it could be. I'm very lucky to have you as my editor and am really excited about working with you on my sixth novel. Thank you, too, to the brilliant team at HQ.

Sam Copeland, my multi-talented agent. Thank you for your swift replies to my emails, for your reassuring phone calls and for putting up with me when I'm being impatient! Thank you, too, to Honor Spreckley and Tristan Kendrick at RCW.

Nicky Sebastian, author of the illustrated guide *Eight Walks on Rathlin Island*. Thank you so much for emailing me your book! I went to Rathlin Island many times as a child but after deciding to set a book there, I only visited the island once before the pandemic scuppered my plans for further research trips! The setting is a vital part of *The Couple at Causeway Cottage* and your guide was a lifesaver!

Gary Holpin, Devon-based photographer. Many thanks for your advice on photography, cameras and tripods! I'm not sure what possessed me to make my main character a photographer, but she wouldn't have been able to take a single picture without your help! www.garyholpin.co.uk

A special thank you to **Louise Mangos**, author of *The Beaten Track*, my writing buddy, friend and partner in crime; to my cousin, friend and beta reader **Anne Nietzel-Schneider**; my mum, **Caroline Maud**, for your encouragement and early feedback on the first draft of this novel.

Thank you to **John Marrs**, author of *The One* and *What Lies Between Us*, for your prompt answers to my weird (research) questions on Aga ovens!

Huge heartfelt thanks, as always, to all the **readers, reviewers and bloggers** who have rated / reviewed / recommended my books. If you enjoyed *The Couple at Causeway Cottage*, please recommend it to a friend, leave a (short) review or consider reading another of my books! I really appreciate your support.

And, above all, my grateful thanks to my family – my husband, **Florent**, our three wonderful children, **Benjamin**, **Amélie** and **Elise**. You're all so supportive and enthusiastic about my books. I couldn't do it without you. A special mention for my black Lab, **Cookie**, who never objects to me wittering on about my storylines and characters on our plot walks and who keeps me company while I write.

Dear Reader,

We hope you enjoyed reading this book. If you did, we'd be so appreciative if you left a review. It really helps us and the author to bring more books like this to you.

Here at HQ Digital we are dedicated to publishing fiction that will keep you turning the pages into the early hours. Don't want to miss a thing? To find out more about our books, promotions, discover exclusive content and enter competitions you can keep in touch in the following ways:

JOIN OUR COMMUNITY:

Sign up to our new email newsletter:
http://smarturl.it/SignUpHQ

Read our new blog www.hqstories.co.uk

https://twitter.com/HQStories

www.facebook.com/HQStories

BUDDING WRITER?

We're also looking for authors to join the HQ Digital family!
Find out more here:

https://www.hqstories.co.uk/want-to-write-for-us/

Thanks for reading, from the HQ Digital team